ALSO BY ADRIENNE YOUNG

Sky in the Deep

The Girl the Sea Gave Back

Fable

NAMES

NAMESAKE

ADRIENNE YOUNG

WEDNESDAY BOOKS
NEW YORK

First published in the United States by Wednesday Books, an imprint of St. Martin's Publishing Group

NAMESAKE. Copyright © 2021 by Adrienne Young.
For information, address St. Martin's Publishing Group, 120 Broadway, New York, NY 10271.

www.wednesdaybooks.com

Designed by Devan Norman

Library of Congress Cataloging-in-Publication Data

Names: Young, Adrienne, 1985– author.
Title: Namesake : a novel / Adrienne Young.
Description: First edition. | New York : Wednesday Books, 2021. | Series: Fable ; 2
Identifiers: LCCN 2020040972 | ISBN 9781250254399 (hardcover) | ISBN 9781250254412 (ebook)
Subjects: CYAC: Adventure and adventurers—Fiction. | Seafaring life—Fiction. | Diving—Fiction. | Treasure troves—Fiction.
Classification: LCC PZ7.1.Y74 Nam 2021 | DDC [Fic]—dc23
LC record available at https://lccn.loc.gov/2020040972

Our books may be purchased in bulk for promotional, educational, or business use. Please contact your local bookseller or the Macmillan Corporate and Premium Sales Department at 1-800-221-7945, extension 5442, or by email at MacmillanSpecialMarkets@macmillan.com.

First Edition: 2021

10 9 8 7 6 5 4 3 2 1

For Mom,
who taught me strength

NAMESAKE

PROLOGUE

My first dive was followed by my first drink of rye.

The sea was filled with the sound of gemstones as I swam after my mother's silhouette, toward the puddle of light rippling on the surface of the water.

My legs burned, kicking against the weight of the dredging belt, but Isolde had insisted I wear it even on my first descent to the reefs. I grimaced, my heart racing in my aching chest, and I surfaced beneath a light-filled sky.

The first thing I saw when my eyes focused was my father peering over the portside of the *Lark,* leaning onto the rail with his elbows. He was wearing one of his rare smiles. One that made his blue eyes flash like the strike of flint.

My mother dragged me through the water, lifting me up to catch the lowest rung of the ladder, and I climbed, trembling with cold. Saint was waiting at the top, sweeping me into his arms as soon as I came over the side. Then he was carrying me across the deck, seawater dripping from my hands and my hair.

We ducked into the helmsman's quarters and Saint pulled the quilt from his bed, wrapping me in the smell of spiced mullein. My mother was coming through the door a moment later, and I watched as my father filled one of his emerald-green glasses with rye.

He set it down in the center of his desk and I picked it up, turning the glass so the sunlight fractured and glittered in its facets.

Saint waited, one side of his mustache lifted on a grin as I brought the glass to my lips and took the rye in one swallow. The burn bloomed in my throat, racing down to my stomach, and I hissed, trying to breathe through it.

My mother looked at me then, with something in her eyes I'd never seen before. A reverence. As if something marvelous and at the same time harrowing had just happened. She blinked, pulling me between her and Saint, and I burrowed in, their warmth instantly making me feel like a child again.

But I wasn't on the *Lark* anymore.

ONE

The knock of a pulley hitting the deck made me blink, and suddenly the white-washed world around me came rushing back. Footsteps on wood. Shadows on the quarterdeck. The snap of rippling sails up the mainmast.

The pain in my head erupted as I squinted against the glare of sunlight and counted. The crew of the *Luna* was at least twenty, probably more with the Waterside strays on board. There had to be a hand or two belowdecks or tucked away into the helmsman's quarters. I hadn't seen Zola since I'd woken on his ship, the hours passing slowly as the sun fell down the western sky at an excruciating pace.

A door slammed in the passageway and the ache in my jaw woke as I clenched my teeth. Clove's heavy steps crossed the deck as he walked to the helm. His rough hands found the spokes as his gaze set on the glowing horizon.

I hadn't seen my father's navigator since that day on Jeval four years ago when he and Saint pushed the tender boat out into the shallows and left me on the beach. But I knew his face. I'd know it anywhere because it was painted into almost every memory I had. Of the *Lark*. Of my parents. He was there, even in the oldest, most broken pieces of the past.

Clove hadn't so much as looked at me since I'd first spotted him, but I could see in the way his chin stayed lifted, keeping his gaze drifting over my head, that he knew exactly who I was.

He had been my only family outside of my parents, and the night the *Lark* sank in Tempest Snare, he'd saved my life. But he'd also never looked back as he and my father sailed away from Jeval. And he'd never come back for me, either. When I found Saint in Ceros and he told me that Clove was *gone,* I'd imagined him as a pile of bones stacked on the silt in the deep of the Narrows. But here he was, navigator of the *Luna.*

He could feel my stare as I studied him, perhaps the same memory resurrecting itself from where he'd had it carefully buried. It kept his spine straight, his cool expression just the tiniest bit thin. But he wouldn't look at me, and I didn't know if that meant he was still the Clove I remembered or if he'd become something different. The distance between the two could mean my life.

A pair of boots stopped before the mast and I looked up into the face of a woman I'd seen that morning. Her cropped, straw-colored hair blew across her forehead as she set a bucket of water beside me and pulled the knife from her belt.

She crouched down and the sunlight glinted on the blade as she reached for my hands. I pulled away from her, but she jerked the ropes forward, fitting the cold iron knife against the raw skin at my wrist. She was cutting me loose.

I went still, watching the deck around us, my mind racing as I carefully slid my feet beneath me. Another yank of the knife and my hands were free. I held them out, my fingers trembling. As soon as her gaze dropped, I pulled in a sharp breath and launched myself forward. Her eyes went wide as I barreled into her, and she hit the deck hard, her head slamming into the wood. I pinned her weight to the coil of ropes against the starboard side and reached for the knife.

Footsteps rushed toward us as a deep voice sounded at my back. "Don't. Let her get it out of her system."

The crew froze and in the second I took to look over my shoulder, the woman rolled out from under me, catching my side with the heel of her boot. I growled, scrambling toward her until I had hold of her wrist. She tried to kick me as I slammed it into the iron crank that stowed the anchor. I could feel the small bones beneath her skin crack as I brought it down again harder, and the knife fell from her grip.

I climbed over her and snatched it up, spinning so that my back pressed against the railing. I lifted the shaking blade before me. All around us, there was only water. No land as far as I could see in any direction. My chest suddenly felt as if it was caving in, my heart sinking.

"Are you finished?"

The voice lifted again, and every head turned back to the passageway. The *Luna*'s helmsman stood with his hands in his pockets, looking not the least bit concerned by the sight of me standing over one of his crew with a knife in my hands.

Zola wove through the others with the same amusement that had shone in his eyes at the tavern in Ceros. His face was lit with a wry grin.

"I said clean her up, Calla." His gaze fell to the woman at my feet.

She glared at me, furious under the attention of her crew. Her broken hand was cradled to her ribs, already swelling.

Zola took four slow steps before one hand left his pocket. He held it out to me, his chin jerking toward the knife. When I didn't move, he smiled wider. A cold silence fell over the ship for just a moment before his other hand flew up, finding my throat. His fingers clamped down as he slammed me into the railing and squeezed until I couldn't draw breath.

His weight drifted forward until I was leaning over the side of the ship and the toes of my boots lifted from the deck. I searched the heads behind him for Clove's wild blond hair, but he wasn't there. When I almost fell backward, I dropped the knife and it hit the deck with a sharp ping, skittering across the wood until it was out of reach.

Calla picked it up, sliding it back into her belt, and Zola's hand instantly let me go. I dropped, collapsing into the ropes and choking on the air.

"Get her cleaned up," he said again.

Zola looked at me for another moment before he turned on his heel. He strode past the others to the helm where Clove leaned into the wheel with the same indifferent expression cast over his face.

Calla yanked me up by my arm with her good hand and shoved me back toward the bow, where the bucket of water was still sitting beside the foremast. The crew went back to work as she pulled a rag from the back of her belt.

"Take those off." She spat, looking at my clothes: "Now."

My eyes trailed to the deckhands working behind her before I turned toward the bow and pulled my shirt over my head. Calla crouched beside me, rubbing the rag over a block of soap and drenching it in the bucket until it lathered. She held the cloth out to me impatiently, and I took it, ignoring the attention of the crew as I scrubbed the suds up over my arms. The dried blood turned the water pink before it rolled over my skin and dripped onto the deck at my feet.

The feel of my own skin brought back to life the memory of West in his quarters, his warmth pressing against mine. Tears smarted behind my eyes again, and I sniffed them back, trying to push the vision away before it could drown me. The smell of morning when I woke in his bed. The way his face looked in the gray light, and the feel of his breath on me.

I reached up to the hollow of my throat, remembering the ring I'd traded for at the gambit. His ring.

It was gone.

West had woken alone in his cabin. He'd probably waited

at the bow, watching the harbor, and when I didn't come, maybe he'd gone into Dern to find me.

I didn't know if anyone had seen me dragged onto the *Luna*. If they had, it wasn't likely they would ever tell a soul what they saw. For all West knew, I'd changed my mind. Paid for passage back to Ceros from some trader on the docks. But if I had, I'd have taken the coin from the haul, I reasoned, trying to carve out every other possibility except the one that I wanted to believe.

That West would look for me. That he'd come after me.

But if he did, that meant something even worse. I'd seen the shadow side of the *Marigold*'s helmsman, and it was dark. It was all flame and smoke.

You don't know him.

The words Saint had spoken in the tavern that morning echoed within me.

Maybe West and the crew of the *Marigold* would cut their ties with Saint and with me. Set out to make their own way. Maybe I *didn't* know West. Not really.

But I did know my father. And I knew what kind of games he played.

The saltwater stung against my skin as I scrubbed harder, and when I was finished, Calla was waiting with a new pair of trousers. I pulled them on and knotted the strings at the waist so they didn't slide from my hips and she tossed me a clean shirt.

I raked my hair up into a knot as she looked me over and when she was satisfied, she turned to the passageway beneath the quarterdeck. She didn't wait for me to follow, pushing past Clove to the helmsman's quarters. But my steps halted when I stepped into his shadow and lifted my gaze, looking up at him through my lashes. The last bit of doubt I had that it was him disappeared as I studied his sun-leathered face. The storm of everything I wanted to say burned on my tongue and I swallowed down the desperate urge to scream.

Clove's lips pursed beneath his mustache before he opened the log on the table beside him and ran a callused finger down the page. Maybe he was just as surprised to see me as I was to see him. Maybe we'd both been pulled into Zola's war with West. What I couldn't put together was how he could be here, crewing for the person my father hated more than anything.

He finished his entry and closed the book, his eyes going back to the horizon as he adjusted the wheel slightly. He was either too ashamed to look at me or afraid someone would see. I wasn't sure which was worse. The Clove I knew would have cut Zola's throat for putting his hands on me.

"Come on, dredger," Calla called from the passageway, one hand holding the edge of an open door.

I let my gaze fall on Clove for the length of another breath before I followed, leaving him and the sunlight behind. I stepped into the cool dark, my boots hitting the wood planks in a steady rhythm despite the shaking that had settled in my limbs.

Behind me, the expanse of sea reached out in an endless blue. The only way off this ship was to find out what Zola wanted, but I had no cards to play. No sunken ship of gems to barter, no coin or secrets that would buy me out of the trouble I'd landed in. And even if the *Marigold* was coming for me, I was alone. The heaviness of the thought sank deep inside me, my fury the only thing keeping me from disappearing with it. I let it rise, filling my chest as I looked back once more to Clove.

It didn't matter how he'd ended up on the *Luna*. There was no forgiveness in Saint's heart for treachery like that. I couldn't find any in mine, either. I had never felt so much of my father inside of me as in that moment, and instead of scaring me, it flooded me with a sense of steadying power. The tide-pull of strength anchored my feet as I remembered.

I wasn't just some Jevali dredger or a pawn in Zola's feud with West. I was Saint's daughter. And before I left the *Luna,* every bastard on this crew was going to know it.

TWO

The door to the helmsman's quarters was an ashen wood burned with the crest of the *Luna*. A crescent moon cradled by three curling stalks of rye. Calla pushed it open and the damp, stale smell of old paper and lamp oil encircled me as I followed her inside.

Dust-filled light cloaked the room in a veil, leaving its corners inked in shadow. The uneven color of the stain on the walls gave away the age of the ship. She was old and she was beautiful, the craftsmanship evident in every detail of the cabin.

The mostly empty space was only disrupted by satin-draped chairs gathered around a long table, where Zola sat at its head.

Silver trays filled with food and gilded candlesticks were neatly arranged down the center of the table. The light danced on glistening pheasant legs and roasted artichokes with blackened skins, piled haphazardly in an opulent feast.

Zola didn't look up as he plucked a round of cheese from one of the bowls and set it onto the edge of his plate. I followed the flickering candlelight to a rusted chandelier that hung above him. It swayed on its hook over Zola's head with a soft creak, most of the crystal baubles missing. The entire scene was a poor man's attempt at majesty, though Zola didn't seem embarrassed by it. That was the Narrows blood in his veins, his pride so thick he'd sooner choke on it than admit to his masquerade.

"I think I have yet to welcome you to the *Luna,* Fable." Zola looked at me, his mouth set in a hard line.

I could still feel the sting on my skin where he'd had his hands around my throat only minutes ago.

"Sit." He picked up the pearl-plated knife and fork on the table, cutting into the pheasant carefully. "And please, help yourself. You must be hungry."

The wind coming through the open shutters caught the unrolled maps on his desk, and their worn edges fluttered to life. I glanced around the cabin, trying to find any clue to what he was up to. It was no different than any other helmsman's quarters I'd seen. And Zola wasn't giving anything away, watching me expectantly from over the candlesticks.

I dragged the chair at the other end of the table out roughly, letting the legs scrape against the floor, and sat down.

He looked pleased, turning his attention back to his plate, and I averted my eyes when the juice of the pheasant began to pool in the center. The salty smell of the food was making the nausea wake inside me, but it was nothing to the hunger that would be in my belly after a few more days.

He stabbed a piece of meat with his fork, holding it before him as he glanced at Calla dismissively. She gave a nod before she ducked out of the quarters, closing the door behind her.

"I trust you've accepted that we're too far from land to take your chances in the water." He popped the bite of pheasant into his mouth and chewed.

The only thing I knew for sure was that we were sailing southwest. What I couldn't figure out was where we were headed. Dern was the southernmost port in the Narrows.

"Where are we going?" I kept my voice even, my back straight.

"The Unnamed Sea." He gave the answer too easily, as if it cost him nothing to do it, and that instantly put me on edge. But I couldn't hide my surprise, and Zola looked pleased at the sight, stabbing a piece of cheese and twirling the fork in his fingers.

"You can't go to the Unnamed Sea," I said, setting my elbows onto the table and leaning forward.

He arched one eyebrow, taking his time to chew before he spoke. "So, people still tell that story, do they?"

I didn't miss that he hadn't corrected me. Zola was still a wanted man in those waters, and if I had to guess, he had no license to trade at the ports that lay beyond the Narrows.

"What are you thinking?" He smirked. He sounded as if he really wanted to know.

"I'm trying to figure out why this fight with West is more important to you than your own neck."

His shoulders shook as his head tipped down, and just when I thought he was choking on the bite of cheese he'd shoved into his mouth, I realized he was laughing. Hysterically.

He hit the table with one hand, his eyes turning to slits as he leaned back into his chair. "Oh, Fable, you can't be that stupid. This has nothing to do with West. Or that bastard he shadows for." He dropped the knife and it clattered against the plate, making me flinch.

So, he did know that West worked for Saint. Maybe that's what started the feud in the first place.

"That's right. I know what the *Marigold* is. I'm not a fool." His hands landed on the arms of the chair.

I stiffened, his relaxed manner making me feel as if there was some greater threat here that I couldn't see. He was too calm. Too settled.

"This is about *you*."

The prick of nerves lifted on my skin. "What is that supposed to mean?"

"I know who you are, Fable."

The words were faint. Only an echo in the ocean of panic that writhed in my gut. I stopped breathing, a feeling like twisting rope behind my ribs. He was right. I *had* been stupid. Zola knew I was Saint's daughter because his navigator was one of three people in the Narrows who knew. That couldn't be a coincidence.

If that was true, Clove hadn't only betrayed Saint. He'd betrayed my mother, too. And that was something I had never thought Clove capable of.

"You really do look just like her. Isolde."

The familiarity that hung in his voice as he spoke of my mother made my stomach sour. I'd hardly believed my father when he told me that Isolde worked on the *Luna's* crew before Saint took her on. She'd never told me about those days, as if the time between when she left Bastian and joined up on the *Lark* had never existed.

Even then, he and my father had been enemies. The war between traders was one that never ended, but Zola had finally found a weapon that could turn the tide.

"How did you know?" I asked, watching him carefully.

"Are you going to pretend like you don't know my navigator?" He matched my icy stare. "Saint has burned a lot of bridges, Fable. Revenge is a powerful motivator."

I pulled in a slow breath, filling my aching chest with the damp air. A small part of me had wanted him to deny it. Some fractured piece of my mind was hoping that Clove hadn't been the one to tell him.

"If you know who I am, then you know that Saint will kill you when he finds out about this," I said, willing the words to be true.

Zola shrugged. "He won't be my problem for much longer." He sounded sure. "Which brings me to why you're here.

I need your help with something." He sat back up, reaching for the bread and tearing a piece from the loaf.

I watched him slather a thick layer of butter onto the crust. "My help?"

He nodded. "That's right. Then you can go back to that pathetic crew or whatever hole in Ceros you were planning to make a home of."

What was so unsettling was that it sounded as if he meant it. There wasn't even a shadow of deceit in the way he met my eyes.

My gaze went back to the window's closed shutters, where slices of blue sea glowed through the slats. There was a deal to be made here. He needed me. "What do you want me to do?"

"It's nothing you can't handle." He peeled back the petal of an artichoke slowly before scraping the flesh between his teeth. "You're not going to eat?"

I leveled my eyes at him. I'd have to have my toes at the edge of death to accept a meal or anything else from anyone on this ship. "Do you always feed your prisoners from your own table?"

"You're not a prisoner, Fable. I told you. I simply need your help."

"You just kidnapped me and tied me to the mast of your ship."

"I thought it best to let your fire die out a little before we talked." The smile returned to his lips and he shook his head. "Like I said, just like her." He gave another raspy laugh before he drained his glass of rye and slammed it down. "Calla!"

Footsteps sounded outside the door before it swung back open. She stood in the passageway, waiting.

"Calla will show you to your hammock in the crew's cabin. If you need anything, you'll ask her."

"A hammock?" I looked between them, confused.

"You'll be given your duties tomorrow and you'll be expected to meet them without question. Those who don't work on this ship don't eat. They don't usually make it back to shore, either," Zola added, a frown breaking his lips.

I couldn't tell if that look was madness or mirth. Maybe it was both. "I want my knife back."

"You won't need it," he said, his mouth full. "The crew's been instructed to leave you alone. As long as you're on the *Luna,* you're safe."

"I want it back," I repeated. "And the ring you took."

Zola seemed to consider it as he picked up the linen napkin on the table and wiped the grease from his fingers. He stood from the ornately carved chair and went to his desk against the far wall, reaching into the neck of his shirt. A moment later, a gold chain surfaced from the collar and a black iron key swung in the air before he caught it in his palm. It clicked as he fit it into the lock of the drawer and slid it open. The ring glinted on the twine as he lifted it from inside and handed it to me.

He picked up the knife next, turning it over in his hand before he held it out. "I've seen that blade before."

Because it was West's knife. He'd given it to me before we got off the *Marigold* in Dern to trade the haul from the *Lark.* I took it from Zola, the pain in my throat expanding as

I rubbed my thumb down the worn handle. The feel of him appeared like a wind blowing over the decks: there one second and gone the next as it slipped over the railing and ran out to sea.

Zola took hold of the door's handle, waiting, and I tucked the knife into my belt before I stepped out into the shadow of the passageway.

"Come on," Calla said, irritated.

She disappeared down the stairs that led belowdecks and I hesitated before I followed, looking back to the deck for Clove. But the helm was taken by someone else. He was gone.

The steps creaked as we came down into the belly of the ship and the air grew colder in the dim glow of the lanterns lining the hallway. Unlike the *Marigold,* it was only the main artery in a series of passages that snaked belowdecks to different rooms and sections of the cargo hold.

I stopped short as we passed one of the open doors, where a man was crouched over a set of tools, writing in a book. Picks, mallets, chisels. My brow creased as the newly fired steel gleamed in the darkness. They were dredging tools. And behind him, the cargo was black.

My eyes narrowed as I bit the inside of my cheek. The *Luna* was a ship made for large inventories, but her hull was empty. And it had to have been offloaded recently. When I'd seen the ship in Ceros, she was drifting heavy. Not only was Zola headed into the Unnamed Sea, he was going in empty-handed.

The man stilled when he felt my gaze on him and he

looked up, eyes like broken shards of black tourmaline. He reached for the door, swinging it closed, and I clenched my hands into fists, my palms slick. Zola was right. I had no idea what he was up to.

Calla followed the narrow hallway all the way to the end, where a doorless passage opened to a dark room. I stepped inside, one hand instinctively drifting back toward my knife. Empty hammocks swung from thick timber beams over jackets and belts hung from the hooks on the walls. In the corner of the room, a sleeping man wrapped in quilted canvas snored, one hand dangling.

"You're here." Calla nodded to a lower hammock on the third row.

"This is the crew's cabin," I said.

She stared at me.

"I'm not crew." The indignation in my voice sharpened the words. The idea of staying with the crew put my teeth on edge. I didn't belong here. I never would.

"You are until Zola says otherwise." The fact seemed to infuriate her. "He's given strict orders that you're to be left alone. But you should know . . ." Her voice lowered. "We know what you bastards did to Crane. And we won't forget it."

It wasn't a warning. It was a threat.

I shifted on my feet, my hand tightening around the knife. If the crew knew I had been on the *Marigold* when West and the others murdered Crane, then I had as many enemies on this ship as people breathing.

Calla let the unsettling silence stretch between us before she disappeared back through the open doorway. I looked around me in the dark room, letting out a shaking breath. The sound of boots pounded overhead, and the ship tilted slightly as a gust of wind caught the sails, pulling the hammocks like needles on a compass.

The eerie quiet made me wrap my arms around myself and squeeze. I sank into one of the dark corners between trunks to get a wide view of the cabin while being hidden by the shadows. There was no getting off this ship until we made port, and there was no way to know exactly where we were headed. Or why.

That first day on the *Marigold* came rushing back to me, standing in the passageway with my hand pressed to the crest on the door. I had been a stranger in that place, but I'd come to belong there. And now everything within me ached for it. A flash of heat lit beneath my skin, the sting of tears gathering in my eyes. Because I'd been a fool. I'd let myself believe, even if it was just for a moment, that I was safe. That I'd found a home and a family. And in the time it took to draw a single breath, it was all torn away.

THREE

Beams of pale moonlight drifted across the wood plank floor throughout the night, creeping closer to me until the warmth of morning spilled through the deck overhead.

Zola had to have been telling the truth about the crew being ordered not to touch me. They hadn't so much as looked in my direction as they came in and out of the cabin overnight, taking their rest hours in staggered shifts. Sometime in the dark hours I'd closed my eyes, West's knife still clutched in my fist.

Voices in the passageway lifted me from the haze between waking and sleeping. The speed of the *Luna* dragged and I tensed as a blue glass bottle rolled across the floor beside me. I could feel the ship slow as I unfolded my legs and got to my feet.

The pounding of footsteps trailed above and I pressed myself to the wall, watching for any movement through the door. But there was only the sound of the wind coming down the passageway.

"Strike sails!" The booming sound of Clove's voice made me flinch.

My stomach dropped as I watched shadows flit between the slats. We were making port.

He called out the orders one after the other, and more voices answered. When the ship groaned again, my feet slid on the damp wood and I reached out to catch myself on the bulkhead.

Either we'd picked up speed and made it out of the Narrows in a single night, or we were making a stop.

I stepped through the door, one hand to the wall as I watched the steps. Calla hadn't told me to stay put in the cabin and Zola said I wasn't a prisoner, but walking around the ship alone made me feel as if I were waiting for someone to stick a blade in my back.

The sunlight hit my face as I came up the stairs and I blinked furiously, trying to focus my eyes against its glare. Two crew members climbed each of the huge masts, taking up the downhauls in a locked rhythm until the sails were reefed.

I froze when I saw Clove at the helm, tucking myself into the mast's shadow. My teeth clenched, a bitter fury covering every inch of my skin as I watched him. I had never imagined a world in which Clove could betray Saint. But the worst part was that she'd trusted him—my mother. She'd loved Clove like a brother and the thought that he could betray *her* was unfathomable. It was something that couldn't exist.

Zola stood at the bow with his arms crossed over his chest, the collar of his jacket pulled up against the wind. But it was what lay beyond him that made me stop breathing altogether. I reached for the nearest railing, my mouth dropping open.

Jeval.

The island sat like a shining emerald in the brilliant blue sea. The barrier islands emerged from the churning waters below like blackened teeth, and the *Luna* drifted into the last bay of the crude docks as the sun peeked over the familiar rise in the distance.

The last time I'd seen the island, I'd been running for my life. I'd thrown myself at the mercy of the *Marigold*'s crew after four years of diving those reefs to survive. Every muscle in my body coiled tightly around my bones as we drifted closer.

A barefoot boy I recognized ran down the dock to secure the heaving lines as the *Luna* neared the outcropping. A deckhand climbed over the railing beside me, reaching for the ties that secured the ladder on the side of the ship, and tugged at their ends until the knots were free. It unrolled against the starboard side with a slap.

"What are we doing here?" I asked, keeping my voice low.

The man arched an eyebrow as he looked up at me, his

gaze dragging over my face. But he didn't answer. "Ryland! Wick!"

Two younger crew members came down from the quarterdeck, one tall and lanky with a fair mop of hair. The other one was broad and muscular, his dark hair shaved down to the scalp.

The deckhand dropped a crate before them and the rattle of steel made me flinch. It was filled with the dredging tools I'd seen last night. "Get these sorted."

From the look of the belts around their waists, they were Zola's dredgers. When he felt my attention on him, the dark-haired one looked up at me, his gaze like the hot burn of rye.

Jeval wasn't a port. The only reason to come here was to offload small over-calculations in inventory. Maybe a crate of fresh eggs that didn't sell in one of the port towns, or a few extra chickens the crew hadn't eaten. And then there was pyre. But pyre wasn't the kind of stone that attracted an outfit like Zola's, and I'd never seen his crest on a ship here before.

If we were stopping in Jeval, Zola needed something else. Something he couldn't get in the Narrows.

I followed the railing toward the bow, fitting myself behind the foremast so I could see the docks without being spotted by anyone who might recognize me. The other ships anchored in the meager harbor were all small vessels and, in the distance, I could see the little boats packed with bodies coming in from the island to trade, carving white trails in the water.

Only weeks ago, I would have been one of them, coming to the barrier islands when the *Marigold* made port to trade my pyre for coin. I woke with a pit in my stomach on those mornings, the smallest voice within me afraid that West wouldn't be there when the mist cleared. But when I stood at the cliff overlooking the sea, the sails of the *Marigold* were there. They were always there.

Zola lifted a hand to clap Clove on the back before he went to the ladder and climbed down. Jeval didn't have a harbor master, but Soren was the man to talk to when something was needed, and he already stood waiting at the mouth of the dock. His cloudy spectacles reflected the sunlight as he peered up at the *Luna*, and for a moment I thought his eyes landed on me.

He'd accused me of stealing on the docks more than once and he'd even made me repay a debt I didn't owe with a week's worth of fish. But his gaze drifted over the ship, leaving me as quickly as it had found me, and I remembered I wasn't the girl who'd leapt for the ladder of the *Marigold* anymore. The one who'd begged and scraped to survive the years on Jeval so she could go searching for the man who didn't want her. Now I was the girl who'd found her own way. And I also had something to lose.

My eyes landed on Zola as his boots hit the dock. Soren walked lazily toward the ladder, tipping his good ear up as Zola spoke. One bushy eyebrow lifted over the rim of his spectacles before he nodded.

The cargo hull was empty, so the only way Zola could be trading was in coin. But there wasn't anything to buy on this island except fish, rope, and pyre. Nothing worth trading in the Unnamed Sea.

Soren left Zola standing at the edge of the walkway before he disappeared into the people crowded on the rickety wood planks. He shouldered back toward the other end, where the skiffs from the beach were slowing to drop barefoot dredgers to trade.

I watched Soren snake through the commotion until he disappeared behind a ship.

Around me, everyone was going about their duties, and from the look of it, not a single crew member was surprised by the stop at the dredger island. My eyes lifted to the mainmast and upper decks, where the deckhands were rolling out the storm sails. Not the ones used in the Narrows. These sails were crafted for the monster gales that haunted the Unnamed Sea.

Behind me, the water stretched out in a bottomless blue, all the way back to Dern. I knew how to survive on Jeval. If I got off the *Luna,* if I found a way to . . . my thoughts flicked from one to the other. If the *Marigold* was looking for me, they'd most likely be following Zola's route back to Sowan. Eventually, they could end up in Jeval.

But there was still a part of me that wondered if the *Marigold* would cut their losses. They had the haul from the *Lark.* They could buy out from Saint and start their own trade. An even softer whisper sounded in the back of my mind.

Maybe they wouldn't come looking at all.

I gritted my teeth, staring at the toes of my boots. I'd sworn that I'd never come back to Jeval, but maybe now it was the only chance I had at staying in the Narrows. My hands tightened on the railing and I peered over it to the water below. If I jumped, I could make it around the barrier islands faster than anyone on this ship. I could hide in the kelp forest at the cove. Eventually, they'd give up looking for me.

When the feeling of eyes on me crept over my skin, I looked over my shoulder. Clove stood on the other side of the helm, watching me as if he knew exactly what I was thinking. It was the first time his eyes had met mine and they didn't waver. His stormy gaze was like the pull of the deep water beneath us.

My fingers slipped from the rail and I leaned into it, staring back. He was older. There were silver strands streaking his blond beard and his skin had lost some of its warm gold color beneath the tattoos covering his arms. But this was still Clove. Still the man that had sung me the old tavern songs as I fell asleep on the *Lark*. The one who'd taught me to pickpocket when we made port and bought me blood oranges on the docks in Dern.

Again, he seemed to read my thoughts, and his jaw ticked.

I was glad. In that moment, I had never hated anyone as much as I hated Clove. I'd never wanted so badly to see anyone dead. The muscles in his shoulders tensed as the words flit across my mind and I imagined him in that crate that West dropped into the black sea. I imagined his deep-throated scream. And the tug at the corner of my mouth filled my eyes with tears, my busted lip stinging.

The dead look in his eyes met mine for only another moment before he went back to work, disappearing beneath the archway that led to the helmsman's quarters.

The burn behind my eyes was matched by the anger still boiling in my chest. If Clove had gone against Saint, then

Zola was probably right. Clove wanted revenge for something, and he was using me to get it.

Voices shouted below and I turned back to the dock, where Soren had returned with a parchment. He unrolled it before Zola and he looked it over carefully. When he was finished, he took the feathered quill from Soren's hand and signed. Beside him, a little boy dripped a pool of wax onto its corner and Zola pressed his merchant's ring into it before it cooled. He was making a deal.

A moment later, a string of dredgers was lining up shoulder to shoulder behind them. My brow creased as I watched Zola walk down the row slowly, inspecting each of them. He stopped when he saw one of the younger ones hide a hand behind his back. Zola reached around him and yanked it free to reveal that the fingers on the boy's right hand were bound in a bandage.

Zola dropped it before dismissing him, and the dredger's place was taken by another who was waiting at the edge of the dock.

It wasn't until that moment that I realized what he was doing. We weren't stopping at Jeval for supplies or trade. Zola wasn't here to buy pyre. He was here for dredgers.

"Make ready!" Clove shouted.

A deckhand shoved me back from the railing. "Out of the way," he growled.

I moved around him, trying to see. But the crew was already lifting the anchor. Calla took the steps to the quarterdeck and I followed on her heel, watching over a stack of crates as Zola came back up over the side of the ship.

The dredgers from the docks spilled onto the deck behind him and the crew of the *Luna* stopped their work, every eye landing on the gold-skinned creatures climbing over the railing.

That's why Zola needed me. He was headed for a dive. But he had at least two dredgers on his crew already, and I made three. There were at least eight Jevalis boarding the *Luna,* with even more coming up the ladder.

In the distance, the surface of the water roughened, the waves bristling as a cold north wind swept in from the sea. It sent a chill up my spine as the heaving lines were pulled up and I turned back to the deck. The last of the dredgers came up onto the ship and I froze when the sunlight hit a face I knew. One I'd feared almost every day I was on Jeval.

Koy stood almost a head taller than the other dredgers as he took his place in the line. And when his gaze fell on me, I could see the same wide look of recognition that I knew was in my own eyes.

My voice was hoarse, hollow on a long breath. "Shit."

FOUR

I watched him.

Koy leaned against the crates secured along the stern, his gaze set on the full sails overhead. The *Luna* was already drifting from the barrier islands and Jeval was growing smaller behind us. Wherever we were headed, Zola wasn't wasting any time.

Koy didn't look up, but I knew he could feel my eyes on him. And I wanted him to.

The last time I'd seen Koy, he was tearing down the docks in the dark, screaming my name. I could still see the way he'd looked beneath the surface of the water, blood trailing in twisting streams. I don't know what had made me jump back in after him. I'd asked myself that question a hundred times, and I didn't have an answer that made any kind of sense. If it were me, Koy wouldn't have hesitated to leave me to drown.

But even if I'd hated him, there was something I had understood about Koy from the start. He was a man willing to do whatever he had to. No matter what, and at any cost. And he'd made me a promise that night I first stood on the deck of the *Marigold*. That if I ever came back to Jeval, he'd tie me to the reef and leave my bones to be picked clean by the creatures who lived in the deep.

My gaze dragged over his form, measuring the height and weight of him. He had the advantage over me in almost every way, but I wasn't going to turn my back or give him a single chance to keep that promise.

I didn't blink until Clove came up the stairs with heavy steps, running both hands through his curling hair to rake it back from his face. The sleeves of his shirt were rolled up to his elbows, and the familiar movement made the pain in my chest flicker back to life.

"Dredgers!" he called out.

The Jevalis lined up along the starboard side, where the dredgers from Zola's crew, Ryland and Wick, stood waiting. The crates of tools were in their hands, and from the look on their faces, they didn't like what was about to happen.

Koy slung his own belt over his shoulder, taking the place on the deck before Clove. That was just like Koy, finding the scariest bastard on the ship and making a point of showing them he wasn't afraid. But when I looked up into Clove's face, his attention was on me.

The steely glint in his eye was unwavering, making my insides feel like I was falling. *"All* of you," he grunted.

I sucked in my bottom lip and bit down to keep it from trembling. In that single look, the years ticked back, making me instantly feel like I was that little girl on the *Lark* he'd chastised for tying a knot wrong. My expression hardened as I took a single step forward, putting me a few feet away from the end of the line.

"While you're aboard this ship, you will not step out of line," he crowed. "You will do as you're told. You will keep your pockets empty." He paused, giving each of the Jevalis a silent look before he continued. I'd seen Clove give a hundred speeches just like it on my father's ship. It, too, was painfully familiar. "You will be given two supper rations a day while you are employed on the *Luna,* and you will be expected to keep your quarters clean."

He was likely repeating the terms on the parchment in his hands—the one Zola signed with the harbor master— and there was no denying it was a generous deal. Two rations a day was decadent living for any Jevali on the deck beside me, and they'd likely be taking home more coin than most of them could earn in months.

"The first of you to break these rules will be *swimming* back to Jeval. Questions?"

"We stay together." Koy was the first to speak, outlining his own terms. He was talking about their sleeping quarters and I suspected it was to ensure they didn't become targets for the *Luna*'s crew. Dredgers were every man for himself on

Jeval, but this was different. There was safety in numbers on this ship.

"Fine." Clove nodded to Ryland and Wick, who looked like they were ready to pull their knives out. They stepped forward, each setting a crate down before the line. "Take what you need for a two-day dive. Consider it part of your payment."

The dredgers lunged forward before Clove had even finished, crouching around the crates to fish out picks and press their callused fingertips to the sharp points. They rooted in the pile for chisels and eyeglasses to add to their belts, and Ryland and Wick watched, disgusted by the way they fumbled through the tools.

I wasn't the only one who'd noticed. Koy stood back behind the others, not taking his gaze off Zola's dredgers. When they locked eyes, the silent tension that flooded the deck was palpable. I felt a shade more invisible then, thinking that maybe the presence of the Jevali dredgers was a good thing. It took the attention off me, if only a little.

"Fable."

I stiffened, hearing my name spoken in Clove's voice.

He took three slow steps toward me, and I drew back, my fingers finding the handle of West's knife.

His boots stopped before mine and I watched the easy way he looked at me. The wrinkles around his eyes were deeper, his fair lashes like threads of gold. There was a scar I'd never seen before below his ear, wrapping around his throat and disappearing into his shirt. I tried not to wonder where it came from.

"We need to worry about any of them?" His chin jerked toward the dredgers on the deck.

I glowered at him, not sure I could believe that he was actually talking to me. What's more, he wanted information, as if we were on the same side. "I guess you'll find out, won't you?"

"I see." He reached into the pocket of his vest, pulling a small purse free. "What'll it cost me?"

"Four years," I answered heavily.

His brow knit in question.

I took a step toward him, and his hand tightened on the purse. "Give me back the four years I spent on that island. Then I'll tell you which one of those dredgers is most likely to cut your throat."

He stared at me, every thought I couldn't hear shining in his eyes.

"Not that it would really matter." I tipped my head to one side.

"What?"

"You never *really* know a person, do you?" I let my meaning fold under the words, watching him carefully. Not a single shadow passed over his face. No hint of what he was thinking.

"We've all got a job to do, don't we?" was his only reply.

"You more than any of us. Navigator, informant . . . traitor," I said.

"Don't make trouble, Fay." His voice lowered. "You do what's asked of you and you'll get paid like everyone else."

"How much is Zola paying *you*?" I snarled.

He didn't answer.

"What's Zola doing in the Unnamed Sea?"

Clove stared at me until the ring of grommets singing on the ropes overhead broke the silence between us. A sail unfolded on the deck, casting Clove and me in its shadow. I looked up to where it was silhouetted against the sunlight, a black square against the blue sky.

But the crest painted on the canvas was missing the curve of the crescent moon that encircled Zola's insignia. I squinted, trying to see it. The crisp outline of three seabirds with wings extended made a tilted triangle. It was a crest I'd never seen before.

If they were raising a new crest, it meant that Zola didn't want to be recognized when we crossed into the waters of the Unnamed Sea.

I looked over my shoulder, but Clove was already disappearing into the helmsman's quarters, the door slamming shut behind him. I could see the ripple of his white shirt behind the wavering glass of the window that looked out over the deck.

I bit down onto my lip again, every quiet thing within me screaming. I'd known the night the *Lark* sank that I'd lost my mother. But I hadn't known I'd lost Clove, too.

FIVE

"Three reefs!" Zola's voice rang out over the ship before he'd even made it through the archway.

He unclasped his jacket, letting it drop from his shoulders, and tossed it to one of the Waterside strays standing at the foot of the mast. His hands caught the anchored ropes stretching from the bow, and he pulled himself up into the lines, looking out over the sea.

But my eyes were on Ryland and Wick. Both stood in the row of Jevalis, every ounce of fury over the disgrace making their muscles tense. They weren't happy Zola had taken on extra dredgers. In fact, they were seething.

"Here, here, and here." Zola followed the line of the reef

crests below with his finger, drawing them on the surface of the water.

In the distance, a crescent-shaped islet was visible, floating like a half-submerged circle.

"Fable will head the dive."

I blinked, turning back to the deck where the dredgers' hard gazes were set on me.

"What?" Ryland snapped, his hands dropping from where they were tucked into the crooks of his arms.

Zola ignored him, looking at the islet. The wind pulled his silver-and-black hair across his rough face as I tried to read it. He said he'd given the crew instructions to leave me alone, but he was giving them plenty of reasons to come after me.

"The fourth reef is picked clean, but there's plenty of tourmaline, palladin, and bloodstone in the others. Probably an emerald or two." Zola jumped back down to the deck, walking down the line of dredgers. "Your hauls will be checked when you surface. First dredger to hit twenty carats of gemstones gets a bonus of double their coin."

Koy stood a little taller as Zola said the words. The other Jevali dredgers looked up at the helmsman with brows raised, and Wick tightened his grip on his belt, his mouth twisting up on one side.

"I need at least three hundred carats of stone. You have until sundown tomorrow."

"What?" Koy stepped forward, his voice finding an edge.

"Ships run on schedules." Zola looked down at him. "You have a problem with that?"

"He's right," I said. Koy looked surprised that I'd agreed

with him, but it was true. "We would have to dive back-to-back while we had the daylight if we were going to dredge enough gems to meet that quota."

Zola seemed to consider it before he pulled the watch from his vest. He flicked it open. "Then I think you'd better be quick about it." He dropped the timepiece back into his pocket and looked up at me. "Now, what do you see?"

He moved over to give me a place at the rail beside him, but I didn't move. Zola was playing a game, but I wasn't sure if anyone on this ship knew what it was. I didn't like that feeling. He was clearly entertained by it all, and that made me want to shove him over the side.

"What do you *see?*" he asked again.

I curled my hands into fists and hooked my thumbs into my belt as I looked out over the water. It was moving smoothly inside the crest of the islet, almost still enough in places to reflect the shapes of the clouds. "It looks good. No riptide that I can see, but we obviously won't know that until we're down there." I eyed the water on the other side of the ridge. The shape of the crater was angled perfectly to protect the interior from the current.

He met my eyes before he stepped around me. "Then get them down there."

The boy holding his jacket held it up for him to slide his arms back in, and then Zola was walking back across the deck without even a glance at us. The door slammed behind him, and in the next breath, the dredgers turned to me. Ryland's face was painted red, his gaze tight.

On the other side of the main mast, Clove stood silent.

There were fourteen of us in all, so the only thing that made sense was to put four or five dredgers on each of the reefs. I took a step forward, studying the Jevalis. They were a range of sizes and length of limb, but I could tell by looking at them who were the fastest swimmers. I also would have to split up the *Luna*'s dredgers if I wanted to keep them from pulling anything underwater.

The smart thing to do would be to have Koy head one of the groups. Whether I liked him or not, he was one of the most skilled dredgers I'd ever seen. He knew gems, and he knew reefs. But I'd made the mistake of letting him out of my sight before and I wasn't going to do it again.

I stopped before Ryland, lifting a chin to him and the Jevali at his side. "You two with me and Koy."

Koy arched one eyebrow up at me, suspicious. I didn't want to dive with him either, but as long as he was on this ship, I needed to know exactly where he was and what he was doing at all times.

I assigned the rest of them, putting together swimmers of varying body sizes in hopes that what one of them lacked, the others might make up for. When they were grouped together on the deck I turned back to the islet, unbuttoning the top of my shirt to pull it over my head. Koy's arm brushed against mine as he came to stand beside me and I stilled, putting more space between us.

"This bastard has no idea what he's doing," he muttered, running his thumb over the picks at his hip and counting them silently. The ones he'd plucked from the crate were shining bright between the rusted ones he'd used on Jeval.

I didn't answer, doing the same on my own belt. Koy and I weren't friends. We weren't even allies. If he was being nice, there was a reason, and one I wouldn't like.

"What? You're not going to talk to me?"

When I looked up into his face, I flinched at the sinister smile that stretched across his lips. "What are you doing here, Koy?"

He leaned into the rail with both hands and the muscles in his arms took shape under his skin. "I'm here to dive."

"What else?"

"That's it." He shrugged.

My eyes narrowed as I studied him. Koy had a skiff and a ferrying trade on Jeval that put coin in his pocket every single day. He was likely the wealthiest dredger on the island, and in the time I'd known him, he'd never once left Jeval. He was after something.

"Come on, Fay. We Jevalis have to stick together." He grinned.

I squared my shoulders to him, stepping so close I had to tilt my head back to meet his eyes. "I'm not Jevali. Now, get in the water."

"Urchins," Wick muttered, moving around us.

Ryland followed on his heels, leaning over me as he hung his shirt on the mast. I had to step back to keep him from touching me. I knew exactly what he was doing. Even if I had the charge from Zola, he wanted me to know who held the power between us. I was no match for him. For any of them, really. And no one on this ship was going to have my back if it came to that.

I felt small beneath him, and that feeling made my stomach turn.

"Better watch yourself down there. Tides are fickle." The look in Ryland's eyes didn't change as he said the words. He climbed up onto the side and jumped, holding his tools in place as he fell through the air. A moment later, Wick jumped in behind him, and they both disappeared beneath the sparkling blue.

Koy watched him surface, his face expressionless. "You're not going to take your eyes off me, are you?" The dark humor bled into the words as he climbed up, and I followed.

I waited for him to step into the air before I sucked in a breath and jumped, crashing into the cold water beside him. The rush of bubbles raced over my skin toward the surface above and my eyes lit with the sting of salt as I turned in a circle, trying to get my bearings. The reef below snaked in a tangled labyrinth, deepening the farther it pulled from the islet in the distance.

Clusters of fish in every color swarmed the crests, catching the light with iridescent scales and rippling fins. The coral was heaped like the domes of an otherworldly palace, some of which I'd never seen before.

We were definitely out of the Narrows now. But the songs of the gemstones were something I knew. They bled together in the water around me and once I began to unravel them from one another, we could get to work.

I broke the surface, sucking in the air and rubbing the salt from my eyes. I could taste it in the back of my throat. "Start on the deeper end of each ridge. We'll use our strength in the first half of the day and can work the shallower crests in the afternoon. The same tomorrow, so mark your tracks. And watch that south side. It looks like the current wraps around the tip of the reef there."

Two of the Jevali dredgers answered with a nod and started their breathing, pulling in the air to fill their chests and squeezing it back out. Koy did the same, tying his hair back, and I kicked against the weight of my belt as I worked my lungs.

The familiar stretch behind my ribs, surrounded by the sound of the dredgers' breath, made me shiver. It was too like my memories of diving the reefs on Jeval and the crippling fear that had followed me in those years.

It wasn't until I stepped foot on the *Marigold* that I felt it lift from me.

I slipped my fingers into the neck of my shirt, pulling West's ring from inside the collar. It sat in the center of my palm, glinting in the sunlight. We were well out of the Narrows, and I could feel the distance like a taut string between me and the *Marigold*.

I pushed the air from my chest, the amber light of West's quarters illuminating in the back of my mind. He tasted like rye and sea wind, and the sound that woke in his chest when my fingertips dragged over his ribs made that night come back to life inside of me.

My breath hitched as I pulled it in and I tipped my head back, taking a last sip of air. And before the thought of him could curl like a fist in my chest, I dove.

SIX

The deck of the *Luna* shimmered with moonlight as we stood shoulder to shoulder in the wind, dripping seawater. Clove was perched on a stool with our hauls organized before him, weighing the stones one at a time and calling out the weights to Zola's coin master, who recorded them in the ledger opened over his lap.

Clove set a raw, bulbous piece of garnet onto the brass scale, leaning forward and squinting to read the dial by lantern light. "Half."

Beside me, Koy let out a satisfied grunt.

I wasn't surprised at his haul. I had often wondered if he'd been taught by a gem sage because he knew how to read the shape of the rock beneath the coral and how to find the crests with the most concentrated stones. I'd be lying if I said I hadn't become a better dredger by watching him on the reefs. But when he started his ferrying business to the barrier islands nearly two years ago, he hadn't needed to dive like the rest of us.

Ryland shook his head bitterly, his jaw clenched. His haul hadn't even registered in the top five. Neither had Wick's. No wonder Zola was looking for a new dredger the day I met him in Dern.

Koy had hit over seven carats and he'd probably do it again tomorrow. He was stronger than me and could hit the mallet in heavier strikes, which meant he needed fewer descents to loose the gems. And I wasn't complaining. He could have the extra coin for all I cared. The sooner we got the haul up, the sooner I could get back to the Narrows and find the *Marigold*.

"Get your gear dry. Supper's up." Clove stood from the stool, handing the scale to the coin master. "Fable." He said my name without looking at me, but his chin tipped up to the archway, signaling me to follow.

I slung my belt over my shoulder as I followed him into the wide breezeway. It was twice the size of the one on the *Marigold*. Work benches were bolted to the deck and walls, where three strykers were cleaning fish. The smell was washed clean by the smoky air pouring out of the helmsman's quarters.

Inside, Zola sat at his desk over a stack of maps, not bothering to look up when Clove set the ledger down before him.

The fragrant scent of the mullein in his pipe hovered in the rafters above us, swirling in the turn of air. The sight almost made me feel as if Saint was there in the cabin with us.

Zola finished what he was writing before he set down the quill and began to read the coin master's ledgers. "So?" he asked, glancing up at me from the page.

I stared at him. "So?"

"I need a report on the dive." His chair creaked as he leaned back, taking the pipe from where it was clenched in his teeth. He held it before him, and the leaves smoldered in the chamber, sending another weak stream of smoke into the air.

"It's right there." The words thinned as my eyes landed on the open book.

He smirked. "*You* led the dive." He slid the ledger toward me. "I want to hear it from you."

I looked to Clove, unsure what Zola wanted. But he only stared at me as if he was waiting for the same answer. I pulled in a long breath through gritted teeth, taking the few steps between me and the desk before I let my belt slide from my shoulder. It landed on the floor hard, the tools clattering together.

"Fine." I picked up the ledger, holding it before me. "Twenty-four carats emerald, thirty-two carats tourmaline, twenty-one carats garnet. Twenty-five and one-half green abalone, thirty-six carats quartz, and twenty-eight carats bloodstone. There are also three pieces of opal, but they're not viable. Might be worth something in trade, but not for coin." I shut the book with a snap, dropping it back onto the desk.

Zola watched me through the haze trailing up from the whalebone pipe. "How'd they do?"

"The dredgers?" My brow pulled.

He gave me a nod.

"I just told you."

His elbows hit the desk and he propped himself up on them. "I mean how'd they *do*. Any problems?"

I glowered at him, irritated. "You're paying me to lead the dives, not report on the dredgers."

Zola pursed his lips, thinking. After a moment, he opened the drawer of his desk and set a small purse on the pile of maps. He fished out five coppers and stacked them before me. "Now I'm paying you for both." I watched the lift of his mouth. The sharpening of his eyes. He was still playing his game. But I still didn't know the rules to it.

Reporting on the other dredgers was the best way to get yanked from my hammock and thrown overboard in the middle of the night. "No thanks," I said flatly.

From the corner of my eye, I thought I could see Clove shift on his feet, but both of his boots were planted side by side, unmoving.

"All right," Zola conceded, scooting his chair up. "We need to hit double those numbers tomorrow."

"Double?" The word leapt from my mouth, too loud.

That got his attention. Both of his eyebrows lifted as he studied me. "Double," he said again.

"That's not what you said. There's no way we can hit that."

"That was before I knew I had such a competent dredger

to lead the dive. I didn't expect you to hit these numbers in a day." He shrugged, pleased with himself.

"It's not possible," I said again.

"Then none of you are getting back to the Narrows."

I set my jaw, willing my face to stay composed. The worst mistake I could make with Zola was letting him shake me. I *had* to get back to my ship. It was all that mattered.

I blinked. When had I begun thinking of the *Marigold* as mine? My home.

But if I didn't find a way to get the upper hand, that was never going to happen. "I know what you're doing."

"You do?"

"You let me loose in the crew's cabin when they all know what happened to Crane. You put me in charge of the dive instead of your own dredgers. You want someone else to get rid of me before we ever make port."

"So, you *were* there when West killed Crane." Zola lifted his brows in revelation. "I wouldn't have pegged you for a murderer. And it wasn't my idea to put you in charge." His attention instantly went to Clove.

I turned to look at him, but Clove was unreadable. His eyes were as empty as a night sky as they stared back into mine. And that was a different kind of threat.

He and Zola were on a tight schedule. One they couldn't afford to break. I was Saint's daughter, sure. But if they wanted to use me against my father, why take me out of the Narrows? There was something more valuable about me than that.

Clove knew what I could do with the gems, and for the

first time I considered *that* was why I was here. Not only to dredge, but to find the gems they needed for whatever they were planning.

"What are you going to do with them?" I asked Zola the question, but my gaze was still pinned on Clove.

Zola half-smiled. "With what?"

"Why is a ship that's licensed to trade in the Narrows sailing under a fake crest and dredging reefs in the Unnamed Sea without a permit?"

His head tilted to one side, surveying me.

"You've dumped your inventory, abandoned your route, and everyone knows that big gem trader in Bastian wants your head."

"And?"

"And it begs the question. What are you going to do with over three hundred carats of gemstones?"

Zola turned the pipe over and tapped it against the bronze bowl at the corner of the desk, emptying its ashes. "Join my crew and maybe I'll tell you." He stood, rolling up the maps.

I glared at him.

"What's it to you? You'd be trading one bastard helmsman for another."

"West is nothing like you," I said.

Zola nearly laughed. "Looks like you don't know your helmsman very well after all." He clicked his tongue.

A chill ran up my spine. That's what Saint said when I saw him in Dern.

"Sorry to be the bearer of bad news, Fable, but West has spilled enough blood to paint the *Marigold* red."

"You're a liar."

He threw up his hands in mock surrender as he came around the desk and found his seat at the table. "You sure you don't want to join me for supper?" The tip of the fork hit the rim of the plate as he picked it up, and that ghoulish, morbid grin returned to his face.

I picked up my belt and started toward the door. Clove didn't move out of my way until I was stopped in front of him, standing so close I could touch him. My mouth didn't open, but I cast every ounce of hatred within me upon him. I let it roll off me in waves until I could see the set of his mouth falter. He stepped to the side and I reached for the latch, flinging the door open and letting it slam against the wall as I left.

I fit the belt back around my waist and tightened it, taking the steps up to the quarterdeck, where Koy was sitting with his legs hanging over the stern. A bowl of steaming stew was clutched in his hands, his hair drying in waves down his back. When he saw me, his brow creased.

I didn't know what had brought Koy onto the *Luna,* and I didn't care. But there was one thing about him I knew I could count on. I stepped on the heel of my boots to slide them off.

He dropped his spoon into the bowl. "What the hell are you doing?"

I checked my tools again, my finger catching on the tip of the chisel. "We have to double today's haul before sundown tomorrow if we're going to get paid."

He stiffened, looking from me to the water. "You're going back in?"

The moon was almost full and its pale light rippled on the calm water around us. As long as the clouds didn't blow in, I could stay in the shallows and work the rock closest to the surface. It would be slow going, but there weren't enough hours of daylight to hit the quota Zola had set.

When he didn't move, I tried again. "I think I can hit those twenty carats before dawn."

He measured me for a moment, his black eyes shining before he groaned, taking his belt from where he'd dropped it on the deck. A moment later we were both back up on the railing. Down on the main deck, Ryland was watching us.

Koy looked over my head, eyeing him. "You watching that one?" he muttered under his breath.

"Oh yeah," I breathed. In the hours since we dropped anchor, I'd felt Ryland's attention on me nearly every time I stood on deck, and I was becoming less convinced Zola's orders to the crew would hold long enough for me to get off his ship alive.

I jumped, and the cold air whipped around me before I plunged into the water, every muscle in my legs burning with fatigue. Koy came up behind me when I broke the surface and we didn't speak as we filled up with breath. The milk-white moon hovered above the horizon, where it was rising at a slow, steady pace.

"I thought you said you weren't Jevali," he said, breaking the silence between us.

"I'm not," I spat.

He arched an eyebrow knowingly, a smirk changing the composition of his face. I'd never admit it, but the most honest part of me knew what he meant. Getting back into the dark water after an entire day of diving was insane. It was something a Jevali would do. That's why I'd known that Koy would come with me.

Whether I liked it or not, there were pieces of me that had been carved by those years on Jeval. It had changed me. In a way, it had made me.

He grinned, reading my thoughts, and gave me a wink before he sank under the surface. In another breath, I followed.

SEVEN

I pulled the mallet through the water and brought it down, hitting the top of the chisel squarely as Koy's shadow moved over me. I could barely feel the burn in my chest anymore, my mind giving way to a wandering train of thought. Memories strung together in unraveling stitches as my hands worked the sunlit rock in a practiced pattern.

I was diving the salty waters of the Unnamed Sea, but in my mind I was standing barefoot on the hot deck of the *Marigold*. Auster at the top of the main mast with a cloud of seabirds around him. The threads of gold lighting in Willa's hair.

West.

Again and again, my mind found its way to him.

It wasn't until the mallet slipped from my numb fingers that I blinked and the reef came rushing back to me. The blue swallowed up the vision, a twist behind my ribs threatening to pull me to the black. I found one of the iron anchors driven into the reef and held on, pinching my eyes closed. The ping of Koy's pick down the ridge sharpened my thoughts enough for me to realize I needed air. He stilled, looking up at me over the waving fronds of red coral for only a moment before he got back to work. There was probably nothing Koy would love more than to see me dead on this reef.

I slipped the mallet back into my belt and pushed off the ledge, kicking toward the light. The reef, and the dredgers on it, grew small beneath me until I broke the surface with a ragged gasp, my vision washed white in the glare of the sun. It hung in the middle of the sky above me, but I couldn't feel its warmth as I drank in the humid air. My skin was ice cold, the blood moving slowly in my veins.

Clove's face appeared over the railing of the *Luna,* and as soon as he laid eyes on me, he vanished again. I squinted, thinking that maybe I had imagined him there. The light was too bright, pulling in glaring beams that splintered and glowed, making my head hurt.

It had been a long night, dredging in the moonlight until it was too dark to see the reef. I'd gotten only an hour or two of sleep before the bell on the deck was ringing again, and I was back in the water by the time the sun appeared on the horizon.

I hooked one arm into the lowest rung of the rope ladder

and untied the purse from my belt with a shaking hand. As soon as it landed in the basket hanging against the hull, the Waterside stray above was hoisting it up for Clove's count.

I stayed there and breathed, willing the feeling to come back into my weak arms. I needed to get my body warm if I was going to keep diving, but the piece of bloodstone I was working on in the reef was almost loose. Three more strikes and I'd have it free.

A splash sounded behind me, and I looked back to see Ryland surface, the sound of his broad chest taking in the air like the howl of wind. He panted, pulling it in and out until it was steady, his face turned up to the sun.

I watched him swim to the ship and set his purse into the next basket. It instantly lifted, dripping as it rose. When the deckhand at the railing fished the haul from inside, he tossed it into the air and caught it again, feeling its weight. "Little light there, Ryland," he said, laughing.

Ryland gave the boy a tight smile, the red beneath his skin blooming. It was one thing to know other dredgers were better than you. It was another for your crew to know it. I wondered if Ryland's place on the *Luna* was becoming just as precarious as mine was.

His burning gaze found me, and I turned away, calling up to the ship. "I need a line!" My voice was hoarse from the burn of salt.

The Waterside stray appeared over the side of the *Luna* again, giving me a nod, and I pressed my forehead into the wet ropes, closing my eyes. My stomach was sour from swallowing the seawater, and the blisters on my hands had all re-opened. But if I wanted to get back to the Narrows, I couldn't afford for this haul to be even one carat short.

The rope landed in the water beside me and I hooked it over my shoulder as I let go of the ladder. My chest was sore when I drew the breath back in, my bruised bones screaming. One more. Then I'd rest. Then I'd climb back up onto the sun-warmed deck and let the trembling in my limbs slow.

I gulped in a last full breath and plunged back under, going still so that I could let myself sink slowly and save as much energy as possible. Koy was coming up again, kicking toward the surface for air, and a stream of bubbles trailed up as he passed me. By the time my feet came down on the reef, he was a fleeting silhouette against the sunlight above.

Floating arms of pink coral pulled into their burrows and fish scattered frantically into the blue as I scaled downward to find the iron anchor. I could tell by the pinch in the center of my throat that the air wasn't going to last long. My body was too tired to regulate it properly, but I could save some of my strength by letting the rope tether me to the reef. This was exactly the point my mother would have told me to get out of the water. And I would. Once I had the bloodstone in my hand.

I threaded the end of the rope through the hold and secured it with a knot before I took the other end and tied it around my waist. The rope was stiff with salt, making it less likely to slip.

The half-dredged gem was the color of sun-dried algae baking on the beach, shining where it was exposed beneath the rock. The voice of the bloodstone was one of the first I'd learned to recognize when my mother began to teach me. Like the soft hum of a familiar tune.

She said stones like that had to be coaxed from the reef. That they wouldn't just answer to anyone.

I took the mallet from my belt and chose the largest pick. If I wasn't short on time, I'd be more careful, using the smallest tools to keep from damaging the edges, but Zola would have to settle for what he got.

I adjusted my angle, working at the corner with quick taps, and when the scrape of rock reverberated around me, I turned, looking up the reef. The dredger working the other end with Ryland had kicked up from an overhang, swimming to the surface.

I hit the chisel again, and the crust of basalt cracked and clouded around me as it fell to the seafloor below. I waited for it to clear before I drifted close, examining the stone's edges. It was larger than I'd expected, the coloring pocked with a crude stripe of bright crimson.

The creak of rock sounded again, and I lifted myself up over the ridge, watching the reef. It was empty. I was only faintly aware of the tingle that crept over my numb skin, the echo of a thought in the back of my mind before the feeling of weight tugged at my hip.

I whirled, the chisel clutched in my hand like a knife before me, and my lips parted when the warmth of him bled through the water. Ryland. He yanked hard at my belt, sliding his knife between my tools and my hip, sawing. I kicked as the belt broke free and fell to the seafloor, trying to push him back. But he pinned me with one hand around my throat, holding me to the reef.

I clawed at his fingers, screaming under water, and the cutting sting of coral sliced into my leg as I thrashed. Ryland looked into my face, watching the air bubble from my lips. The sharp tinge of fear raced over my body, reawakening the cold skin and bringing the heat back into my face.

He was waiting for my lungs to empty. He was trying to drown me.

I pressed my lips together, willing my heart to slow before I burned through the last bit of my air. He had himself wedged against the rock, holding me in place with his weight. No amount of kicking was going to shift him. I searched above us for a shadow. For anyone who might be able to see. But there was only the shimmer of light on the surface.

I watched helplessly as my hold loosened on him, and a desperate cry broke in my chest. My hands couldn't move. I could hardly even bend my fingers.

Ryland's eyes flickered over my head to the reef. His grip clamped down harder before he suddenly let me go and kicked off the outcropping. I watched him disappear over me, and I launched myself from the rock, carving through the water as fast as I could. I kicked, watching the light on the surface spread as the darkness of my mind pushed forward.

Forty more feet.

My arms slowed, the resistance of the water heavier each time my heart beat in my chest.

Thirty feet.

A sharp jerk stopped me, throwing my arms and legs forward, and my mouth opened, letting the cold water pour down my throat.

The rope. It was still tied around my waist. Anchored to the reef below.

I screamed, panicked. The last of my air rippled up in strands of bubbles as my hands raced to the knot, pulling weakly at the tight fibers. When it wouldn't budge, I reached around my back for my knife. But it was gone. My belt was at the foot of the ridge.

Inky darkness flooded my mind as my chest caved in, my stomach turning. I tried to shift the rope over my hips, but it was no use. Below, a dark head of hair peeked up over the reef, and Koy's black eyes looked up at me.

Blood trailed up before me in ribbons, floating like threads of smoke, and I suddenly felt lighter. Empty. The ache in my chest disappeared, leaving my insides hollow.

There was only the heartbeat pounding in my ears as I looked down at my leg, cut in a single bloody stripe. The shadow wrapped itself around me, folding my mind within it, and when it came, I let it swallow me whole.

EIGHT

Breathe!"

The roaring voice tore me from the deep. A sting lit on my cheek and a sound rattled in my throat.

"Breathe!"

My eyes cracked open just enough to see a man's face before me, darkened in the shadow of the ship's hull beside us. A face that only pulled the faintest recognition. A deckhand. His gray eyes ran over me, but I couldn't move. I couldn't draw a breath.

His hand rose up out of the water, lifting into the air, and came down again. He slapped me across the face and my chest exploded in pain as I gasped, swallowing the air and choking on the warm seawater in my mouth. The blurry edges of my vision came together, and the world around me focused, filling me with panic. I leapt for the rope beside me, hooking my arm around it to keep me above the water.

"Get her up!" The deckhand's voice rang painfully in my ears.

And then I was moving. The crank on the deck of the *Luna* screeched and clicked, pulling me up with it, and the weight of my body made me slip down the wet rope until I wrapped my legs around its length.

When I looked up, Clove was watching from the quarterdeck, and I blinked when he wavered, the world turning on its side. I coughed until my lungs ached and he came down the steps two at a time, landing on the deck beside me.

"What happened?"

But I couldn't speak. I fell to my knees, retching the saltwater from my belly until there was nothing left. A pool of warm red crept over the wood slats, touching my hand, and I looked down to my leg, remembering the blood in the water. The gash from the coral was still bleeding.

I sat back heavily, opening the torn skin with my fingers to inspect it. It wasn't deep enough to see bone, but it needed to be closed. Another wave of nausea washed over me and I fell back onto the hot deck, running my hands through my hair and trying to remember what had just happened.

The crew of the *Luna* stood around me, staring, but Ryland was nowhere to be seen, probably still cowering on the reef and waiting to find out if I was going to snitch.

Koy came over the railing a moment later, landing with two heavy feet beside the foremast.

"What happened?" Clove said again, taking a step toward him.

But Koy was looking at me, and I put together the question in his eyes. He was playing by the rules of Jeval, waiting to see what I'd say first before he answered.

"I ran out of air," I said hoarsely. My throat was on fire. "Lost my belt and couldn't cut myself from the line I anchored to the reef." I glanced back to Koy.

Clove followed my gaze to him, his mustache twitching. "Who saw it?" He turned in a circle, watching the faces of the other dredgers on the deck. But no one answered.

"What do you care?" I snapped, getting back to my feet. I steadied myself against the mizzen, breathing through the urge to retch again.

The knotted rope was still heavy on my hips, the length of it trailing over the side and disappearing into the water. I pulled, winding it up until the end fell onto the deck, and I crouched to pick it up. The fibers were sliced cleanly, not frayed.

It was the work of a blade.

I stood, the rope clutched in my hand as I looked to the bow. Koy's eyes dropped to the deck and he turned, fitting his belt back around him. The last thing I'd seen before I blacked out was his face, peering up over the reef. If I didn't know better, I'd think that he'd cut me loose.

I snatched a knife from the belt of a dredger standing next to me and sawed at the rope around my waist. One of the strykers came up the steps from belowdecks with a tin box of needle and thread in one hand, a bottle of rye in the other.

He reached out to steady me, but I tore my arm away. "Don't touch me," I snarled, snatching them from his hands and pushing past him to the archway.

I could feel the stares of the crew pinned to my back as I limped down the stairs, leaning into the wall to stay on my feet. I took a lantern from the hook and moved down the passage until I made it to the cargo hold, the tears lighting in my eyes as soon as I was cloaked in the darkness. I sniffed, willing the pain in my chest to stay put. I wasn't going to let them hear me cry.

My leg stung, but it was nothing a few stitches couldn't fix, and more importantly, it wouldn't keep me from diving. I'd seen worse.

I closed the door and sat on an empty crate, moving the lantern close to me before I uncorked the rye. I pulled a deep breath in and let it go before I poured it over the wound. A growl erupted in my throat as I clenched my teeth. The burn shot up my leg, finding my belly, and the urge to vomit returned, making me feel dizzy.

I brought the bottle to my lips and drank, welcoming the warmth in my chest. Another second or two under water, and I wouldn't have taken another breath. I wouldn't have woken.

The passageway outside the door was silent and dark. I stared at the ground, trying to remember what I'd seen. The only two people on that reef were Koy and Ryland. And the look in Ryland's eyes when he wrapped his hand around my throat had been clear. He'd wanted me dead.

That meant that Koy had cut the rope. That he'd saved my life. But that couldn't be true.

I threaded the needle with trembling hands and pinched the deepest part of the cut together. The needle went through my skin without so much as a prick, and I was grateful that I was still so cold I could barely feel it.

"Through and over. Through again." I found my lips moving around the words silently, the tears falling from the tip of my nose as I worked.

Clove had taught me to stitch a wound when I was a girl. He'd cut himself on a grappling hook and when he caught me spying on him on the quarterdeck, he demanded that I sit and learn.

"Through again." I whispered.

The wide cargo hold seemed to close in, making me feel small in the darkness as one crystal clear memory surfaced after the other. My father at his desk. My mother lining up the gemstones on the table before me.

Which are the fakes?

The first time I got it right, she took me to the top of the mainmast and we screamed into the wind.

I stared into the dark, watching the image of her twist in the shadows. The shape of her moved with a bend of light coming from the deck, flickering like a lantern's flame. She was a ghost. And for a moment, I thought that maybe I was too. That I was existing in some in-between space where Isolde had been waiting for me. That maybe I hadn't made it out of the water. That I'd died with the cold sea in my lungs.

In that moment, I wanted my mother. I wanted her the way I had as a little girl, waking from a nightmare. In all the years on Jeval and in the time since, I'd hardened the way Saint wanted me to. I'd become something not easily broken. But as I sat there stitching up my leg, a quiet cry escaping my lips, I felt young. Fragile. More than that, I felt alone.

I wiped at my slick cheek with the back of my blood-ied hand and made another stitch. The creak of floorboards sounded and I raised the lantern. Beneath the closed door, the shadow of two feet broke the light. I watched the latch, waiting for it to lift, but a moment later, the shadow disap-peared.

I drew a few steadying breaths, taking West's ring into my hand and squeezing. It had been six days since the morn-ing I climbed down the ladder of the *Marigold* in Dern. Five nights since I'd slept in his bed. Willa, Paj, Auster, Hamish. Their faces were illuminated hazily in my mind. They were followed by Saint's. I swallowed, remembering him in the tavern in Dern, a teacup in his hand. I would have given any-thing to see him in that moment. Even if he was cold. Even if he was cruel.

I tied off the last stitch and poured the rest of the rye over the wound, inspecting my work. It wasn't the cleanest of stitches and it would leave a nasty scar, but it would do.

I stood, dropping the bottle. It rolled across the cargo hold as I took up the lantern and walked back to the door. I lifted my chin as I pulled it open and stepped into the empty passageway. When I came back up onto the deck, the deckhand whose voice I'd woken to was watching me with wide eyes from where he stood before the helm.

I shoved the lantern into his hands. "I need a new belt."

He looked confused.

"A belt," I repeated, impatient.

He hesitated, looking to Clove, who was still perched on the stool, weighing stones. I could have sworn I saw him smirk before he gave the deckhand a nod.

The boy shuffled belowdecks, leaving me there shivering in the wind. Seawater still dripped from my hair, hitting the deck beside my feet. When I looked up, Koy was watching me from the bow, where he was fishing a new pick from the crate.

I stalked toward him, trying to hide the limp in my gait. "Why did you do that?"

"Do what?" He slipped the pick into his belt.

"You . . ." I said, my words uneven. "You cut the rope."

Koy laughed, but it was thin. "I don't know what you're talking about."

I stepped closer to him, lowering my voice. "Yes, you do."

Koy scanned the deck around. He towered over me as he looked into my face, his black eyes meeting mine. "I didn't cut the rope."

He shoved past me as the boy returned with a belt full of

tools. I wound it around me, fastening the buckle tightly. A hush fell over the deck as I stepped up onto the anchor crank and balanced on the side of the ship with one foot. I stood against the wind, looking down at the rippling blue below. And before I could think twice, I jumped.

NINE

The distant ring of a harbor bell found me deep beneath the surface of a dream painted with honey-gold ships, winged sails, and the sound of strung adder stones clinking in the wind.

My eyes opened to pitch black.

The crew's cabin was silent except for the rake of snores and the creak of the trunks as the *Luna* slowed. My hand frantically searched for my knife as I sat up, unfolding my legs from the fabric and letting my toes touch the cool floor.

I hadn't meant to fall asleep. I'd watched Ryland's hammock above me in the dark until he was still, and though my

eyes were heavy and my bones ached, I'd been determined to
stay awake in case he decided to finish what he started.

On the other side of the cabin Koy was still sleeping, one
of his hands hanging from the canvas and nearly touching
the ground. I stood, breathing through the pain in my leg,
and felt along the floor for my boots. When I had them on, I
opened the door, slipping into the passageway.

I followed the wall with my hand until I reached the
stairs, peering up to the patch of gray sky above.

Zola's voice was already calling out orders as I stepped
onto the deck. I wrapped my arms around myself when the
chill in the air made me shiver. The *Luna* was enveloped in
a bright white fog so thick I could feel the caress of it on my
face.

"Slow, slow!" Voices shouted in the mist and Clove tilted
his head, listening before he turned the helm just slightly.

I went to the rail, watching the swirling mist. I could hear
the dockworkers, but the slip didn't appear until we were
only feet away. At least a dozen sets of hands were reaching
out, ready to catch the hull before it scraped.

"There now!" the voice called again as the ship stopped,
both anchors dropping into the water with a staggered
smack.

Clove stepped around me to unroll the ladder and Zola
appeared a moment later, his coin master on his heels.

Only the black, spindly crests of rooftops were visible,
poking up out of the fog like reeds in a pond. But none of
them looked familiar.

"Where are we?" I asked, waiting for Zola to look at me.

He pulled his gloves on methodically, tugging until his fingers were tight in the leather. "Sagsay Holm."

"Sagsay Holm?" My voice rose and I squared my shoulders to him, my mouth dropping open. "You said we were going back to the Narrows."

"No, I didn't."

"Yes, you did."

He leaned into the mizzen, eyeing me patiently. "I said that I needed your help. And we're not finished yet."

"I brought up that haul in two days," I growled. "We met the quota."

"You brought up the haul, and now it's time to turn it over," he said simply.

I cursed under my breath. That's why we were in Sagsay Holm. Turning the haul over meant commissioning a gem merchant to clean and cut the stones to get them ready for trade. "I didn't agree to that."

"You didn't *agree* to anything. You're on my ship and you'll do what you're told if you want to get back to Ceros." He leaned in close to me, daring me to argue.

"You bastard." I gritted my teeth, muttering.

He swung a leg over the side and caught the ladder with his boot, climbing down.

"You're with me." Clove's grating voice sounded beside me.

I turned on him. "What?"

He pushed a locked chest into my hands, throwing a hand to motion to the rail. "You're coming with me," he said again.

"I'm not going anywhere with you."

"You can stay on the ship with them if you want." He tipped a chin up to the quarterdeck, where several members of the crew were watching me. "Your call."

I sighed, staring into the fog. If no one was on the ship to make sure Zola's orders were followed, there was no telling what would happen. Koy had saved my neck once, but something told me he wouldn't do it again if it came down to him and me against an entire crew.

I could see in Clove's eyes that he knew I didn't have a choice. "Where are we going?"

"I need you to make sure the merchant doesn't try to pull anything with the haul. I don't trust these Saltbloods."

I shook my head, smirking incredulously. He wanted a gem sage to make sure the merchants didn't swap any stones. "I'm not my mother." Isolde had begun to teach me the art of the gem sage before she died, but I'd needed many more years of apprenticeship if I was ever going to have her skill.

Something changed on Clove's face then, and it made my fingers curl tighter around the handles of the heavy chest. "Better than nothing." The tone of his voice had changed too, and I wondered if the mention of my mother had gotten beneath his skin.

I took a chance in saying it. "You know Isolde would hate you, right?" I took a step toward him.

He didn't blink as I looked him in the eye, but the courage I'd had flickered out the moment I invoked her name. He wasn't the only one who wasn't immune to Isolde's memory. It snaked around me and squeezed.

Clove's hands slid into the pockets of his jacket. "Get on that dock. Now."

I looked at him for another moment before I shoved the chest back into his hands and pulled the hood of my jacket up. I said nothing as I climbed over the rail and down the ladder into a crowd of dockworkers on the slip. Zola stood at the edge before the harbor master, unfolding a parchment with the fake crest imprinted at its corner. I watched the man closely, wondering if he would catch it. Sailing under a false crest was a crime that would get you barred from stepping foot on another ship for as long as you lived.

The harbor master scribbled into his book, double checking the document before he closed it. "I don't like unscheduled ships on this dock," he grunted.

"We'll be in and out. Just need a few supplies before we get to Bastian," Zola said, his manner civil and cool.

The harbor master was ready to argue, but a moment later Zola pulled a small purse from the pocket of his jacket, holding it between them. The harbor master looked over his shoulder to the main dock before he took it without another word.

Clove landed on the dock beside me, and Zola gave him a nod before he started toward the village. I followed on Clove's heels, weaving in and out of the hucksters and shipwrights until we made it to the street.

The cobblestones were wide and flat, unlike the round ones in Ceros, but more than that, they were clean. Not a single smear of mud or even a pile of discarded harbor supplies lay on the street, and the windows of every building sparkled.

The mist was beginning to thin in the brightening sunlight, and I looked up to the redbrick buildings as we passed. Round windows were set into their faces, reflecting Clove and me as we passed. It was a familiar scene, the two of us. One that I didn't want to look at.

I'd heard almost nothing about the port town of Sagsay Holm except that my father had been here a few times when the Trade Council of the Narrows met with the Trade Council of the Unnamed Sea. Back then, he'd been playing hand after hand to get a license to trade in these waters. Whatever he'd done to finally make it happen probably wasn't legal, but in the end, he'd gotten what he wanted.

Clove shouldered through the crowd and I stayed close, following in the wake of his steps. He seemed to know exactly where he was going, taking turn after turn without looking at the hand-painted signs that marked the streets and alleys. When he finally stopped, we were standing beneath a faceted, circular window. The panes were fit together like a puzzle, reflecting the deepening blue of the sky behind us.

Clove shifted the chest beneath one arm and reached up to tap the brass knocker. The sound of it echoed with a ping around us, but it was quiet behind the door, the window dark. When he knocked again, it suddenly opened.

A small woman clad in a worn leather apron stood before us. Her face was flushed red, a bit of dark hair sticking to her wide forehead. "Yes?"

"Looking to turn over," Clove answered, not mincing words.

"All right." She let the door swing open, pulling a stack of papers from the pocket of her apron. Her nose scrunched until her spectacles fell into place. "We're a little tight this week."

"I need them today."

Her hands froze, and she looked at him over the rim of her spectacles before she laughed. "Not possible." When he said nothing, she set one hand on her hip. "Look, we have a *schedule*—"

"I understand." Clove was already reaching into his jacket. He pulled out a sizable purse, holding it out without a word. "For the trouble." When her eyes narrowed, he pushed it toward her. "In addition to the fee, of course."

She seemed to think about that, her mouth twisting up on one side.

It was one of many purses I'd seen him and Zola pull from their pockets, and I was beginning to wonder if Zola had wagered his entire fortune on this venture. He was clearly in a hurry, and he was willing to take chances. What required a two-day dive and a rush turnover in Sagsay Holm? He'd risen a fake crest over the *Luna* and whatever documents he used to make port had to be forgeries. What could possibly be worth losing his trade license?

The woman hesitated for another breath before she finally took the purse and disappeared in the doorway. Clove climbed the steps, following her inside, and I closed the door behind us.

Immediately, the hum of gemstone woke in the air. The deep reverberation of carnelian and the high-pitched song of amber. The low and steady buzz of onyx. The sounds pressed around me like the pressure of water on a dive.

She led us to a small sitting room lit only by a large window.

"Tea?" The woman pulled the apron over her head and hung it on the wall. "It's going to be a while."

Clove answered with a nod and she opened a sliding door, where a man was sitting at a wooden table in the workshop.

"It's a rush." She dropped the purse onto the wooden table and he looked up, eyeing us through the open door.

The woman leaned over the table, speaking too low for us to hear, and the man set the piece of quartz he was working on into the box in front of him. The stone in his merchant's ring flashed. The metal was worn and scraped, which meant he'd been a merchant for some time.

I took the seat beside the cold fireplace so I had a good view of him. It wasn't unheard of for low-level gem merchants to make swaps here and there when they cleaned and cut hauls. It was one of a few ways fakes made it into the gem trade.

He cleared the table quickly, looking us up and down. "You just come from the Narrows?"

A teapot lid clinked on the other side of the wall.

"We did," Clove answered, clearly suspicious.

"You better not be bringing any of that trouble here," he grunted.

"What trouble?" I asked, but Clove gave me a sharp look as if to silence me.

"That business with the burning ships," the man said. "Was all I heard about yesterday at the merchant's house."

Clove's eyes drifted back to me.

"Some trader in the Narrows is going port to port, setting fire to ships. Looking for a vessel called the *Luna*."

I froze, my heart jumping up into my throat.

Saint. Or West. It had to be.

But West and the crew of the *Marigold* wouldn't be able to do anything so brazen without catching the Trade Council's retribution. If they were looking for me, they'd do it quietly. But ships burning at every port in the Narrows . . . that was something my father would do.

I let out a shaking breath. A timid smile lifted on my trembling lips, and I turned toward the window to brush a tear from the corner of my eye before Clove caught sight of me. He couldn't be surprised. He knew my father better than even I did.

I hadn't even let myself hope for it, but somehow I'd known deep down that he would come for me.

The man at the table opened the chest, and his eyes widened before he picked up the first stone—a piece of black tourmaline. He didn't waste any time, lowering the eyeglass and getting straight to work with a fine pick.

Clove sank into a chair beside the bricked fireplace across the room, setting one foot up onto his knee. "You going to tell me what happened on that dive yesterday?"

I kept my voice low, not taking my eyes off the merchant. "You going to tell me what Saint did to make you join up with Zola?" I could feel Clove's stare narrow on me. "That's what happened, right? Saint betrayed you somehow and you thought you'd get revenge. No one knows Saint's operation like you do, and no one else knows about the daughter he fathered. That makes you quite the prize for Zola."

The woman pushed back into the sitting room with a tray of tea, setting it on the low table with a clatter. She filled Clove's cup before she filled mine, but I only stared into it, watching the ripple of light on its surface.

"Anything else I can get you?"

Clove dismissed her with a flick of his hand, and she took the apron from the hook before making her way into the workshop. She sat across the table from the man, picking up the next stone on the pile.

"I saw Saint. In Ceros," I said. "He told me you were *gone*."

Clove brought the cup to his lips, sipping sharply.

"I thought that meant you were dead." The words fell heavy in the silent room.

"Well, I'm not."

I picked up the cup, following the vine of hand-painted flowers along the rim with the tip of my finger. "Can't help but think," I said, bringing it to my lips and meeting his eyes through the wisp of steam curling into the air between us, "you might as well be."

TEN

The deck of the *Luna* was washed in lantern light by the time we made it back to the ship.

Clove had me check the gems twice before we left the merchant, putting us well after sundown. They'd done a good job in the time they'd been given, so I didn't point out that a few of the edges and points weren't as sharp as they should be. Gems were gems. As long as they weighed out, I couldn't care less what they looked like.

"Make ready!" Sagsay Holm glittered behind us as Zola called out the orders and the crew snapped into rhythm, unleashing the ship from the harbor.

Three figures climbed the masts in lockstep, working the

lines to bring down the sheets, and before we'd even cleared the dock, the wind filled them into perfect white arcs against the black sky. The sails on the *Luna* made the ones on the *Marigold* seem small, and as soon as I thought it, I pushed the vision of the golden ship from my mind, ignoring the feeling that writhed inside me.

When the ship made it out of the bay, Zola murmured something under his breath to his navigator, and Clove dropped his hands from the helm and followed Zola into his quarters. The door closed behind them, and I studied the string of stars lifting up over the horizon. We were bearing north, not south.

I watched the shadows slide beneath the door of the helmsman's quarters, thinking. We were farther from the Narrows than I'd ever been. The Unnamed Sea was a thing painted in my mind by the bright colors of my mother's stories, but like the Narrows, it was filled with cutthroat traders, devious merchants, and powerful guilds. By the time Zola finished what he was doing, he'd probably be dead. And when the price for his sins was called in, I didn't want to be anywhere near the *Luna*.

I went up the steps to the quarterdeck and leaned over the stern. The ship carved a gentle wake in the sea below, folding the dark water into white foam. Calla was stowing the lines, watching me warily as she wound the ropes. When she was finished she took the steps down to the main deck, and I looked around me before I flung one leg over the rail.

The ornate carving of the *Luna*'s wooden hull rose and fell in sweeping waves around the window of the helmsman's quarters. I followed its shape with the toes of my boots, sliding across the stern until I could see the light from Zola's cabin slicing through the dark between the slats of closed shutters.

I reached up, finding the lip of the window, and held close to the ship so I could wedge myself against the wood. The candlelit room came into view, and I squinted, eyeing the mirror that hung beside the door. In its reflection I could see Clove standing beside the small wooden table in the corner, a green glass of rye clutched in his big hand.

Zola sat at the desk before him, looking over the ledgers carefully. "It's enough."

"How do you know?" Clove asked, his worn voice barely audible over the sound of the water rushing below.

"Because it has to be enough."

Clove answered with a silent nod, bringing the rye to his lips. The light glinted off the glass like a stone in a gem lamp.

Zola picked up the rye bottle. "What else?"

It took me a moment to realize that Clove was hesitating, staring into the corner of the room absently before he spoke. "There was talk in the village."

"Oh?" Zola's tone turned up, and when I caught his reflection in the mirror again, his face was lit in sly humor.

"Word reached Sagsay Holm yesterday that someone's going port to port in the Narrows." He paused. "Burning ships."

Zola paled, and I wasn't sure why. He had to know it wasn't safe to leave his fleet behind in the Narrows. Whatever had brought him to the Unnamed Sea had to have been worth it to him. His hand shook just enough to spill a little of the rye on the desk, but he didn't look up.

"*Your* ships, I suspect," Clove added.

My fingers clamped down harder on the sill of the window. "Saint?"

"West," Clove breathed.

My breath hitched, the swift flare of fear making me still. If West was burning ships in the Narrows, he was putting the *Marigold* and its crew at risk. He couldn't hide something like that from the Trade Council like Saint could.

"At least six ships gone," Clove said. "Several crew dead. Probably more by now."

I breathed through the sting lighting my eyes. Zola said that night in his quarters that West had enough blood on his hands to paint the *Marigold* red. I didn't want to believe it, but there was some small part of me that already did.

"It doesn't matter." Zola was doing a poor job of keeping his fury at bay. "Our future and our fortune both lie in Bastian."

"Bastian." My mouth moved around the word.

We weren't headed south because we weren't taking this haul back to the Narrows. The *Luna* was going to Bastian.

"I want every inch of this ship cleaned and polished before we dock, understand? Every set of hands better be working from the time the sun comes up to the moment I see land on the horizon. I'm not making port in Bastian looking like a Waterside stray," Zola muttered, taking the rye in one shot and pouring another.

Clove looked into his glass, swirling what was left of the amber spirit. "She'll know the moment we dock. She knows everything that happens in that harbor."

"Good." Zola smirked. "Then she'll be expecting us."

I studied Zola's face, confused. But slowly, the pieces began to fit together, the thoughts swirling in my mind before landing.

Holland.

He wasn't using the haul to start a new venture beyond the Narrows. Zola was paying a debt. For years, he hadn't been able to sail these waters without getting his throat cut by Holland. He'd finally found a way to make good with her, but how? Three hundred carats of gemstone was nothing to the most powerful gem trader in the Unnamed Sea.

Zola wasn't lying when he said that this wasn't about me or West. It wasn't even about Saint.

My fingers slipped on the dew-slicked frame and I caught myself on the shutter, clinging to the hull.

When I looked back up, Clove's eyes were on the window, and I held my breath, hidden in the darkness. His eyes narrowed, as if they were pinned on mine. He was stalking across the cabin in the next moment, and I swung back, pressing myself to the carving beside the window. The shutter swung open, slamming on the wood, and I watched his hand appear on the sill, the moonlight catching the gold ring on his finger. I tried not to move, the pain in my leg throbbing as I pushed the heel of my boot into the ledge to keep myself still.

But a moment later, the shutters closed, locking in place.

He hadn't seen me. He couldn't have seen me. But the beat of my heart faltered, my blood running hot.

I reached up, hauling myself back to the railing, and threw myself onto the quarterdeck. I raced to the steps and swung myself over them, landing on the deck with both feet, and the stitches in my thigh pulled, stinging. The men at the helm looked up at me wide-eyed as I walked to the passageway and slipped into the darkness.

The door to the helmsman's quarters was already opening, and I stepped around the light it painted on the deck before I made my way below. Footsteps sounded overhead as I ran down the hallway to the crew's cabin, weaving between the hammocks until I found the third row. Ryland was asleep and I ducked under him, not bothering with my boots as I sank back into the quilted fabric of my own hammock. I pulled my knees to my chest, shaking.

The shadows in the darkened doorway moved, and I found the knife at my belt, waiting. Zola had taken great care to hide what he was doing in the Unnamed Sea, and if he thought I'd found him out, there was no way he was letting me go back to the Narrows. There was no way he was going to let me leave this ship alive.

I stared into the darkness, clutching the knife against my chest as a figure took shape beneath the bulkhead. I squinted my eyes, trying to make it out. When a beam of light flashed over a head of silvery blond hair, I swallowed to keep from crying out.

Clove. He *had* seen me.

His shadow moved slowly through the hammocks, his footsteps silent as he crept closer. He peered into each one before he moved on, and when he made it to the next row, I pressed a hand over my mouth, trying to stay still. If I was quick enough, I could strike first. Drive the blade of my knife up into his gut before he could get his hands on me. But the thought made my stomach roil, a single tear rolling from the corner of my eye.

He was a bastard and he was a traitor. But he was still Clove.

I swallowed down a cry as he stopped at the hammock beside mine. Another step, and his legs were next to me as he looked into Ryland's hammock. He stopped then, and I lifted the knife, measuring the angle. If I stabbed him beneath the ribs, catching a lung, it would be enough to keep him from running after me. I hoped.

The blade shook as I lifted it, waiting for him to come low, but he wasn't moving. The glint of a knife shone in the darkness as Clove lifted his hands, reaching into Ryland's hammock. I went still, watching his face from below and trying not to breathe. But Clove's eyes were expressionless, the cool set of his mouth relaxed, his eyes soft.

The hammock shook above me and something hot hit my face. I flinched, reaching up to wipe it from my cheek, and another drop fell, hitting my arm. When I held my fingers to the light, I went still.

It was blood.

The hammock swung silently above me, and Clove sheathed his knife before he reached back up and heaved

Ryland from inside. I watched in horror as he took him onto his shoulder and his limp hands fell beside my face, swinging.

He was dead.

I didn't move as the sound of footsteps trailed to the door. Then he was gone, leaving the cabin quiet. As soon as the light stopped moving I sat up, staring into the black passageway, my eyes wide.

There was no sound except deep, sleeping breaths and the creak of swaying rope. The hushed hum of water against the hull. For a moment, I thought maybe I'd dreamed it. That I'd seen the work of spirits in the dark. I looked over my shoulder, searching the cabin, and froze when I saw him.

Koy was still in his hammock, his open eyes on me.

ELEVEN

I waited for the others to wake before I dared to move. I lay awake for hours in the dark, listening for the sounds of footsteps coming back down the passageway, but the ship had been quiet through the night until dawn summoned the first shift of crew.

I couldn't feel the tiredness that had pressed down on me the day before. I could hardly even feel the pain in my leg, where my skin was puckered and red around the stitches. Ryland was dead, and the comfort of relief unraveled the tension wound around me. I wasn't safe on the *Luna*, but Ryland was gone, and I didn't think Koy would be the one to kill me in my sleep.

The real question was what had happened last night, and why.

I scanned the deck before I came up the last few steps, instinctively looking for Ryland to be sure I hadn't dreamed it. Wick was up on the mizzen, replacing a grommet at the corner of a sail, the wind pulling his winding hair across his forehead. But there was no sign of Ryland.

At the bow, Clove was recording numbers in his log, and I studied the calm, unconcerned way he looked over the pages. It was the same look he had the night before, when I watched him take the knife to Ryland and haul his body from the cabin.

"Crew check!" the bosun called out, his voice echoing.

Everyone on deck grudgingly obeyed, leaving their work to line up against the port side. The last of the deckhands and dredgers came up from belowdecks, the sleep still dragging on their faces. I took my place at the end, watching the bosun look up from his book, marking names as he went.

"Where's Ryland?" He set his hands on his hips, gaze trailing over each of our faces.

I caught Koy's eyes across the deck. He didn't flinch.

"Bastard never got back on the ship last night." Clove grunted from behind him, his attention still on the logs.

My hands found each other behind my back, fingers tangling together. There was only one reason I could think of that Clove would go after Ryland, but it didn't make any sense. He'd been the one to tell Zola who I was. He'd pitted me against the crew. Why would he try to protect me?

Tears welled and I tried to blink them away, wiping at

the corner of my eye before one could fall. I was afraid to believe it.

I watched Wick for any sign that he was going to object, he'd probably seen the blood in Ryland's hammock when he woke that morning. But even if he didn't know who might have put it there, he didn't want to cross them. He kept his mouth shut.

The bosun made another mark in his book, dismissing each of the crew, and a few minutes later everyone on the *Luna* was back to work.

Clove didn't look at me as I went to the helm, his shoulders hunching as I came closer. I looked up into his face, studying the wrinkles that framed his deep-set eyes, and he glanced over my head nervously for a fraction of a moment, to the deck. He was making sure no one was watching us, and that was the only answer I needed.

He reached for the peg on the mast beside us, leaning over me. "Not here." His voice ground, making me swallow hard.

If Clove was looking out for me, then he hadn't turned on Saint. He hadn't turned on *me*. And that could only mean one thing. Zola wasn't the only one who was up to something.

My father was, too.

"Dredger!" The bosun shouted over the wind, his hands cupped over his mouth. "Helmsman wants to see you! Now!"

I tried to meet Clove's eyes, but he snapped the book shut, crossing the deck. He walked through the open door to the helmsman's quarters and I stopped before it, watching Zola. He stood at the window, his hands clasped behind his back.

Clove took a seat at the end of the table, setting one foot up on his knee and leaning back into the chair beside a basin filled with suds.

Zola looked over his shoulder to me when I didn't move. "Well. Come in."

I glanced between them, searching for any hint of what was coming. But Clove looked unconcerned. He'd done a good job of convincing Zola, but there had to have been a price for that trust. Clove had never been an innocent man, but I wondered what he'd done to get on this ship.

"The haul?" Zola lifted the tails of his coat to sit on the stool beside the window.

"Sorted and itemized with the letter of authenticity from the merchant in Sagsay Holm," Clove reported, rote. "He put total worth around six thousand coppers."

I flinched at the number. Six thousand coppers in one trade. That was the kind of sum that launched entire trade routes.

"And you checked them?" Zola looked up to me.

"Twice," Clove answered.

But Zola was still looking at me. "I want to hear it from you. Did you check the stones?"

"Twice," I repeated, irritated.

"The person these stones are going to will catch it if you missed anything. And I don't think I need to tell you what will happen if she does."

"Guess you'll have to wait and see," I said flatly.

"Guess we will," Zola said. "I want you cleaned up and ready before we make port." He motioned to the basin.

I stood up off the wall, dropping my arms. "Ready for what?"

"You've got business in Bastian."

"No, I don't. I got your haul. I checked your stones. I've earned my coin three times over."

"Almost," Zola said.

I stared at him. "I'm done playing this game. When am I going back to the Narrows?"

"Soon."

"Give it to me in days." My voice rose.

Zola tipped his chin up, looking down his nose at me. "Two days."

My hands curled into fists at my sides. I let out a frustrated breath.

"I have one more thing I need you to do. After that, your fate is in your own hands."

But I wasn't going to rely on the *Luna* to get me home. I had a better chance with just about any other ship in Bastian's harbor. I could buy passage from another helmsman and sail back to the Narrows with fewer enemies than I had here. "Give me my coin now and I'll do whatever you want."

"That's fair." Zola shrugged. "But you're only getting half. The other half, you can have tomorrow night."

"What's tomorrow night?"

"It's a surprise." He opened the drawer of his desk and took out a purse, counting out twenty-five coins quickly. When he was finished, he set his hand on the pile and slid them over the maps toward me.

Clove got back to his feet.

"I need you dressed and down on that dock by the time Bastian is in sight." Zola closed the drawer and stood, coming around the desk to face me.

"Boots." Clove held out a hand, waiting.

I looked down to my feet. The leather of my boots was still scuffed and muddy from the streets of Dern. I muttered a curse, sliding my feet from each one and leaving them on the ground for him to pick up himself. The tick of a smile twitched at the corner of his mouth before he bent down to snatch them up.

Zola opened the door and waited for Calla to enter before he and Clove left. She had a change of clothes draped over her arms, and I glowered at the ruffled cuff of the shirt's sleeve.

"You can't be serious," I hissed.

Calla tipped her head to one side impatiently.

I tugged the shirt over my head and unbuttoned my trousers before I went to the basin. My blistered knuckles stung as I slid my hands slowly into the hot water. The bubbles smelled like herbs, and I raked the water up my arms, scrubbing before I moved to my face and neck. When I was finished I went to the mirror, wiping at the places I'd missed with the corner of a cloth.

My mouth twisted as I looked at my reflection in the glass. Once, my mother might have stood before this mirror. Isolde couldn't have been much older than me when Zola first took her on, and I wondered how long it had taken her to find out what kind of man he was. Her days on the *Luna* were ones she'd never told me about, and part of me didn't want to know anything about them. In my mind, her spirit lived on the *Lark*. I didn't like the idea of any piece of her being left here.

I pulled my fingers through my hair to untangle as much as I could, and wound the length of it up until I could tuck the end underneath to make a tight knot. I didn't bother trying to tame the loose waving pieces that fell around my face. Zola may have needed someone to play the role of a Saltblood, but he'd have to settle for me.

Calla tossed the shirt onto the bed and I picked it up, examining the cloth. It wasn't one that traders usually wore. The linen was newly spun and thin, falling down the arms softly to the wrists. The trousers, too, were new, made of a thick black wool fit with whalebone buttons. Zola had obviously been prepared when he stepped into that alley in Dern. He'd had a very detailed plan. The thought made a tingle run up my spine.

Two days, I told myself. Two days and I would be on my way back to the *Marigold*.

There was a knock at the door before I'd even finished tucking in the shirt, and Calla opened it to one of the Waterside strays. He held my boots in his small hands. They were cleaned and shined, the laces replaced with new ones made of a tightly knit cord. I stared down at them, and emotion curled thick in my throat, remembering the night that West had given them to me.

I'd stood in the rain at the village gambit, watching him and Willa in the alley. The light from the streetlamps carved the angles of West's face, and his voice had changed when he said my name. That was the first time I'd seen the underneath of him, if only for a moment. And I missed him so badly I could hardly breathe.

I couldn't help but wonder at what my father and Zola had said. That there was a darkness to West that went deeper than I'd known. A part of me didn't want to know. To believe that it didn't matter. Anyone who'd survived the Narrows had that same darkness. It was the only way to stay alive.

But that night in Dern, when we said we wouldn't lie to each other, he hadn't told me the whole truth. And I was afraid of what I might find if he did. That when I saw him again, he would look different to me. That he would look like Saint.

TWELVE

The faint flicker of sprawling lights glowed like stars on the shoreline ahead.

Bastian.

I stood at the bow of the *Luna,* watching the city come closer. It was a place I knew only in stories. Streets and lights and colors that formed memories that weren't my own.

My mother had loved Bastian. The way the wet streets shone in the moonlight. The roll of buildings up the hill and the smell of the markets. But in the end, she left and she'd never gone back.

The hands of the dockworkers below slowed on their

tasks as the *Luna* made port, and the crew pulled up her sails, stowing them neatly on the masts. She looked beautiful in the cloak of night, the dark wood gleaming and polished. But there was no amount of scrubbing or ruffled shirts that could hide where we'd come from. We were Narrows-born traders through and through and from the look of everyone in the harbor, they knew it.

Every other ship anchored in the bays looked as if they were carved from rays of daylight, crisp and clean against the wide sky. The cities of the Unnamed Sea prided themselves on their opulence, and none more than Bastian. My mother had never carried the same air, but it was still there in little things. Like the way she kept her dredging tools pristine on her belt or the way her fingernails seemed to always be clean.

There are some things that can't be carved from a person, no matter how far from home they've sailed.

The harbor master appeared in the distance, followed by a throng of dockworkers trailing behind him. His severe brow made his eyes look squinted and the parchments in his hand fluttered as he waved his arms over his head. But Zola didn't waste any time making himself at home. He didn't even wait for approval before having the crew secure the hauling lines.

"Who's that there?" the harbor master called out, stopping to look up and study the crest on the foresail.

Zola met Clove's eyes before he took the ladder down, and the crew of the *Luna* watched over the side of the ship as he walked up the dock to meet him.

"Time to go." Clove tucked an extra knife into his belt.

I eyed him suspiciously. He hadn't even glanced in my direction since we'd stood in Zola's quarters and I realized there was more to his place on the *Luna* than even Zola knew. But he'd given me no hint of what was going on or what part I was supposed to be playing. Everything had been on a racing clock since we'd left Dern, and I wanted to know what happened when it finally ticked down. Jeval. The dive. Sagsay Holm. Zola was meticulously making each move with careful precision. I knew it had something to do with Holland, but that's where my revelations had stopped.

Koy watched me from the quarterdeck as I disappeared over the side of the ship. The crew had been instructed not to leave the *Luna* for any reason, and the Jevali dredgers didn't seem to mind one bit. Their eyes studied the city on the hill warily, as if something about it scared them. Bastian itself was bigger than the entire island of Jeval.

Zola was still talking to the harbor master with an easy smile when Clove and I slipped around them, headed for the wide stone staircase that led to the merchant's house. This wasn't anything like the rusted structure the Narrows merchants traded in. It was built with clean white stone, the corners studded with ornate statues of seabirds that unfolded their wings over the street below.

I stopped when we reached the top step, and the street widened to reveal the rolling expanse of the vast city. I turned in a circle, trying to take it in, but Bastian was immense. Overwhelming. I'd never seen anything like it.

Clove disappeared around the corner of the merchant's house as I turned back to the street. When I stepped into the alleyway, he was already waiting. He leaned against the brick, the glow of streetlamps lighting half his face. Even standing in the middle of the street, surrounded by buildings that hid most of the sky, he looked like a giant.

The harsh coldness that had been in his eyes since I first saw him on the *Luna* softened when he looked up at me from beneath the brim of his hat. It was a look that was so familiar that my shoulders drew down my back, the tension that had me wound tight for the last ten days uncoiling itself from me. In an instant, I felt as if I were unraveling. One side of his mustache slowly ticked up and a crooked grin illuminated his eyes with a spark.

I took the four steps between us, my boots hitting the cobblestones in an echo, and I threw my arms around him. The cry that had been trapped in my throat finally escaped, and I leaned into him, my fingers clutching his jacket. I didn't care that it was weak. That it was an admission to how scared I was. I only wanted to feel like for a moment, I wasn't alone.

Clove stood rigid, watching around us warily, but after a moment his huge arms came around me, squeezing. "There now, Fay," he said, one hand rubbing my back.

I curled my arms into my chest and let him hold me tighter, closing my eyes. "Does he know where I am?" I couldn't say my father's name without my voice fully giving way.

Clove pulled me back to look up at him and one rough

hand brushed the tears from my flushed cheek. "He knows exactly where you are."

If Saint was in on this, he'd known the morning I saw him in Dern. He'd sat across the table from me drinking his tea without so much as a hint about what was waiting for me in the alley.

I gritted my teeth. I was so tired of my father's games. But the anger I felt was immediately replaced by desperation. I took hold of Clove's jacket, pulling him toward me. "I have to get out of here. I have to get back to the Narrows."

"You're not going anywhere until we finish this." Clove planted a kiss on the top of my head before he started up the street again, his hands finding his pockets.

"Finish what?" My voice rose as I followed after him. "You haven't told me anything."

"We've been working a long time for this, Fay. And we can't finish it without you."

I stopped in my tracks, gaping at him.

When he could no longer hear my footsteps, the gate of Clove's stride broke and he halted, looking back.

"Tell me what's going on or I'm bartering with the first ship down in the harbor for passage back to the Narrows," I said, my voice tired.

He stopped beneath the faded sign of a fishmonger, sighing. "In a day's time, you'll know everything."

I could see that I wasn't going to sway him. If this was the work of my father, then there were a lot of moving pieces and I was one of them.

"You swear it?" I took a step closer, daring him to lie to me.

"I do."

I searched his face, wanting to believe him. "On my mother's soul?"

The words made him flinch and his lips pressed into a hard line before he answered. "I swear it." He shook his head with an irritated smirk. "Same stubborn ass as her," he muttered.

The collar of his jacket was pulled up around his neck and his fair hair curled out from beneath his cap. For the first time since Dern, I felt like I could exhale. He felt like home. As long as I was with Clove, he wouldn't let anything happen to me. And the truth was, if he and my father were taking down Zola, I was in.

We walked until the street opened abruptly to a square of shops, all clad with huge, clean windows. Each one was fit with flower boxes and fresh, bright paint. Clove stopped before the first shop on the corner, straightening his hat. The sign that hung over the street read FROCKS & LIVERIES.

He pushed open the door and I followed him into the warm shop, where a woman was crouched beside a dress form, needle in hand.

She looked up with her head tilted to the side, eyes raking over us from top to bottom. "May I help you?" The question sounded like an accusation.

Clove cleared his throat. "We need a frock. One fit for a gala." I rounded on him, stunned, but before I could object, he was speaking again. "And we'll need it tomorrow."

The woman rose, sticking the needle into a cushion on

her wrist with a flick. "Then you had better have the coin to pay me to sew through the night."

"It's not a problem," Clove answered.

She seemed to consider it for a moment before she wove through the bolts of cloth piled on the long wooden counter. "New silks just came in yesterday. No one in Bastian has anything like this yet."

Clove ignored my icy stare, following her to the window that looked out over the street.

"What is this?" I whispered, pulling on the sleeve of his jacket.

"You're just going to have to trust me."

I was as angry with myself as I was with him. I should have known the moment I saw Clove on Zola's ship that Saint was up to something. Now I was entangled in whatever scheme they'd hatched and it wasn't likely that I'd come out unscathed.

His hand moved over the different fabrics carefully, his lips pursing before he picked one up. "This one."

It was the richest of blues, the color of the sea on sunny days when it was too deep to see the bottom. The dark fabric shimmered as it caught the light. I couldn't imagine what Clove could possibly have planned that would warrant a frock made of something so fine, but I had a feeling I wouldn't like it.

"All right, let's get you up there. Everything off." The woman wrapped her arms around the dress form, tipping backward to set it against the wall.

The curtain in front of the mirror closed with a whoosh, and then she was staring at me, both hands on her hips. "Well? Come on."

I groaned before I pulled my shirt over my head and unclipped the wrap over my breasts. She hung it up, *tsk*ing as she smoothed out the trousers and rubbed at the creases in the wool.

"Now let's look at you." Her eyes moved over my naked body, and she frowned when she saw the scar on my arm and the stitches in my leg. They weren't my only marks. "Well, I suppose we can cover those. Turn."

I reluctantly obeyed, giving her my back, and when I met Clove's eyes over the curtain, he was smirking again. I flinched when her cold hands took my waist, running up the length of my ribs.

"All right," she said.

She pushed out of the curtain and returned holding a roll of stiff white fabric with laces. I cringed. "Is that . . . ?"

"Corset, my dear." She smiled sweetly. "Arms up."

I bit down onto my bottom lip to keep from cursing and turned again so she could fit it around me. She jerked at the laces until my sore ribs were screaming and I pressed my hands against the wall to steady myself.

"You've never worn a corset?" The woman's tone turned up.

"No," I snapped. My mother had never put me in one and I'd had no need for one on Jeval.

She fit the panniers around my waist next, tying the strings so the shape of the hoops bulged at each of my hips.

Then she started on the silk, cutting and draping and pinning until the form of a frock took shape. It wasn't until she pulled the curtain open that she turned me around and I saw what she was doing.

My reflection appeared in the gold-framed mirror and I sucked in a breath, stepping back.

The garment was fitted at the bodice, wrapping closed in the front so the skin between my breasts came to a sharp point beneath the folds of the fabric. The sleeves were no more than shredded blue silk waiting to be pinned, but the skirt was full, rippling like waves around me.

"I'll need pockets," I said, swallowing.

"Pockets?" she huffed. "Why on earth would you need pockets?"

I didn't answer. I wasn't going to tell her it was for my knife, or explain why I'd need one at a gala.

"Just do it," Clove called from behind her.

"Wait here." The woman sighed before she disappeared into the back of the shop.

Clove sat in the chair, taking in the sight of me. When he saw my face, he tried not to laugh.

"Enjoying yourself?" I muttered.

His mouth twisted up on one side again. "Your mother wouldn't have been caught dead wearing that thing."

I was struck by the ease with which we'd slid into the old rhythms between us when only hours ago I'd been ready to kill him. Growing up, there wasn't a day I wasn't stuck to his side on the ship or at port. Looking at him now, I felt like I was ten years old again. And that feeling made me miss my mother.

"What happened between Zola and Isolde?" I asked softly, not sure I really wanted the answer.

Clove sat up straighter, pulling at the collar of his shirt. "What do you mean?"

"Saint told me they had history. What kind of history?"

He gave away more than he knew when he wouldn't meet my gaze. "I think you should talk to Saint about that."

"I'm asking you."

He rubbed his hands over his face, letting out a long breath. When he leaned back into the chair, he looked at me for a long moment. "Zola had just established trade in Bastian when he met Isolde. She was trading at the merchant's house, and I guess she saw a way out."

"Out of what?"

"Whatever she was running from." He clenched his jaw. "She struck a deal with Zola and took a place on his crew as one of his dredgers. But he wanted more from her than her skill with the gems. I don't know what happened between them, but whatever it was, it was bad enough for her to pay him everything she'd saved to get off the *Luna*."

I cringed, trying not to imagine what it could have been. "And then she met Saint."

"Then she met Saint," he repeated. "And everything changed."

"How did she get him to take her on?"

"I don't think he really had a choice. He was ruined for Isolde the first day she sat down beside him at Griff's tavern."

Griff's. I couldn't help but grin at that.

"They were friends. And then they were more," he said, his eyes drifting like he was lost in thought. "And then there was you."

I smiled sadly. The earliest memories I had were of both of them—Saint and Isolde. And they were cast in warm, golden light. Untouched by everything that came after. They'd found each other.

I took West's ring from where it hung around my neck, holding it before me. I'd felt that way when he kissed me in Tempest Snare. Like we were a world of our own. We had been, in that moment.

If the rumors in Sagsay Holm were true, West was ready to give up the *Marigold* and everything else. I had to finish what my father started if I was going to keep that from happening.

"He couldn't have planned this," I said, almost to myself.

"What?"

"Saint. He didn't know I'd left Jeval until I saw him in Ceros." I was putting it together slowly. "I wasn't a part of his plan until West took me on."

Clove stared at me.

"Am I right?" But I didn't need an answer. The truth of it was in his silence. "When I showed up at his post, Saint didn't want anything to do with me. But when he saw me leaving the harbor on the *Marigold* that night, he wanted me off that ship. And he saw a way to use me."

I shook my head, half-laughing at the absurdity of it. There was more to the story than I knew. "What did Zola mean when he said that West is like Saint?"

Clove shrugged. "You know what it means."

"If I knew, I wouldn't be asking."

"He's got a lot of demons, Fay."

"We all do." I gave him a knowing look.

"I guess that's true enough."

I crossed my arms, ignoring the way the silk threatened to pull open at the seams. I was so tired of secrets. So tired of lies. "I'm here, Clove. For you and for Saint. You owe me a hell of a lot more than this."

His eyes narrowed. "*Owe* you?"

I lifted both eyebrows, looking down my nose at him. "Saint's not the only one who left me on that beach."

His jaw ticked. "Fay, I'm—"

"I don't want an apology. I want the truth."

His eyes dropped for a moment to West's ring hanging around my neck. "I was wondering if the two of you were . . ." He didn't finish, hesitating before he went on. "West does what Saint needs done. Whatever it is. And it's usually pretty dirty work."

"Like Sowan?" I asked in a low voice.

He nodded. "Like Sowan. He's been Saint's guy for a long time."

"That's why Saint let him have the *Marigold*," I mumbled. He'd *earned* it.

Clove leaned forward to set his elbows onto his knees. "He's dangerous, Fay," he said more gently. "You need to be careful with that one."

I told myself it wasn't anything I didn't already know. The *Marigold* was a shadow ship, and that came with shadow work. But I had a feeling that even the crew didn't know about everything West did for my father.

The night West told me he loved me, he'd also told me about Sowan. About a merchant whose operation he'd sunk on Saint's request. What he hadn't said was that it was one of many similar stories or that my father's deeds were the heaviest of the burdens he carried.

Don't lie to me and I won't lie to you. Ever.

The only promise we'd made to each other West had already broken.

THIRTEEN

I watched the drip of water into the basin where the shape of me was rippling. The deep blue of the frock set the red in my hair aflame, my cheeks glowing with rouge.

My skin was too warm beneath the dress. The room Zola had put me in at the tavern had a hearth stacked with a blazing fire and a bed stuffed with soft down on which I hadn't been able to bring myself to sleep.

I wasn't sure who he was trying to impress. There was no amount of luxury that could wash him clean of what he was. If I had to guess, I'd say the scar on Willa's face and the *Marigold*'s slashed sails were probably the least of his sins.

The silk hugged my body tightly, the skirts swishing as I made my way down the steps into the tavern. Clove and Zola sat at a table in the farthest corner drinking rye. They were both dressed in fine tailored coats fit with shining brass buttons, unruly hair trimmed and combed back away from their windblown faces. A flicker of recognition flashed before my eyes. Clove had always been rough around his edges, but he looked younger in the expensive green wool, his blond hair shining.

He sat up straighter when he saw me, setting down the rye glass he was sipping from, and I was instantly embarrassed, catching my reflection in the window. My hair was pulled up in loose curls, pinned to make a halo around the crown of my head, and the light shimmered over the frock.

I looked utterly ridiculous.

"Well, well . . ." Zola's eyes dragged over me from head to toe. "What do you think?" He stood from the chair, showing off his coat with a flourish of his hand.

I gave him a withering look. "I think I'm ready to get this over with so I can get the hell out of here."

Clove drained his glass before he stood and opened the door of the tavern. The cold wind rushed in, making me shiver. I'd decided to leave the cloak Clove purchased for me in the room because when I'd set it on my shoulders, I felt like I was suffocating beneath its weight. Still, the cold was a welcome relief from the heat simmering under my skin.

Clove had given me his word that in a few hours, he would tell me the truth. Tomorrow, I'd be on my way back to the the Narrows. I'd be able to find the *Marigold* before West did even more damage than what was already done.

The heels of my shoes clicked as I walked in Zola's wake. Despite his attempt at arrogance, I could see he was nervous. He was missing the usual rock to his gait, his mouth pressing into a hard line as he moved down the street. He watched the ground, thinking. Measuring. Calculating.

He led us through the city, and the farther we walked, the more beautiful it became. Dusk painted Bastian in soft pinks and purples, and the white stone buildings caught their hues, making everything look like it was from a dream.

The cobblestones bled from rough, paved rectangles to polished granite squares as we made another turn, and Zola stopped, looking at the shining marble face of a grand building in the distance.

A series of enormous arches stood over wide, gleaming steps, where three sets of double doors were flung open to the night. Lantern light spilled out onto the street from inside, the race of shadows slipping into the dark.

The ornate plaque above the center doors read AzIMUTH HOUSE.

The first word was one I knew. It was a term used in celestial navigation to describe the bearing of the sun or moon or stars from one's position. But *house* didn't begin to describe what this was. Stone carvings covered every inch of the edifice in flowers and vines, and above them all, an expanse of night sky was adorned with a pearl-faced moon.

Zola was quiet, his gaze dropping from the arches to his boots.

My brow knit when I realized he was summoning up his courage and a wicked smile stretched up my cheek. I liked this version of Zola. He was unsure. He was afraid.

"Ready?" He glanced back at me but didn't wait for an answer. He took off up the steps without us.

I looked to Clove. He was missing the hesitation that saddled Zola. And that could only mean one thing. Everything was going according to his plan.

He lifted a hand, gesturing for me to go first, and I picked up the heavy skirts, taking the stairs up to the doors. A gust of air whipped around me, pulling a few strands of hair from where they were pinned, and for a moment I felt like I was up on the mast of the *Lark,* leaning into the heavy wind. But the *Lark* had never felt more far away than it did now.

We slipped through the open doors and the warmth of the hall enveloped me as my eyes drifted up to the ceiling. Panes of painted murals set with gemstones looked down on us, too many to count. They were framed by stained glass windows in a kaleidoscope of colors that soaked the light of the hall with saturated hues. The people gathered below reflected their brilliant shades, dressed in colorful, shining fabrics. Coats in the richest reds and golds and expertly draped frocks moved like bleeding ink across the mosaicked floor. I looked down to the toes of my shoes. Beneath my feet, chips of amethyst and rose quartz and celestine fit together in the shape of a flower.

"What is this place?" I whispered to Clove.

He spoke low beside me, his eyes scanning the room. "Holland's home."

"She *lives* here?"

My fingers curled into my silk skirts. Large candelabras were lit throughout the hall, where trays of sparkling glasses floated through the crowd on the fingers of servers dressed in white. The gala's guests filled the room, encircling glass cases that were framed in brushed bronze. Inside the one nearest to us, a glimmer caught my eye.

I could feel the gemstone before I could see it. The deep reverberation of it woke in the center of my chest, my lips parting as I walked toward the case and leaned over the glass. It was a piece of red beryl almost as big as my hand.

"What the . . ." The words dissolved.

I'd never seen anything like it. The color was a pale red, its face cut into intricate facets so my reflection was broken into pieces on the stone. There was no telling what it was worth.

The hall was an exhibit of some kind, designed to showcase the expansive collection of gems. It looked like a museum.

"Find her," Zola muttered, looking to Clove.

Clove met my eyes for a moment before he obeyed, shouldering through the people gathered between the next two cases.

Zola fell quiet, studying the room.

"You look nervous." I folded my hands together behind my back, letting my head tip to one side.

He gave me a weak smile. "Do I?"

"Actually, you look terrified," I said sweetly.

His jaw tightened as a silver tray appeared beside me. It

was set with delicate etched glasses filled with a pale, bubbling liquid.

"Take one," Zola said, plucking one up by the rim.

I untangled my fingers to reach up and take one of the drinks, giving it a sniff.

"It's cava." He grinned. "Saltbloods don't drink rye."

I took a sip, grimacing at the way it fizzed on my tongue. "When are you going to tell me what we're doing here?"

"We're waiting for the woman of the hour." Zola rocked back onto his heels. "Should be any minute now." I watched him gulp down the glass and reach for another.

The light cast his skin in a warm brown that made his face almost handsome, and I couldn't help but think he didn't look like a monster. Maybe that was why Isolde stepped onto the *Luna* that day. I wondered how long it took her to find out she was wrong.

"I want to ask you a question," I said, cupping my hands around the narrow glass.

"Then ask it."

I watched him carefully. "What were you to my mother?"

A twinkle lit in his eyes as he surveyed me. "Ah. That depends on who you ask." His voice lowered conspiratorially. "A helmsman. A savior." He paused. "A villain. Which version of the story do you want to hear?"

I took another long drink and the cava burned in my throat. "Why did she leave the *Luna*?"

"If she hadn't gotten herself killed, you could ask her yourself," he answered. "Though there's no telling which tale she would have given you. I never should have trusted her."

"What is that supposed to mean?"

"Isolde didn't just take *her* fate into her own hands when she left Bastian. She took mine too. Letting her onto my crew is the worst mistake I've ever made."

My brow creased. Saint had said the same thing about her, but for different reasons.

"But tonight, I'm going to fix that. Thanks to you."

There was some faint echo in the back of my mind, trying to string the words together. None of it made any sense. "How could my mother have anything to do with this?"

"Isolde is the reason Holland has had a bounty on my head all these years. She's the reason I lost any chance I had at trading in the Unnamed Sea and the reason I haven't been back since."

"What are you saying?"

"I'm saying that when I helped Holland's daughter escape Bastian, I fell out of her good graces."

The silk of my dress pulled tight across my chest as I drew in a breath, my head swimming. "You're lying," I snapped.

Zola shrugged. "I don't need you to believe me."

I pressed a hand to my ribs, feeling as if my lungs didn't have room behind my bones. What he was saying couldn't be true. If Isolde was Holland's daughter . . .

A group of women floated past us arm in arm, talking in hushed whispers as they made their way to the back of the room. Zola drained his glass, setting it down on the case between us and I wiped my brow with the back of my hand, feeling dizzy. Everything suddenly looked as if we were underwater. I needed air.

When I tried to step past him, he caught my arm, squeezing. "What do you think you're doing?"

The man beside us looked over his shoulder for just a moment, his eyes landing on Zola's grip on the sleeve of my dress. "Get your hand off me," I growled through clenched teeth, daring him to make a scene.

I wrenched my arm free and gave the man a timid smile before I stepped into the aisle of cases, Zola's hot stare pinned to my back. Zola was a liar. I knew that. But there was some uneasiness that had lifted within me when he'd said the words. I searched through the candlelit memories I had of my mother. Of her stories. She'd never told me anything of her parents. Nothing of her home.

But why would my mother leave *this*?

I looked around the room, biting down on my lip. In every direction, people laughed and talked, at ease in their fancy clothes. But no one seemed to notice how much I didn't fit in that dress or in that room. The hall was filled with the songs of the gems, resounding so loud that it made me feel off balance. No one seemed to notice that either.

I drifted past the cases, my eyes flitting over their glass tops, and stopped short when the melody of the stone in the next case caught my ear. It was one I'd only ever heard once.

Larimar. I stilled, listening. Like the ringing call of birds or the whistle of wind in a cavern. It was one of the rarest gems in existence. And that was the point. This gala wasn't just a party. It was a display of wealth and power.

The slide of a hand moved over my hip, hooking my

waist, and my fingers immediately went for the knife inside my skirts. The cava splashed from my glass as I whirled and I pressed the tip of the knife into the crisp white shirt before me, pulled over a broad chest.

But a scent I knew poured into my lungs as I inhaled and looked up into green eyes, the glass shaking furiously in my hand.

West.

FOURTEEN

I sucked in a breath, swallowing down the cry in my throat as I stared up at him. His gold-streaked hair was combed back from his face, the color of his skin aglow in the candlelight. Even the sound of the gems quieted, snuffed out by the violent winds roaring inside of me.

West reached up between us, wrapping his hand around the handle of the knife in my hand, and I watched him swallow, his eyes changing. They were weighed down by dark circles, making him look worn and thin.

I took hold of his jacket, crumpling the fine fabric as I pulled him toward me and pressed my face to his chest. I instantly felt as if my legs would give out beneath the heavy dress. As if I were going to sink to the floor.

"Fable." The sound of his voice summoned the pain under my ribs again, and my heartbeat kicked up, my blood running hotter in my veins.

Something in the back of my mind was whispering in warning. Telling me to look for Zola. To pick up my skirts and run. But I couldn't move, leaning into the warmth of West, afraid that he would disappear. That I'd imagined him there.

"Are you all right?" he breathed, tilting my face up to look at him.

I nodded weakly.

He took the glass from my hand and set it onto the case beside us. "Let's go."

And then we were walking. The eyes in the room drifted toward us as we passed, and West's fingers wound into mine. I let him pull me through the crowd, toward the night sky cast beyond the open doors. I didn't care anymore about what plan Saint and Clove had. I didn't care if Zola was watching or whether it was true what he'd said about my mother.

"The *Marigold*?" I whispered frantically, squeezing West's hand so hard that my knuckles hurt.

"In the harbor," he answered, walking faster.

"Fable!" Zola's deep voice echoed over the sound of the chatter.

I caught sight of Clove against the far wall, Zola at his side as they both pushed through the crowd toward us. But it was the sharp, skittering sound of glass shattering that made my pulse stop in its tracks, and I froze, West's hand slipping from mine.

A hundred thoughts erupted chaotically in my mind as my eyes landed on the vision of a woman. An old woman. Her face was stricken, her eyes wide beneath silver hair that was braided in an intricate labyrinth over the top of her head. It was studded with fanned combs of pink tourmaline that matched the rings covering her fingers. At her feet, the broken pieces of a crystal glass were scattered around her violet gown.

The deep, breathy resonance of her voice shook the room around us when she said it. "Isolde?"

West's hand found mine again and he wrapped one arm around me, pulling me away. I stumbled beside him, looking over my shoulder to see her, my brow knitting in recognition.

The doors ahead slammed shut and men in dark blue coats filed in along the wall, calling out orders. The room filled with the sound of voices as the guests pushed back, taking West and me with them.

"You!" one of the men shouted, and it took me a moment to realize that he was talking to me.

"Shit," West rasped behind me.

The woman turned on her heel, walking toward another set of doors that opened on the other side of the room. A hot hand grabbed me, yanking me forward and West lifted a fist into the air, swinging. When it came down, it caught the man in the jaw.

He stumbled, falling into the crowd as he pulled a short

sword from his hip, and a woman screamed. More guards emerged from the crowd, surrounding us, and the candle-light gleamed on four blades all pointed at West. But their eyes were on me.

West slipped the knife from his belt, holding it at his side with a look of eerie calm. My eyes widened, watching him. It was the face I'd seen the night he threw Crane into the sea. There were four guards surrounding us, but West took a step forward. By the time he took another, he would be dead.

"Don't." I reached for his knife, but he moved from my reach, stepping around me. "Don't, West!" He blinked, as if only just remembering I was there and I took hold of his jacket, pulling him back.

I pushed into his chest until he moved back against the wall. "I'll come with you!" I said over my shoulder. "Don't touch him."

West grabbed my arm, squeezing, but I slipped out of his reach.

The swords pointed at us lowered a little, and the man with a bloody nose gave a nod in West's direction. "She wants both of you."

I looked up to West, but he was as confused as I was. His green eyes were like glass in the dim light. Narrowed and focused.

The guard stepped back, waiting, and I pushed into the crowd with West close behind me. The room was silent as we followed the blue jackets to the open door where the woman had disappeared. A few seconds later they were closing be-hind us, and the distant sound of music started up again.

Lanterns washed the ceiling over us in light, illuminating more murals and carvings as our footsteps echoed in the corridor.

"What the hell is going on?" West growled behind me.

A set of huge wooden doors opened in the dark down the hall, where I could see the shape of Clove slipping into a lit room.

The guard stopped, motioning us forward before he went back the way we came, and West and I stood in the empty hall, staring at each other.

"Join us. Please," a soft voice called from beyond the doors.

The sound of the gala bled away behind us as I let go of West's hand and stepped inside. His shadow followed mine as he came to stand beside me, his eyes moving over everything in the room until they found Zola.

The guard shoved him forward and Zola stumbled, catching himself on the wall as the doors groaned shut behind us.

The woman in the violet gown stood beside a polished mahogany desk. Behind her, the wall was covered in gold-painted paper and the brush strokes curved and dipped, making a maze of ocean waves all the way up to the ceiling. Her frock looked like it was made of cream, rippling around her slight form until it pooled on the floor.

"I'm Holland." She clasped her hands before her and the light caught the stones in her rings. She was looking at me.

West took a step closer to me as I stared at her, not sure what to say.

Holland's eyes ran over my face in fascination. "You're Fable," she said softly.

"I am," I answered.

In the corner, Clove had his arms crossed over his chest, leaning into the wall beside a glowing fireplace. A framed portrait was set onto the mantel and all the air seemed to leave the room as my eyes focused on a girl in a red gown, a gilded halo around her head.

It was Isolde. My mother.

"And you must be West," Holland said, her eyes drifting up to him. "Runner of Saint's shadow ship."

West went still beside me. He was smart enough not to deny it, but I didn't like the look in his eye. I was terrified that at any moment he was going to do something that put a knife to his throat.

"Yes, I know exactly who you are." Holland answered his unspoken question. "And I know exactly what you do."

I looked between them. How could someone like Holland know anything about West when no one in the Narrows did?

"What do you want?" West said flatly.

She smiled. "Don't worry. We'll get to that."

"Holland." Zola's voice swallowed the silence, but he shut his mouth when Holland's sharp eyes landed on him.

The crack in his cool facade was now a canyon. Zola didn't have any power here and every one of us knew it. Clove was the only one who didn't seem to be worried. I wasn't sure if that made me afraid, or relieved.

"I don't think you were on the invitation list for this gala,

Zola." Holland spoke, and the sound of her voice was like music. Soft and lilting.

"My apologies," Zola answered, standing up straighter. "But I thought it was time we dealt with our business."

"Did you?" Holland's tone flattened, "I made it clear if you ever made port in the Unnamed Sea again, it would be the last time you made port anywhere."

"I know we have history—"

"History?" she said.

"It's been almost twenty years, Holland."

I looked back to Holland, catching her eyes on me before they shot back to Zola.

He unbuttoned his jacket methodically, not taking his eyes from hers, and Holland's guard stepped closer to him, knife drawn. Zola took hold of the lapels and pulled them open, revealing four pockets. From each one hung the strings of a leather pouch.

Holland jerked her chin at the table against the wall, and Zola set them down one at a time. She didn't move as he poured the gemstones out onto the mirrored tray, lining them up neatly for inspection.

Zola waited, letting Holland look over the haul. "Consider it a gift."

"You think a few hundred carats of gemstones can buy my forgiveness for what you did?" The words were so low they sent a chill into the air, despite the blazing fire.

"That's not all I brought you." Zola's eyes landed on me.

I instinctively took a step backward, pressing myself

against the wall as he looked at me. But Holland's attention didn't leave Zola. "You think this was *your* idea?"

Zola's lips parted, staring at Holland. "What?"

"Pay him." Holland's command fell like a stone in the quiet.

The guard walked around the desk and took a silver box from the shelf. He set it onto the tray before he opened it carefully, revealing more coppers than I'd ever seen in my life. Thousands, maybe.

Clove finally moved then, stepping out of the shadows. "No need to count it," he said. "I trust you." He was talking to Holland.

The ice cold of the sea found me and I reached for the arm of West's jacket, trying to ground myself. Trying to put it all together.

Clove wasn't spying on Zola. He was *delivering* Zola. To Holland.

"A mother never heals from the loss of a child. It's a wound that festers," Holland said simply. "One that not even your death will soothe."

Zola was already shuffling backward toward the door, his eyes wide. "I brought her back. For you."

"And I appreciate that." She lifted a finger into the air and the guard opened the door, where two other men were waiting.

They stepped into the room without a word, and before Zola even knew what was happening, they had him by the jacket, dragging him into the dark hallway. "Wait!" he shouted.

Clove closed the lid of the box with a snap as Zola's screams echoed, and I realized the sound in my ears was my own breath coming in and out in panicked gusts. Zola's voice suddenly vanished, and I heard his weight fall to the floor.

My fingers were slick around the handle of the knife inside my skirts as I stared into the dark, blinking when a trail of fresh, bright blood seeped across the white marble and into the light spilling from the room. Then there was only silence.

FIFTEEN

He was dead. Zola was dead.

I tried to fit that bit of truth together with everything that had happened over the last ten days. This was why Clove had taken the job on Zola's crew. It was all leading to this very moment.

Zola wasn't just a problem for Saint or West. He was a problem the Narrows needed solved. Saint planted Clove on the *Luna* to get him into Holland's hands. He'd convinced Zola he could be rid of her threats once and for all. But how had he done it?

The coin she'd given Clove looked like a bounty, and my gut told me Saint's name had stayed out of it. To Holland,

Clove was just a trader from the Narrows looking to make a lot of copper.

It was brilliant, really. My father used Zola's feud with Holland to get him to sail to his own death. And why kill a trader and risk the fallout with the Narrows Trade Council when a powerful merchant in the Unnamed Sea could do it instead?

"Why didn't you tell me?" I asked, my voice far away.

Clove looked at me with an expression that echoed sympathy. But he kept his mouth shut, his eyes sliding to Holland. He didn't want her knowing more than she needed to.

Clove took orders from Saint, and Saint had a reason for everything he did. The bottom line was that even if I trusted him, Saint didn't trust *me*. And why would he? I'd worked my own schemes against him to free the *Marigold*.

My gaze drifted back to Zola's blood on the white marble floor, and I watched the way it gleamed as the firelight moved over it. Only moments ago he'd stood next to me. I could still feel his grip on my arm, squeezing.

The deafening silence made me blink and I realized that Holland was staring at me, as if she expected me to say something. When I didn't, she looked disappointed.

"I think that's enough for one night, don't you?" she said.

I wasn't sure how to answer that. I wasn't even sure what she was asking.

"You'll stay here." There was no invitation in her tone. She wasn't asking. Her eyes were still studying me, moving over my hair, my shoulders, my feet. "We'll talk in the morning."

I opened my mouth to argue, but West was already speaking. "She's not staying," he said, clipped.

Clove picked up the box of coin lazily, tucking it under one arm. "I'm afraid I'm going to have to agree with him."

He and West didn't seem the slightest bit afraid of Holland, but I was terrified enough for all of us. At the lift of Holland's finger, they'd be dragging West or Clove into the dark next.

"You're all staying," Holland said. "Fable's not the only one I have business with." But that calm in her eyes was the same one that had been there a moment ago when she'd lifted that finger.

In the hallway, I could hear something being dragged over the marble. I swallowed hard.

"I hope you'll make yourself at home," Holland said, reaching for the shining handle of another door. She pulled it open and a hallway lit with bright lanterns appeared.

She waited for me to walk through, but I didn't move. I was staring at the portrait of my mother over the mantel, the firelight catching her eyes.

The rings on Holland's fingers sparkled as she took a step toward me. The fine fabric of her dress rippled like melted silver, and the combs in her hair twinkled. I couldn't help but think that she was like someone from one of the old tales. A specter or a sea fairy. Something not of this world.

The same had been true of my mother.

Holland reached for my hand, taking it into hers, and she held it between us, turning it so my palm faced up. Her thumbs spread over the lines there, and her hold on me tightened when she saw the tip of my scar peeking out from beneath my sleeve.

Her pale blue eyes lifted to meet mine and she let me go. "Welcome home, Fable."

Home.

The word stretched and folded, the sound of it strange.

I clutched my skirts with both hands and walked through the door, biting back the turn of my stomach. Saint may have gotten what he wanted, but now Holland was the one with the upper hand, and she knew it.

The guard led us into another corridor that ended at the foot of a winding staircase, and we followed it up to a salon that overlooked the bottom floor. He didn't stop until we reached a door at the end of the row. It was painted pearly pink with a bouquet of wild blooms at its center.

"Someone will come for you at the first bell," he said, letting the door swing open.

The room was bathed in pale moonlight cast through a large window. Beneath it was a bed, half of it shrouded in shadows.

West stepped inside first, and the man caught him in the chest with a hand. "This room is for her."

"Then I'm staying here too." West shoved past him, holding the door open for me to follow.

I looked over my shoulder to Clove. He leaned against the banister, giving me a reassuring nod. "See you in the morning." His manner was cool, but there was an unsteady look in his eye. I wasn't the only one who could see that Holland was the oil in a lamp, ready to catch flame.

The guard who'd dragged Zola into the dark appeared at the top of the staircase. He walked toward us with quick steps, and I studied his jacket and hands for any sign of blood. But he was crisp and clean, just like the gala and its guests below.

He took a place beside the door and West closed it behind me, stilling to listen when the latch fell into place. When footsteps faded into the distance, his shoulders relaxed. He leaned into the door, crossing his arms over his chest as he faced me.

"What the hell is going on, Fable?" he grated.

My throat ached, seeing him washed in the icy blue moonlight. "Saint." My father's name felt foreign to me, somehow. "He used me to lure Zola here so that Holland would kill him." I wasn't even sure I understood it all, but those were the pieces I'd put together.

"Lure him how? What is Holland to *you*?"

"I think . . ." I searched for the words. "I think she's my grandmother."

West's eyes widened. *"What?"*

The word sounded odd and misshapen as he said it, and I realized that the darkness was moving around me. I couldn't draw the air into my chest.

The ghost of my mother hovered between these walls, some echo of her in the air.

In the flood of memories that danced in my mind, I searched for anything Isolde may have told me about this place. But there was nothing but tales of dives and the streets of the city where she was born. Nothing of Azimuth House or the woman who lived here.

"When Isolde ran away from Bastian, she took a place on Zola's crew." I pressed my hands against the blue silk wrapped around my torso. "Holland is her mother. That's why Zola lost his license to trade in the Unnamed Sea. That's why he hasn't sailed here in over twenty years."

He fell silent, but the room was filled with his racing thoughts. He was looking for a way out of this. An escape from the trap we'd both walked into.

I went to the window, looking out to where the harbor would sit in the darkness. "What about the crew?"

West stood and the shadows found his face, making the darkness under his eyes more severe. "They won't make a move."

"You sure about that?" I asked, thinking of Willa. When we didn't show up at the harbor, she'd be ready to tear the city apart.

I sat on the edge of the bed and he stood before me, looking down into my face. His hand lifted as if he was going to touch me, but then he froze, his eyes focusing on the shine of gold tucked beneath the fabric of my dress. He slid the tip of a finger beneath the twine and pulled until the ring dangled in the air between us.

He stared at it for a moment before his green eyes flickered up to meet mine. "That's what you were doing in Dern?"

I nodded, swallowing hard. "I'm sorry." The words broke in my throat.

The crease in his brow deepened. "For what?"

"For all of this."

I wasn't just talking about what happened that morning at the gambit. It was everything. It was Holland and Bastian and West burning Zola's ships. It was for everything he didn't want to tell me about what he'd done for Saint. When I'd stepped off the *Marigold,* I'd set our course to this moment. And I didn't want to admit that West looked different to me now. That he looked more like my father.

He touched my face, fingertips sliding into my hair.

I didn't know what he'd done in the Narrows, trying to find me. But the weight of it was heavy on him. He was darkened with it. In that moment, I only wanted to feel his rough hands on my skin and swallow the air around him until I could taste him on my tongue. To feel as if I were hidden in his shadow.

His face lowered until his mouth hovered over mine, and he kissed me so gently that the burn of tears instantly erupted behind my eyes. My hands moved down the shape of his back and he leaned into me, inhaling deeply, as if he was pulling the warmth of me inside of him. I put what Clove told me out of my mind, closing my eyes and imagining that we were in the lantern light of West's quarters on the *Marigold.*

His teeth slipped over my bottom lip and the sting resurfaced from where the skin was still healing. But I didn't care. I kissed him again and his hands reached for the skirts, pulling them up until I could feel his fingers on my legs. His touch dragged up, and when his hand wrapped around the stitches in my thigh, I winced, hissing.

West pulled away from me suddenly, his eyes running over my face.

"It's nothing," I whispered, pulling him back to me.

But he ignored me, pushing the skirts up to my hips so he could look at it. The clumsy stitches puckered in a jagged line at the center of a trailing purple bruise. He brushed a thumb lightly around it, his jaw clenching. "What happened?"

I pushed the frock back down between us, embarrassed. "One of Zola's dredgers tried to make sure I didn't come back up from a dive."

West's eyes were bright and sparkling, but the set of his mouth was still. Calm. "Who?"

"He's dead," I murmured.

He fell quiet, letting me go, and the space between us again grew wide and empty. The warmth that had been in his touch was gone, making me shiver. The last ten days flashed in his eyes, showing me a glimpse of that part of West I'd seen the night he told me about his sister. The night he hadn't told me about Saint.

I don't need to know, some part of me whispered. But the lie in the words echoed behind them. Because eventually, we would have to unearth those buried bones, along with whatever else West was hiding from me.

SIXTEEN

I sat on the floor against the wall, watching the beam of morning light crawl across the tassel-edged rug until it touched my toes. The hours had passed in silence, with only the occasional sound of boots outside the closed door.

West stood at the window watching the street, and I could see the finery of his coat much better in the light. The burgundy wool fell to his knees, the color making his hair look even more fair, and I wondered how in the world anyone had gotten him into it. Even his boots were shined.

I hadn't slept, watching West's tired eyes stare out the window. He looked as if he hadn't closed them in days, the cut of his cheekbones sharper.

As if he could feel my attention on him, he looked over his shoulder. "You all right?"

"I'm all right," I said, my eyes dropping to his hands. The last time I'd seen West, he told me he'd killed sixteen men. I wondered how many it was now. "You're worried about them," I said, thinking of the *Marigold*.

"They'll be fine." I could tell he was reassuring himself, not me. "The sooner we get out of here, the better."

A soft knock sounded at the door and we both stilled. I hesitated before I got to my feet, grimacing when the stitches in my leg pinched. My wrinkled skirts rustled as I walked barefoot across the carpets, and when I opened it, a small woman stood in the hall with a fresh frock in her arms. It was a delicate pale pink fabric, almost the same hue that colored the walls of the room.

Clove still stood against the banister out on the salon, his box of coin sitting at his feet. He'd stayed out there all night.

"I've come to dress you," the woman said, looking up at me.

"I'm not a doll," I snapped. "I don't need to be dressed."

Behind her, Clove stifled a laugh.

The woman looked confused. "But the hooks—"

I snatched the frock from her hands and closed the door before she finished. The garment shimmered as I held it up, inspecting it. It was garish, with a high neck and a pleated skirt.

West seemed to be thinking the same thing, wincing as if looking at it hurt him.

I dropped it on the bed with a huff and reached back for the closures of the blue frock I was wearing. The fastenings at the top came undone with a snap, and when I couldn't reach the ones at the center, I groaned.

I reached into the pocket of my skirts and found the knife. West watched from where he stood at the window as I slid the blade along the seam at my ribs, jerking. The tailored waist loosened with the tear and I rolled the bodice down until the entire thing dropped to the floor in a heap. My sore ribs and shoulders ached, finally free of the constricting silk.

West eyed the underdress and panniers fitted around my hips. "What the—"

I stopped him with a sharp look, stepping into the new frock and fastening the buttons in the back as far up as I could. When my fingers couldn't get to the next one, West finished them with a scowl on his face. The short sleeves would show my scar, and for a moment the thought unnerved me. I was used to covering it up.

I pulled the pins from my hair and let the length of it fall around me before I shook it out. The deep auburn strands spilled over my shoulders, dark against the pale color of the bodice. When I opened the door again, the woman was still standing there, a pair of shoes in the same pink fabric clutched in her delicate hands.

Her eyes went wide when she saw the shredded blue silk on the floor behind me. "Oh my."

She composed herself, setting the shoes down, and I stepped into them one at a time with the frock bunched in my arms. She bristled when she caught sight of the scar on my arm, and I dropped the skirts, waiting for her to stop staring.

Her cheeks bloomed crimson. "I'll show you to breakfast." She gave an apologetic bow of her head.

West was already waiting in the hall with Clove. The woman stepped around them carefully, as if she was afraid to touch them, and Clove looked pleased. He moved aside, letting her pass, and she led us back down the staircase. The corridor we'd walked down the night before was now filled with sunlight coming through the floor-to-ceiling windows. Painted portraits lined the inner wall, their deep, saturated colors depicting faces of men and women wrapped in robes and adorned with jewels.

The coin in Clove's box jingled as we followed the woman, side by side, down the turning steps.

"It's time to tell me what the hell is going on," I said in a low voice.

Clove's eyes cut to West warily. "You know what's going on. I took on Holland's bounty and brought Zola back to Bastian from the Narrows."

"But why?" Clove was loyal to Saint, but he wasn't stupid, and he hadn't risked his neck for nothing. There was something in it for him. "Why would you come all this way on Saint's order?"

He arched an eyebrow, irritated. "He made it worth my while." He tapped the silver box under his arm. "I'm using the coin to start a new fleet under Saint's crest."

"What? Why not strike out on your own?"

Clove laughed, shaking his head. "Would you want to be in competition with Saint?"

I wouldn't. No one in their right mind would. This was a way for everyone to get what they wanted.

"I'd been trying to convince Zola to come back to Bastian for over a year, but he wasn't interested. He was too afraid of Holland."

"Until you used me as bait," I muttered. "If Saint wanted to use me to get Zola to Holland, he knew where I was. He could have come to get me from Jeval any time." Clove kept pace beside me, silent. "Why now?"

Clove glanced over his shoulder, looking to West again, and I stopped short, the skirts slipping from my fingers.

"So, I was right." I glared at him. "This is about West."

West looked between us, but he said nothing. He'd likely already been thinking the same thing.

Saint had been working against Zola for some time, but when he realized I'd used him to help West, he'd seen a way to solve not one problem, but two. He'd get Zola to Bastian and me off the *Marigold*.

"That bastard," I growled, gritting my teeth.

West watched me from the corner of his eye, the muscle in his jaw ticking. Once, he'd said he'd never be free of Saint. I was beginning to wonder if he was right.

We took two more turns before we were standing at a wide set of doors that opened to an enormous solarium. Walls of glass rose to a ceiling that framed the blue sky, making the light so bright that I had to blink to let my eyes adjust.

At the very center of the room sat a decadently dressed round table, where Holland was waiting.

The belt around her waist was studded with trailing swirls of emerald, the same stone that hung from the gold chain around her neck. It caught the light as she faced the windows looking over the city, a teacup in her hand.

West studied her, an undecipherable question in his eyes.

Our escort stopped at the door, gesturing for us to enter, and I stepped into the room with West at my side, Clove trailing behind.

"Good morning," Holland said, her eyes on the golden landscape before us. "Sit, please."

The solarium was filled with plants, making the air warm and humid. Wide leaves and choking vines crawled up the windows, and blooms of every color were scattered along fronds and branches.

I reached for the chair but a young man appeared from behind us, pulling it out for me. I sat cautiously, taking in the contents of the table.

Pastries and cakes were arranged in ornate patterns atop silver platters and stands, and fresh berries were piled into white porcelain bowls. My mouth watered at the smell of sugar and butter, but West and Clove kept their hands in their laps. I did the same.

"Like looking into the past." Holland gingerly set her cup onto the saucer before her. "You're a perfect rendering of your mother."

"So are you," I said.

That made her mouth twist a little, but it was true. I could see my mother in all of her angles, even with her years and silvered hair. Holland was beautiful in the same wild, untamed way Isolde had been.

"I take it she never told you about me." Her head tilted to the side inquisitively.

"She didn't," I answered honestly. There was no point in lying.

"I admit, when Zola sent me a message saying he was bringing me Isolde's daughter, I didn't believe him. But there's no denying it." Her eyes ran over me again. "I'm still trying to figure out how you slipped my notice. Nothing happens on the sea that I don't know about."

But I knew the answer to that question. No one but Clove knew who I was, and I'd spent four years on Jeval, far removed from anyone's curiosity. For the first time, I wondered if that was one of Saint's reasons for leaving me there.

"Isolde was a stubborn girl," she breathed. "Beautiful. Talented. But so very stubborn."

I stayed silent, paying close attention to the corners of her mouth. The shifting of her eyes. But the surface of Holland gave away nothing.

"She was seventeen years old when she left on the *Luna* without so much as a goodbye. I woke one morning and she didn't come down to breakfast." She picked up her cup, and it shook in her hand as she took another sip of hot tea. "If her father hadn't already been dead, it would have killed him."

She selected a pastry from the platter, setting it onto

the plate before her as the doors opened behind us. A man stepped into the room, his jacket buttoned all the way up to his neck and his hat in his hands. It took me a moment to place him. The harbor master.

West seemed to realize it in the same moment, turning just a little in his chair to keep his back to him.

He stopped beside the table before he handed Holland a roll of parchments. "The *Luna* is being stripped as we speak. There's a good bit of supplies, but no inventory. Sails are good."

"Well, we can always use sails," Holland murmured, looking over the parchments. "The crew?"

"Down on the docks looking for work," he answered.

I glanced at Clove, thinking of the dredgers. If Holland took the *Luna*, they likely hadn't been paid. They'd all be looking for passage back to Jeval.

"Strike the berth from the log. I don't want anyone digging around," Holland said.

West's hand tightened on the arm of the chair. She hadn't just killed Zola. She was sinking the ship and covering up the fact that he'd ever been in Bastian. By the time she was through, it would be as if he'd never made port.

"I want the *Luna* at the bottom of the sea before the sun goes down. I don't need the Trade Council getting wind of this before the meeting."

Clove met my eyes across the table. My only guess was that she was talking about the Trade Council meeting that took place between the Narrows and the Unnamed Sea in Sagsay Holm.

The harbor master grunted in answer. "One unscheduled ship is noted there, too." He pointed to the page in Holland's hands. "The *Marigold*."

I instantly went rigid, my cup hitting the saucer a little too hard. Beside me, West's stillness made me shiver. He looked like he was about to launch himself from the chair and cut the man's throat.

Holland glanced up at me. "I don't think we need to worry about them. Do you?"

"No," I said, meeting her eyes. There was an exchange to be made here. I just wasn't sure what it was.

She handed the harbor master the parchments dismissively and he gave a nod before he turned on his heel and headed back toward the doors.

I watched him leave, gritting my teeth. If the harbor master was in Holland's pocket, then nothing happened down on those docks without her knowing.

"Now," she said, folding her hands on the table as she looked back to Clove. "I trust you can get back to the Narrows."

"Sounds like you just told him to sink the ship I came in on," Clove said, annoyed.

"Then I'll take care of it. But I have one more thing I need you to do."

"I brought in the bounty." He gestured to the silver box. "And you've already paid."

"I'm willing to double it," she said.

Clove's eyes narrowed, suspicious. "I'm listening."

She picked up a berry, holding it before her. "Saint."

The sound of my heart pounded in my ears, my fingers gripping the handle of the cup tightly.

Clove leaned both elbows onto the table. "What do you want with Saint?"

"The same thing I wanted from Zola. Restitution. My daughter died on his ship and he'll be held responsible. He's expected at the Trade Council meeting in Sagsay Holm. I want you to make sure he doesn't make it."

Clove stared at the table, thinking. I could almost hear his mind turning, formulating. Trying to weave together some kind of plan that would get us all out of this mess. When I opened my mouth to speak, he silenced me with the slightest shake of his head.

It dawned on me then that Saint's involvement in the bounty wasn't the only thing Clove had kept secret. He'd also kept hidden the fact that Saint was my father.

"Do you want the job or not?" Holland pressed.

I held my breath. If he turned it down, she'd commission someone else.

Clove's eyes met hers. "I want the job."

I set my hands into my lap, my fingers twisting into the skirts. Holland had found a way to reach across the sea, into the Narrows, and draw Zola out. Now she wanted Saint.

"Good." She popped the berry into her mouth, chewing. "And that brings me to you." She looked to West.

He leveled his gaze at her, waiting.

"Once Saint is out of the way, there will be an entire trade route left behind. If anyone knows Saint's operation, it's the helmsman of his shadow ship."

And there it was—the other part of her plan. Holland didn't just want revenge. This was also business.

"I'm not interested," West said flatly.

"You will be," Holland said, staring back at him. "Someone like me could always use the talents of someone like you. I'll make it worth your time."

I bit the inside of my cheek, watching West carefully. His stoic expression hid whatever he was thinking.

"If what I've heard about you is true, then it's nothing you can't handle."

"You don't know anything about me," he said.

"Oh, I think I do." She smiled. An uncomfortable silence filled the space between the four of us before her eyes fell on me again. She stood, folding her napkin neatly and setting it onto the table. "Now, Fable. There's something I want to show you."

SEVENTEEN

The doors to Azimuth House opened to the blinding light of late morning. Holland stood at the top of the steps, a shimmering silhouette. She was ethereal, her long silver hair spilling down the gold embroidered cloak that floated out behind her as she made her way to the street.

West hesitated on the top step, watching her. His coat was unbuttoned, the collar of his white shirt open, and the wind blew his unruly hair from where it had been combed the night before.

"I don't like this," he said, keeping his voice low.

"Me either," Clove muttered behind me.

West's eyes flicked up to the harbor in the distance. But from here, it was impossible to make out the ships. By now, the crew of the *Marigold* would be worried, and if the harbor master was in Holland's pocket, he'd be watching them closely. I could only hope that they would lay low and wait it out like West had ordered.

Holland looked between the three of us with a question in her eyes that made me uncomfortable. We weren't in the Narrows anymore, but the same rules applied. The less she knew about who West and Clove were to me, the better.

We followed her down the staircase to the street. It seemed the whole city was already doing business. I didn't miss the way people looked up as Holland passed, and neither did West. He watched around us, glancing up to windows and down alleys as we walked, and his silence was making me more nervous by the minute.

Clove hadn't told me what West had done for my father in detail, but he'd said enough to make me worry about what West was capable of. What he'd be willing to do if he thought Holland was dangerous, and what it would cost him.

Not even a day ago, I'd been afraid I might never see him again. The sinking feeling returned, dropping down the center of my chest, and I moved closer to him. His hand drifted toward mine but he didn't take it, his fingers curling into a fist. As if at any moment, he would take hold of me and start for the harbor.

There was a part of me that wished he would. But there was a shift in power happening in the Narrows. Zola was gone, and Holland's sights were set on Saint. Blood aside, that didn't bode well for the *Marigold*. If we were going to get ahead of this, we needed to know what was coming.

The coin in Clove's chest rattled as he walked beside me. He hadn't taken Holland's offer to stow the coin in her study, and now he was drawing the eye of nearly everyone on the street as we made our way to the farthest pier on the south side of Bastian. Holland's crest was painted on its brick, with private slips stretching far enough from shore that each could easily dock three ships. It wasn't like any I'd ever seen in the Narrows. It looked more like a small port than a shipping pier.

The men standing at the doors pulled them open as we reached the entrance. Holland didn't slow, walking down the center aisle where countless stalls filled the floor. The rectangular workspaces were sectioned off with polished wood beams, each worker clad in an apron that had Holland's crest burned into the leather.

These weren't the kinds of workers that filled Ceros. They wore clean white shirts, their hair combed or braided, and were freshly bathed. Holland liked her post the way she liked her home. Tidy. And the way they didn't meet her eyes as she passed gave away their fear of her.

My gaze flitted over the people in the stalls as we passed. Some of them looked to be gem merchants cleaning stones, chipping away at the outer rock on crude rubies or tumbling the smaller, broken pieces of sapphires. I slowed when I spotted a man cutting a yellow diamond. He worked with quick movements, making the splice in the stone by muscle memory more than sight. Once he was finished, he set it aside and started on another.

"This is everything I've built over the last forty years." Holland's voice sounded behind me. "Everything Isolde left behind."

The question was why. It was the same one I'd been asking myself since the moment the *Luna* drifted into port.

Bastian was beautiful. If there were slums, I had yet to see any. It was well known that there were more than enough jobs, and many people left the Narrows for apprenticeships and opportunities here. What had taken Isolde from the Unnamed Sea?

I looked back at West. He stood in the center of the aisle, his eyes moving over the huge pier.

"We shouldn't be here," he said suddenly. He ran a hand through his hair, raking it back from his face in a familiar movement that told me he was on edge. It wasn't just Holland. Something else was bothering him.

The aisle opened to a long corridor, and Holland didn't wait for us, walking with paced steps toward three men who stood before a doorway draped with thick velvet. Holland pulled the gloves from her hands and unbuttoned her cloak as she went inside. When Clove sank down into the leather chair beside the door, she glared at him.

The dark room illuminated as one of the men struck a long match and lit the candles along the walls. The space looked like a polished, more luxurious version of Saint's post in The Pinch. Maps hung over the walls, red ink marking the edges of the land, and I resisted the urge to reach up and follow the trail of them with my fingers. They were diving maps.

"You're a dredger," Holland said, watching me study them. "Like your mother was."

"I am."

She half-laughed, shaking her head. "That's not the only thing I didn't understand about that girl." Her voice quieted. "She was always restless. I don't think there was anything in this world that could calm the sea inside of her."

But I knew that wasn't true. The Isolde I'd known had been steady, made of deep waters. Maybe Holland was telling the truth about her, but that was before Saint. That was before me.

I read the spines on the books that lined the shelves until my eyes landed on a glass case behind the desk. It was empty. A small satin cushion sat inside, behind an engraved plaque I couldn't read.

Holland looked pleased with my interest. "Midnight," she said, following my gaze to the case. She set one hand on top of it, tapping a ring against the glass.

I tipped my head to one side, eyeing her. Midnight was a stone that only existed in legend. And if she had one, she would have had it on display at the gala.

"She didn't tell you that either?" Holland smirked.

"Tell me what?"

"The night Isolde disappeared, so did the midnight that was in this case."

I crossed my arms, scowling. "My mother wasn't a thief."

"I never took her for one." Holland sat in the plush chair, setting a hand on each arm. "Have you ever seen it? Midnight?"

She knew the answer. No one had. The little I knew about the stone was what I'd heard in the stories of superstitious deckhands and merchants.

"It's quite a peculiar gem. An opaque black with violet inclusions," she said. "It was discovered on a dive in Yuri's Constellation."

I knew the name from maps of the Unnamed Sea. It was a cluster of reefs.

"Isolde is the one who found it."

My hands fell to my sides from where they were tucked into my elbows. Beside me, West was studying my face, looking for any evidence of its truth.

"That's a lie. She would have told me." My eyes went to Clove, who was being careful to stay inconspicuous. When he finally caught my eyes, his head tipped to one side.

It *was* true.

"Are you sure about that?" Holland pressed, "Every merchant worth their salt and both Trade Councils attended the unveiling at Azimuth House and every one of them would tell you it's not myth." Holland lifted her chin. "It would have changed everything. Taken the trade by storm. But a few days later, Isolde was gone. So was the midnight."

I stared at her, unsure of what to say. There was accusation in her voice. Suspicion.

"I don't know anything about midnight," I answered.

"Hmm." Holland pursed her lips.

I couldn't tell if she believed me, but I wasn't lying. I'd never once heard my mother mention it.

A knock at the door broke the silence between us and Holland's tension unraveled. "Come in."

The door opened and on the other side, a young man not much older than I stood waiting with a roll of leather-bound parchments tucked under his arm.

"You're late," Holland said scornfully. "Did anyone see you?"

"No." His icy stare settled on her as he came in. I hadn't seen anyone so much as look at Holland in the eye, but he did. Without reservation.

He stopped before her desk, waiting with the parchments in his scarred hands. They were the scars of a silversmith, striping over his knuckles and wrapping around his palms. I followed them up his arms, where they disappeared beneath his rolled sleeves.

There, just below his elbow, a black tattoo was inked into the skin of his forearm. The twisted shape of two entangled snakes, each eating the other's tail.

I took a step forward, studying the shape of it. It was the exact same tattoo that Auster had. In the same exact place.

West's eyes dragged over the man quietly. He noticed it too.

I had never asked Auster about the mark. It wasn't unusual for traders to have tattoos. But if he was from Bastian, it couldn't be a coincidence.

"Show me," Holland muttered.

He tipped his head toward me and West. "I don't know them."

"That's right. You don't," Holland said, coldly. "Now show me."

He hesitated before he untied the leather strap around the parchments, unrolling them carefully across the desk. The page opened to a drawing penned in thin black ink in the style of a ship diagram. But it wasn't a ship. I took a step closer, eyeing the parchment.

It was a teapot.

Holland leaned forward, studying the rendering carefully. "You're sure you can do this kind of work?" Her finger moved over the written dimensions.

But there was no way anyone could. I had never seen anything like it. The pot was set inside a silver chamber with geometric cutouts, the design set with several different faceted gemstones. The margin listed them in alphabetical order: amber, fluorite, jade, onyx, topaz. It looked as if the chamber would spin, creating a myriad of color patterns.

"If you don't think I can do it, get one of your apprentices to."

I liked the way he glared at her, unyielding. So did Clove. He watched the young man with a wry grin.

"If I had anyone skilled enough to make it, I wouldn't have commissioned you, Ezra." Her voice lowered. "Henrik says you can do it. If he's wrong, he'll be paying *me* for the mistake."

Ezra closed the parchments, knotting the leather ties. "We done?"

My attention drifted to the tattoo again, and when I looked up, Ezra was watching me, his eyes glancing down to the mark.

Holland tapped a finger on the desk methodically. "You

have ten days. I need it in hand before the Trade Council meeting in Sagsay Holm."

I stiffened, remembering what she said that morning. That was also her deadline for dealing with Saint.

Ezra answered with a nod. He met my eyes one more time before he turned, pushing through the door and disappearing back into the corridor.

"What is it?" I asked, watching the door close.

"A gift." She set her hands back onto the desk. "For the Trade Councils of the Narrows and the Unnamed Sea."

The tea set had to be worth a ton of coin. If it was a gift, she was getting ready to make a request of the Trade Councils. One that required persuasion. But I still couldn't figure it out. She'd dealt with Zola, leaving only Saint to contend with in Ceros. But she didn't even trade there. I'd never seen a ship with her crest at a single port. After seeing her operation, it didn't make sense that her route excluded the Narrows. She was known far beyond the Unnamed Sea, her power and wealth legendary. So, why didn't she trade in Ceros?

The only explanation was that for one reason or another, Holland *couldn't* sail the Narrows.

"You don't have license to trade in the Narrows, do you?" I said, putting it together.

She looked impressed. "The Trade Council in the Narrows thinks that if I'm allowed to open my route to Ceros, it will sink the Narrows-born traders."

And it would.

"I built this empire with my own two hands, Fable," she said. "I had nothing when I started, and now I'll leave the

Unnamed Sea with the most powerful gem trade anyone has ever seen."

I could see in her eyes that this was what she'd wanted me to witness. The success. The power.

"There's only one problem. This empire has no heir."

West went still beside me, the tension rolling off him in the deafening silence. Clove, too, watched me. But my attention was on Holland. My eyes narrowed, my lips parting as I tried to peel back the words. "You don't even know me."

She gave me an approving smile. "I want to change that."

"I don't need an empire. I have a life and a crew. In the Narrows." The words stung as I spoke them. I was so desperate to get back to the *Marigold* that I could feel the tears threatening to rise.

"The offer isn't just for you." She looked to West. "I'd like you to consider coming onto my fleet."

"No." West spoke his answer so quickly that Holland had barely finished when he opened his mouth.

"You're not even going to hear me out?"

"No, I'm not," he said, unblinking.

She didn't look amused anymore. She looked angry. I took an involuntary step closer to West and she noticed, looking between the two of us. I'd given too much away.

"I'd like you to take an evening to think about my offer. If you still don't want it by the time the sun rises, you're free to go."

I bit the inside of my cheek, watching the sharp spark of light in her eye. In only a night I'd learned more about my mother than I had in my entire life. Saint wasn't the only one with secrets, and I couldn't help but feel betrayed.

If Holland was telling the truth about Isolde, then she was a thief. A liar. She'd never told me about my grand-mother in the Unnamed Sea or the single most important gem discovery she was responsible for. But there were some things about my mother I knew were true. Things I trusted. If she destroyed the only chance Holland had at pushing into the Narrows, she had a reason.

And there was more going on here than Holland was showing us. Taking out Zola and Saint wasn't just revenge. It was strategy. They were the two most powerful traders, both posted from Ceros. She was clearing the playing field before she made her move with the Council.

Saint wasn't the only one working a long game.

EIGHTEEN

Holland's man led us back up the staircase, and I ran a hand along the banister, looking up to the window-paned skylight above us. Dust glinted off the glass like the facets of a gem.

"Fable." West's voice made me blink. He stood at the end of the corridor with Clove, his face cut sharp with apprehension.

My fingers slipped from the bannister and I curled them into a fist. He waited for me to step inside the room and closed the door behind us, leaving Clove outside.

I searched the table for a match and lit the candles. Through the window, I could see the sun setting beyond the horizon. When it rose again, we'd be on our way to the harbor.

"Are you going to take it?" West's words filled the quiet.

My stomach dropped as I looked up at him, the smoking match still in my hand. He was shut up tight, the hardness in him showing. "What?"

"Are you going to take the offer from Holland?"

I turned to face him. "Are you really asking me that?"

But he didn't hold my gaze. His eyes dropped to the floor between us. "I am."

I caught the crook of his arm and waited for him to look at me. "I told her I didn't want it."

The look of relief on his face was more obvious than I knew he wanted it to be. But he didn't appear to be convinced.

"You can't trust her, Fable," he breathed. "But that doesn't mean you shouldn't take her offer."

"You sound like you *want* me to take it." I sank into the chair beside the window. "What is it?" I asked softly.

He was unreadable, silent for a long moment before he finally answered. "We need to talk."

But I wasn't sure I was ready for what he might say. "We don't have to."

"Yes, we do."

"West—"

"We should talk about it before you decide."

"I told you. I've already decided," I said again.

"You might change your mind when you hear what I have to say."

My pulse beat under my skin rapidly, my mind racing.

I wasn't sure why I suddenly felt afraid of him. Since the moment Saint told me West wasn't who I thought he was, I'd been holding my breath. Waiting to see where the break would be between us. Maybe this was it.

"There's more to my position with Saint than I told you. I'm sure you've figured that out by now." He slid his hands into his pockets, pressing his lips together before he continued. "I was crewing as a Waterside stray on a ship. The helmsman was the one I told you about. He wasn't a good man."

I still remembered the way West's face looked when he told me the helmsman had beat him in the hull of the ship.

"Our route put us in Ceros for two days every three weeks, and one night, when we made port, I went to Waterside to see Willa. When I got there, I knew something was wrong, but she wouldn't tell me anything. I had to ask around before I found out someone who worked at the tavern was coming around while I was gone and stealing from her and my mother. Every time I left port, he would show up. He knew there was no one to stop him, and Willa didn't tell me because she was afraid of what I would do."

I'd seen that look on Willa's face before, the fear of West taking matters into his own hands. That's what she was trying to avoid when she sold her dagger to the gambit in Dern. She was trying to keep West out of it.

"It was nearly morning when I made it to the tavern, and when I found him, he was drunk. If he wasn't, I don't think I would have been able to . . ." He paused, his eyes moving over the floor as if he was seeing the memory. "He was sitting at a table alone. I didn't even think about it. I wasn't afraid. I just walked up to him and put my hands around his throat and this quiet came over me. It was like . . . it was so *easy*. He fell out of his chair and he was kicking and trying to pull my hands away. But I just kept squeezing. I kept squeezing even after he stopped moving."

I didn't know what to say. I tried to imagine him, maybe fourteen years old, strangling a grown man in the middle of an empty tavern. His pale waving hair in his face. His golden skin in the firelight.

"I don't know how long it took me to realize he was dead. When I finally let him go, I just sat there, staring at him. And I didn't feel anything. I didn't feel bad about what I'd done." He swallowed. "When I finally looked up, there was only one other person in the tavern sitting at the bar. I hadn't noticed him until that moment. And he was watching me." West met my eyes. "It was Saint."

I could see him, too, sitting at the bar in his blue coat with a green glass in his hand. Wheels turning.

"I knew who he was. I recognized him. At first, he didn't say anything. He just kept drinking his rye, and when he was finished, he offered me a place on his crew. Right there, on the spot. Of course, I took it. I thought that anything had to be better than the helmsman I was working for. And he was. Saint was fair to me. So, when he started asking me to do him favors, I did them."

"What kind of favors?" I whispered.

He let out a deep breath. "We'd make port and sometimes, there was something that needed to be done. Sometimes there wasn't. Carrying out punishments for unpaid debts. Hurting people who wouldn't be intimidated. Sinking operations or sabotaging inventories. I did whatever he asked."

"And Sowan?"

His eyes flashed. He didn't want to talk about Sowan. "That was an accident."

"But what happened?"

His voice was suddenly quieter. "Saint asked me to take care of a merchant there who was working against him. I set fire to his warehouse when we stopped there on our route. The crew didn't know," he said, almost to himself. But that was the part of the story he'd already told me. "When we made port in Dern, I found out someone was in the warehouse when I started the fire."

I'd been there when the merchant told him. I'd seen the look of confusion that passed between Paj and the others, but there had to be some part of them that knew what West did for Saint. They were too smart to have missed it.

A million things flitted through my mind, but too fast. I couldn't grab hold of a single one. Saint was right that I didn't know West. So was Zola. I'd only seen the sides of him that he'd chosen to show me.

"We've all done things to survive," I said.

"That's not what I'm trying to tell you." The air around him changed as he spoke, "Fable, I need you to understand something. I did what I needed to do. I didn't like it, but I had a sister and a mother who needed my wages, and I had a place on a crew that treated me well. I know it's not right, but if I could go back, I think I would do it all again." He said it so earnestly. "I don't know what that makes me. But it's true."

It looked as if those were the words that had cost him most of all. Because he was telling the truth. There was no blame to be placed on anyone else's shoulders. *This* was West, and he wasn't lying about it.

"That's why Saint doesn't want to lose you. Why he gave you a shadow ship to run." I rubbed a hand over my face, suddenly so tired. "But why didn't you tell me?" I asked. "Did you think I wouldn't find out?"

"I knew I was going to have to tell you about my work with Saint. I just wanted to . . ." He paused. "I was afraid you'd change your mind. About me. About the *Marigold*."

I wanted to say that I wouldn't have. That it wouldn't have made a difference. But I wasn't sure if that was true. Crewing for my father was one thing. I *knew* him. There was no mystery about who he was or what he wanted. But West was different.

"We're going to have to figure out how to trust each other," I said.

"I know."

I knew that West was in deep with my father, but this was something different. West was the reason people feared Saint. He was the shadow Saint cast on everything around him. The haul from the *Lark* wasn't just buying West's freedom from my father. It was buying his soul.

"If you hadn't known about the *Lark* . . . if you hadn't needed it to save the *Marigold*, would you have taken me onto the crew?"

"No." He answered without a breath of hesitation.

My heart sank, tears springing to my eyes.

"I don't think I would have. I would have wanted you to get as far away from me as possible," he admitted. "In a way, a part of me still wishes that we hadn't voted you on."

"How can you say that?" I said, indignant.

"Because you and I have cursed ourselves, Fable. We will always have something to lose. I knew it that day in Tempest Snare when I kissed you. I knew it in Dern when I told you that I loved you."

"Then why did you do it?"

He was silent for so long that I wasn't sure he would answer. When he finally did, his voice was hollow. "The first time I ever saw you, you were standing on the dock at the barrier islands. We'd made port at Jeval for the first time, and I'd been watching for you. A girl with dark auburn hair and freckles with a scar on the inside of her left arm, Saint said. It was two days before you showed."

I remembered that day, too. It was the first time I'd traded with West. The first time I'd ever seen the *Marigold* at the barrier islands.

"You were bartering with a trader, arguing for a better price on the pyre you were hocking. And when someone called from the deck of his ship and he looked up, you slipped a blood orange from one of his crates. As if the whole reason you'd been standing there was to wait for the moment when he wasn't looking. You dropped the orange into your bag and when he turned back around, you went right on arguing with him."

"I don't remember that," I said.

"I do." The shadow of a smile lifted on his lips. "Every time we dropped anchor at Jeval after that day, I had this constricting pain in my chest." He reached up, tucking a hand into his open jacket as if it were there now. "Like I was holding my breath, afraid you wouldn't be on the docks. That you'd be gone. And when I woke up in Dern and you weren't there, it came back. I couldn't find you." His voice wavered, splintering the words. He looked so heavy. So tired.

"You did find me. And I don't want Holland's offer."

"You're sure?"

"I'm sure."

He softened, the look in his eye more familiar. The sound of wind whistled outside the window, and ease finally found the set of his shoulders.

"But what are we going to do about Saint?" I asked, my mind drifting to my father.

"What do you mean?"

"Holland is after him, West. It's only a matter of time before she figures out Clove isn't going to deliver. She'll find another way."

"We cut our ties to him." West shrugged. "Saint can take care of himself."

My brow creased. I tried to understand his meaning.

"We can't get involved, Fable. He left us to deal with Zola when we were dead in the water. Now he can deal with Holland. You don't owe him anything."

"It's not about owing. This is about the future of the Narrows." It was mostly true.

He sighed, raking a hand through his waving hair. "Which is why we need to get back to Ceros."

For me, it wasn't that simple. If Holland got license to trade in the Narrows, it didn't matter how much coin the *Marigold* had. She'd wipe out every trader within a matter of years.

More dangerous than that was the fact that the idea of something happening to Saint made me feel panicked. Afraid. I didn't like that I was still instinctively loyal to him when he hadn't been loyal to me. But this went beyond me begging for a place on his crew, or him abandoning me on Ceros. If Holland got ahold of Saint, I was going to lose him forever. And it didn't matter what he'd done, or why. I couldn't let that happen.

West couldn't see that. He never would.

"Tomorrow, we'll leave Bastian and go home," he said.

I nodded, reaching up to take his hand.

He stared at me, his eyes dropping to my mouth. But he didn't move.

"Are you going to kiss me?" I whispered.

"I wasn't sure if you still wanted me to."

I stood, lifting onto my toes. He pressed his forehead to mine before he parted my lips with his, and I let out the breath I'd been holding since I woke up on the *Luna*. I wanted to cry, the ache in my chest breaking open and filling me with relief. Because I'd been here before, over and over in my dreams since I'd left the Narrows. But this time, it was real. This time, I wouldn't wake. West was living and breathing, warm in my arms. And the feel of him touching me was humming in every drop of my blood.

I don't know what I had expected him to say or what explanations he would have for the past. But West had none.

More than that, he didn't even have regrets.

I don't know what that makes me.

His words whispered back to life in my mind as I touched his face and his arms tightened around me. But I didn't feel afraid of him the way I thought I would. I felt safe. I didn't know if I could love someone like my father, but I did. With a love that was deep and pleading. With a love that was terrifying.

And I didn't know what that made *me*.

NINETEEN

I laid awake listening to West's breathing. It sounded like the waves lapping the shore of Jeval on warm days, rushing in and then dragging out.

I didn't think I'd remember any of those things when I left Jeval—the color of the shallows, the stretch of the sky, or the sound of the water. Those four years had been so shadowed by the pain of losing my mother and the yearning for my father that it had consumed both light and dark. Until West. Until the day the *Marigold* showed up at the barrier islands, her strange winglike sails bowed in the wind. It took almost six months for me to believe that every time I saw it sail away wasn't the last time. I had begun to trust West long before I realized it. But I wasn't sure yet if he trusted me.

A flash of light ignited along the crack beneath the door, and I watched as it disappeared. Out the window, dawn was more than an hour away, leaving the sky black.

I slipped out of West's heavy arms and sat up, listening. Azimuth House was silent, except for the sound of quiet footsteps on the staircase down the hall. My bare feet found the plush rug, and I stood, holding my skirts in my arms so they didn't rustle. West was lost in a deep sleep, his face soft for the first time since I'd seen him at the gala.

The handle to the door creaked softly as I lifted it, opening the door. Clove was snoring against the wall, his legs crossed in front of him and the chest of coin under his arm.

The glow of a lantern was bobbing along the wall, and I peered over the bannister to see a head of silver hair below. Holland was wrapped in a satin robe, making her way down the corridor.

I looked back to the dark room before stepping over Clove's legs and following the light. It washed over the floor before me as I took turn after turn in the dark, and when I reached the end of the corridor, it flickered out.

Ahead, a door was open.

I walked with silent steps, watching Holland's shadow move over the marble, and the light hit my face as I peered through the crack. It was a wood-paneled room with one wall covered in overlapping maps, the others all set with mounted bronze candelabras. Holland stood in the corner, staring up at a painting that hung over the desk. My mother was wrapped in an emerald green dress fit with a violet gem brooch, her face aglow in the candlelight.

I pushed the door open and Holland's gaze dropped to meet mine.

She lifted a finger, wiping the corner of her eye. "Good evening."

"Almost morning now," I answered, stepping inside.

Holland's eyes fell down my wrinkled dress. "I come down here when I can't sleep. No use in lying in bed when I can get some work done."

But it didn't look as if she was working. It looked as if Holland had come down to see Isolde.

She pulled a long match from a box on the desk and I watched as her hand floated over the tapers. When the last wick was lit, she blew out the match and I studied the illuminated maps pieced together on the far wall. They showed a detailed system of reefs, but this wasn't just any chain of islands. I'd seen it before.

Yuri's Constellation.

I took a step closer, reading notes written in blue ink along the margins of the diagrams. Different areas were crossed out, as if someone had methodically marked them. It was an active dive chart, like the ones my father would hang up in his helmsman's quarters on the *Lark*. And that could mean only one thing.

Holland was still looking for the midnight.

Behind her, another large portrait of a man was hung in a gilded frame. He was handsome, with dark hair, gray eyes, and a proud set to his chin. But there was a kindness in his face. Something warm.

"Is that my grandfather?" I asked.

Holland smiled. "It is. Oskar."

Oskar. The name seemed to fit the man in the portrait, but I was certain I'd never heard my mother speak it.

"He apprenticed as a gem sage with his father, but he'd given his heart to the stars. Against your great-grandfather's wishes, Oskar took an apprenticeship as a celestial navigator."

I guessed that's where Azimuth House had gotten its name, as well as its design.

"He was the best of his time. There wasn't a trader in the Unnamed Sea who didn't revere his work, and nearly every navigator out on those waters was an apprentice of his at one time or another." She smiled proudly. "But he taught Isolde the trade of a gem sage when he realized what she could do."

The tradition of a gem sage was something that was passed down, and only to people who had the gift. My mother had seen early on that I had it. I wondered how long it had taken Oskar to see it in my mother.

I reached up, touching the edge of another portrait. It looked like the same man, but he was older. His white hair was cut short, curling around his ears.

"Odd that your mother never told you about him. They were quite close from the time she was a little girl."

"She didn't tell me a lot of things."

"We have that in common." Holland smiled sadly. "She was always a mystery to me. But Oskar . . . he understood her in a way I never could."

If that was true, then why hadn't she ever told me about him? The only explanation I could think of was that maybe she didn't want to risk anyone knowing she was the daughter of the most powerful people in the Unnamed Sea. That would bring its own kind of trouble. But I couldn't shake the feeling that the reason my mother hadn't told me about Holland was because she didn't want to be found. That maybe, Isolde had been afraid of her.

"I didn't know she had a daughter until I got a message from Zola. I didn't believe him, but then . . ." She drew a breath. "Then I saw you."

I looked again to the portrait of my mother, measuring myself against it. It was like looking in a mirror, except that there was something gentle about her. Something untouched. Her eyes seemed to follow me about the room, never leaving me.

"Did she tell you where she got your name?" Holland said, breaking me from the thought.

"No. She didn't."

"Fable's Skerry," she said, walking back to the desk. She moved a pile of books, revealing a map of the Bastian coast painted onto the desktop. She ran a finger along the jagged edge of the land, dragging it into the water to what looked like a tiny island. "This was her hiding place when she wanted to get away from me." She laughed, but it was faintly bitter. "The lighthouse on Fable's Skerry."

"A lighthouse?"

She nodded. "She was no more than eight or nine when she started disappearing for entire days. Then she'd reappear out of nowhere as if nothing had happened. It took almost two years for us to figure out where she was going."

My chest felt tight, making my heart skip. I didn't like that this woman, a stranger, knew so much about my mother. I didn't like that she knew more than I did.

"How did she die?" Holland said suddenly, and the look in her eye turned apprehensive. As if she'd had to summon up the courage to ask.

"Storm," I said. "She drowned in Tempest Snare."

Holland blinked, letting out the breath she'd been holding. "I see." There was a long silence before she spoke again. "I lost track of Isolde for years after she left Zola's crew. I didn't hear that she'd died on the *Lark* until a year ago."

"That's why you want Saint?"

"It's one reason," she corrected.

I didn't know what she knew about Saint and Isolde, but there'd been a stone in my stomach since that morning, when she'd said his name. If Holland wanted Saint dead, it was likely that she'd get what she wanted. And that thought made me feel as if I were sinking, no air in my lungs, watching the surface light pull farther away above me.

West had made it clear that Saint would have to fend for himself, but even if she didn't kill him, Saint would die before he let her take his trade. It didn't matter what had happened four years ago, or that night on the *Lark*. It didn't matter what had happened the day he left me on Jeval. The moment he handed me that map of the Snare, or the morning I fleeced him with my mother's necklace. Everything focused in clear, crisp colors.

Saint was a bastard, but he was mine. He belonged to me. And even more unbelievable, I really did love him.

"I changed my mind." I spoke before I could think better of it.

Holland arched an eyebrow as she looked up at me. "Reconsidering my offer?"

I bit down on my lip, the vision of Saint at his desk resurfacing. The hazy, dim light. The glass of rye in his hand. The smell of pipe smoke as he looked over his ledgers. I took a step toward her. "I want to make a deal."

She leaned closer, smirking. "I'm listening."

"I wasn't lying when I said that Isolde never told me about the midnight. But I know you're still looking for it." I glanced up to the maps. "And I know I can find it."

That made her quiet. There was a sudden stillness in her, pulling the shadows from the room into her eyes. "I've had crews looking for that cache for years. What makes you think you can find it?"

"Dredging isn't the only thing my mother taught me."

She didn't look the least bit surprised. "So, you *are* a gem sage. I was wondering about that."

"You could have just asked."

She half-laughed. "I suppose you're right." She stood from the chair, coming around the corner of the desk. "You said you want to make a *deal*. What do you want from me?"

"Your word." I met her eyes. "If I find the midnight for you, you leave Saint alone."

That seemed to catch her off guard. Her eyes narrowed. "Why? What business do you have with him?"

"I owe him," I said. "That's all."

"I don't believe you."

"I don't care if you believe me."

Her mouth twisted up on one side as she tapped a finger on the desk.

"I don't want your empire, but I will find the midnight. When I do, I'll have your word that you won't touch Saint. Or his trade." I held out my hand between us.

Holland stared at it, thinking. I could see her sizing me up, trying to see what I was made of. "I think perhaps Saint is more to you than I realized. I think he was more to Isolde than I realized."

She wasn't stupid. She was putting it together. She knew that Saint was Isolde's helmsman, but she didn't know he was her lover. And I wasn't going to tell her she was right.

"Do we have a deal or not?" I lifted my hand between us.

She took it, smiling so that the candlelight flashed in her eyes. "We have a deal."

TWENTY

Bastian was beautiful in the predawn dark.

I stood at the window with my fingertips pressed to the cold glass, watching the glimmer of streetlights below. Azimuth House sat at the top of the hill, overlooking the landscape like a sentinel, and it was fitting. Holland had her eye on everything that happened in this city. The docks. The merchants. The Trade Council. And now she had her sights set on Ceros.

It was only a matter of time before she was doing the same thing in the Narrows.

The maps from the walls in Holland's office were rolled up tight and tied with twine on the table beside the door.

She'd looked me in the eye when she gave them to me, a spark of recognition making me still. In that moment, I'd felt as if I were looking at my mother.

There was a break in the rhythm of West's breaths and I turned from the window. He lay on top of the quilts, one arm tucked beneath a pillow, and even in the low light, I could see that the color was coming back into his cheeks.

That's why I hadn't woken him, I told myself. Why I'd stood in the dark silence for the last hour, waiting for him to open his eyes. But really, I was afraid.

I climbed onto the end of the bed, watching his chest rise and fall. His brows pulled together, his eyes still closed, and he sucked in a sharp breath with a jolt. His eyes fluttered open and I watched them focus frantically. He dragged his bleary gaze over the room until he spotted me. When he did, he let the breath go.

"What's wrong?" I reached out, hooking my fingers into the crook of his arm. His skin was hot, his pulse racing.

He sat up, pushing the hair back from his face. His eyes went to the window and I realized that he was looking for the harbor. For the *Marigold*. "We should go. Get on the water before the sun rises."

My heartbeat pounded in my ears as he got to his feet, my teeth clenching. "We can't." I folded my fingers together to keep my hands from shaking. "*I* can't."

Almost instantly, West's face changed. He turned toward me, his back to the dark sky. "What?" The sound of his voice was deepened with sleep.

I opened my mouth, trying to find a way to say it. I'd

turned the words over in my head again and again, but now they escaped me.

The look in his eye slowly transformed from concern to fear. "Fable."

"I can't go back to the Narrows with you," I said. "Not yet."

His face turned to stone. "What are you talking about?"

I'd known the moment I made the deal with Holland that it would cost me with West. But I had to believe that it was something I could fix.

"Last night," I swallowed. "I made a deal with Holland. One you're not going to like."

The color drained from his cheeks. "What are you talking about?"

"I . . ." My voice wavered

"What did you do, Fable?"

"I'm going to find midnight. For Holland."

"In exchange for what?" The words were clipped.

This was the moment I'd been dreading. That flash of fury in his eyes. The tight clench in his jaw.

I pressed my tongue to my teeth. Once I said it, there was no going back. "Saint." I unfolded my legs, sliding from the bed, and West took a step back from me. "If I find the midnight for Holland, she'll leave Saint alone."

It took a moment for me to place the look on West's face. It was disbelief. "What the hell were you thinking?"

I didn't have an answer to that. Not one he could understand. "I have to do this, West."

"We agreed," he breathed. "We agreed that we'd cut ties with him."

"I know." I swallowed.

He turned to the window, staring out at the sea in the distance.

"It's in Yuri's Constellation. I can find it."

"What if you can't?"

"I can. I know I can." I tried to sound sure. "I'll take one of her crews and—" The words cut off when he turned to look at me.

West's silent rage filled the room around us. "I'm not leaving Bastian without you."

"I'm not asking you to stay." I twisted my fingers into the underdress. "Take the *Marigold* back to Ceros and I'll meet you."

He took the jacket from where it was hung on the back of the chair and slipped his arms into the sleeves. "When you made that deal, you made it for both of us."

I'd been afraid he would say that. It's exactly what I would have said if West had done the same thing. But the crew would never agree. He'd be outvoted before he even finished telling them what I'd done. "West, I'm sorry."

He went still, searching my eyes. "Tell me all of this has nothing to do with what I told you last night."

"What?"

He sucked in his bottom lip. "I think you agreed to this deal because you're not sure you want to come back to the Narrows."

"The Narrows is my home, West. I'm telling you the truth. This is about me and Saint. Nothing else."

He muttered something under his breath as he buttoned his collar.

"What? What are you thinking?"

"I don't think you want to know what I'm thinking," he said lowly.

"I do."

He hesitated, letting a long silence stretch out between us before he finally answered, "I'm thinking that I was right."

"Right about what?"

A bit of red bloomed beneath his skin. "When you asked me to take you onto this crew, I told you that if you had to choose between us and Saint, that you would choose him."

My mouth dropped open, a small sound escaping my throat. "That's not what's happening, West."

"Isn't it?" His eyes were cold when they lifted to meet mine.

I recoiled, the words cutting deep.

"I'm not choosing him over you," I said again, louder. Angrier. "If it was Willa, you'd do the same thing."

"Saint's not Willa," he shot back. He was rigid, still slightly turned away from me. "He left you, Fable. When you went to him in Ceros, he didn't want you."

"I know," I said weakly.

"Then why are you doing this?"

I could hardly get the words out. Looking at West in that moment, it felt as if they'd lost their meaning. "I just can't let anything happen to him."

West stared at me, his gaze growing colder. "Look me in the eye and tell me that *we* are your crew. That the *Marigold* is your home."

"It is," I said, the conviction in my voice making pain erupt in my chest. I didn't blink, willing him to believe it.

He picked up the frock from the end of the bed and handed it to me. "Then let's go."

TWENTY-ONE

L amplight still glinted on the docks, reflecting in the glass of shop windows on the hill. West stayed close to me, his long strides hitting the wood planks beside mine. He'd said almost nothing since we left Azimuth House, but the air between us rang with his silence. He was angry. Furious, even.

I couldn't blame him. He'd left the Narrows to come find me, and I'd trapped him in Holland's net.

Clove had been enraged when I told him, too. Mostly because he was the one who'd have to deal with my father. He followed us through the narrow streets, his precious chest of coin still pinned beneath his arm. I hadn't seen it leave his hands since Holland gave it to him.

My stomach was in knots as we stood at the entrance to the harbor and my heart jumped into my throat when the *Marigold* came into view.

She was beautiful, her honey-hued wood aglow in the morning light. The sea was clear and blue behind her, and the new sails were as white as fresh cream, rolled up neatly on the masts. More than once, I'd wondered if I'd ever see her again.

That same feeling I had each time I saw her at the barrier islands—deep relief—came over me, making my bottom lip tremble. When he realized that I'd stopped, West turned back, looking up at me from the bottom of the steps. His hair caught in the wind, and he tucked it behind his ears before he pulled the cap from his pocket and tugged it on.

I took up the skirts and followed him. The docks were bustling with inventory to be logged and helmsmen waiting for their approvals from Bastian's harbor master. He stood at the mouth of the longest slip, bent over a table of parchments as I passed. The ledger he'd shown Holland was open, recording the ships that had come in through the night. In another hour, the logs would likely be sitting on Holland's desk.

My steps faltered when a face I recognized was lit with the glow of a barrel fire. Calla had her head wrapped in a scarf, the muscles in her arms taking shape under her skin as she pried the lid off a crate with one hand. The other was still tucked into a sling from where I'd broken her fingers.

I searched the other docks for any sign of Koy, but I didn't see him. He and everyone else on the *Luna* would be looking for work like the harbor master said, scraping together what coin they could until they got onto another crew or purchased passage back to the Narrows.

Ahead, the bow of the *Marigold* was dark except for a single lantern that flickered with a yellow flame. A slight silhouette was painted against the sky.

Willa.

She leaned over the railing, looking down at us. Her twisted locks were pulled up on top of her head like a coil of rope. I couldn't see her face, but I could hear the long exhale that escaped her lips as she spotted us.

The ladder unrolled a moment later, and Clove climbed up first. West held it in place for me to take hold of the rungs. When he didn't look at me, I squared my shoulders to him, waiting. "Are we all right?" I asked.

"We're all right," West said, meeting my eyes. But he was still cold.

I wished he would touch me. Ground me to the dock so the feeling of the restless sea inside me would calm. But there was a distance between us that hadn't been there before. And I wasn't sure how to close it.

I climbed the ladder and when I reached the top, Willa was standing before the helm, staring apprehensively at Clove. But he was entirely uninterested in her, finding a crate at the bow to sit and prop up his boots.

When she looked up at me, her face was twisted up, her mouth hanging open. "*What* are you wearing?"

I looked down at the frock, mortified, but before I could answer, a wide smile spread her lips. The scar on her cheek glistened white. I dropped over the railing and she threw her arms around me, holding me so tight that I could hardly breathe.

She let me go, leaning back to look at me. "It's good to see you."

I nodded in answer, sniffling, and she grabbed my hand, squeezing it. My eyes burned at the show of affection. I'd missed her. I'd missed all of them.

Footsteps pounded below and a moment later Paj was coming up the steps, Auster behind him. He was missing his shirt, his long, shining black hair spilling over his shoulders.

"Our bad luck charm is back!" Paj called to the open door of the helmsman's quarters as he crossed the deck toward me. "And she's wearing a skirt!" He clapped me on the back hard, and I stumbled forward into Auster's arms. His bare skin was warm as I pressed a flushed cheek to his chest. He smelled like saltwater and sun.

Behind him, Hamish was glowering at Clove from where he stood in the breezeway. "What is he doing here?"

"Come for a cup of tea." Clove winked at him.

Hamish tipped his chin up at me and then at West. "You're late. Two days late." The set of his mouth was grim.

"Things didn't exactly go as planned," West muttered.

"We heard about Zola," Paj said. "People on the docks have been talking and yesterday someone came to tear apart the *Luna*."

"Bastard got what was coming to him." Willa huffed. "Where have you been?"

"You can tell us later." Paj started for the helmsman's quarters. "Let's get the hell out of here."

Willa nodded, moving toward the mainmast.

"Wait." My hands clenched into fists inside the pockets of my jacket, and when I felt West's eyes on me, I didn't look up. I didn't want to see his face when I said it.

But he cut me off, stepping forward to face the crew. "There's something we have to do before we go back to Ceros."

"West—" I grabbed hold of his arm but he pulled away, turning to Paj.

"Set course for Yuri's Constellation."

Each of the crew looked as confused as I was. "What?"

"Yuri's Constellation?" Willa glanced between us. "What are you talking about?"

"West," I lowered my voice, "don't."

"And what exactly are we doing in Yuri's Constellation?" Hamish asked, with his best attempt at patience.

"We aren't doing anything there. I am," I answered. "It's a dredging job. A one-time thing. When I'm done, I'll find you in Ceros."

"What's the cut?" Hamish put his spectacles back on, comfortable as long as we were talking numbers.

I swallowed. "There isn't one."

"What's going on, Fable?" Paj took a step toward me.

"As soon as I take care of this, I'll be back in the Narrows. You can take my share of the *Lark* and—"

"Fable made a deal with Holland," West's voice rolled over the deck between us.

The confusion in the crew's eyes instantly turned into suspicion.

"What deal?" Auster pressed.

"I'm going to find something for her."

Paj scoffed. "Why?"

I ran a hand over my face. "Holland is . . ."

"She's Isolde's mother," Clove finished, exasperated.

The four of them looked to West, but he was silent.

"Holland is your *grandmother*?" Hamish pulled the spectacles from his face. They dangled from his fingertips.

"I didn't know until the night of the gala," I said, staring at the deck. "She's after Saint and I told her I'd find something for her if she left him alone."

Another sudden, howling silence fell over the ship.

"You can't be serious," Paj rasped. "Is there a bastard from here to the Narrows you're *not* related to?"

"No way are we taking on a job to save Saint's neck," Willa snapped.

"I agree," Hamish echoed.

"I know." It was exactly what I expected them to say. "That's why I'm doing this on my own."

"No, you're not. And we're not taking a vote," West said. "Set course for Yuri's Constellation."

Every eye snapped up to him.

"West," I whispered.

"What is that supposed to mean?" Willa almost laughed.

"We're going to Yuri's Constellation. We'll do the dive and then go home."

Paj pushed off the railing, crossing his arms over his chest. "Are you telling me we don't have a say in this?"

"No. That's not what he's saying," I said.

"That's exactly what I'm saying," West interrupted. "The *Marigold* is going to Yuri's Constellation."

"What are you doing?" I gaped at him.

"I'm giving orders. Anyone who doesn't want to follow them can find passage back to the Narrows."

The crew stared at him in disbelief.

"Do you have any idea what we've done to get here? To find you?" Willa spat. This time, she was talking to me. "And now you want to save the man who's made our lives hell for the last two years?"

At the bow, Clove watched with an air of amusement. He crossed his arms over the chest in his lap, eyes jumping from West to the others.

"You still haven't told us what we're supposed to be dredging," Auster said calmly. He looked as if he was the only one not ready to punch West in the face.

"Before my mother left Bastian, she stole something from Holland," I said. "Midnight."

Paj's eyes went wide, but Willa's narrowed.

Auster laughed, but it bled to silence when he met my eyes. "What, you're serious?"

"It's in Yuri's Constellation. All we have to do is find it."

"There is no *we*," Paj growled. "Not in this."

I bristled, taking a step back. But Paj didn't blink.

"No one's even seen it!" Hamish shrieked. "It's probably not even real. No more than a story some drunk Saltblood bastard told at a tavern."

"It's real," Clove said, his deep voice silencing them.

Hamish shook his head. "Even if it is, another piece of midnight hasn't been dredged since it was unveiled by Holland."

"My mother found it. So can I," I said.

The familiar fire reignited in Willa's eyes. "You're insane. Both of you."

"I want everything together by the end of the day. We shove off at dawn," West said.

All four of them stared at him, furious. After another moment, he pushed off the mizzen, running one hand through his hair before he started for the breezeway. I watched him disappear into the helmsman's quarters before I followed.

The light from the room crept through the open door and the floorboards creaked as I stepped inside. The familiar smell of West's cabin poured into my lungs, and I wrapped my arms around myself, eyeing the string of adder stones hanging in the window.

"What was that?" I said.

West pulled a green rye glass from the drawer of his desk and reached up to the bulkhead, feeling down the length of it. The hem of his shirt came up, showing a sliver of bronze skin, and I bit the inside of my cheek.

His hand finally hit what he was looking for and pulled an amber bottle from the rafter. He uncorked it, filling the glass. "I've been having this dream," he said. "Since Dern."

I watched him pick up the glass and the uncomfortable silence stretched between us.

He shot the rye, swallowing hard. "About that night that we killed Crane." He held the glass out to me.

I took it, wondering if that's why he'd woken with a start this morning in Azimuth House.

He picked up the bottle, refilling the glass. "We're standing on the deck in the moonlight and I pry up the lid of the crate." He set the rye onto the desk, his jaw clenching. "But Crane's not in it. You are."

The cold pricked my skin, making me shiver, and the rye shook in the glass. I brought it to my lips and tipped my head back, draining it.

"You're angry at me. Not them."

He didn't deny it.

"You can't make them go to Yuri's Constellation."

"Yes, I can," he said firmly. "I'm the helmsman of this ship. My name is on the deed."

"That's not how this crew works, West."

He looked past me to the dark window. "It is now."

The ache in my throat made it hard to swallow. He'd made up his mind the moment I told him about my deal with Holland. Nothing I said was going to change it now. "This isn't right. You should take the *Marigold* back to the Narrows."

"I'm not taking the *Marigold* anywhere unless you're on it," he said, and it looked as if he hated the words.

This is what he was talking about when he said we were cursed. West was willing to defy the crew if it meant he didn't have to leave me in the Unnamed Sea. He was already paying the price for that day in Tempest Snare and that night in his cabin, when he told me he loved me.

We'd both be paying as long as we lived.

TWENTY-TWO

He's got 'em!"

Hamish's voice calling from the window made me drop the quill on the table. I slid out of the booth and went to the doors of the tavern, propped open to the street. Paj was walking up the cobblestones with three rolled parchments under his arm, his collar pulled up against the bitter wind. He shoved past a group of men headed for the merchant's house, almost knocking one of them over.

Clove had volunteered to be the one to go to the mapmaker, not trusting Paj to do it. He hadn't hidden the fact that he didn't think our navigator could get the *Marigold* to Yuri's Constellation and back again. But I'd had other errands for Clove.

I looked out to the street again, watching for any sign of him. He was late.

I slid my hands into the pockets of the new trousers Willa had begrudgingly gone to buy for me. It felt good to be out of that ridiculous frock and back in a pair of boots.

Paj was barreling through the doors a moment later. He made his way to the booth where we'd set up and dropped the maps haphazardly on the table. He didn't bother looking at me. In fact, none of them had so much as glanced in my direction all day.

West ignored Paj's display of indignation, rolling up the sleeves of his shirt. "All right. What have we got?"

"Look for yourself," Paj grunted.

"Paj," Auster warned, raising an eyebrow.

Beside him, Willa looked as if she approved of Paj's protest. She huffed, stirring another cube of sugar into her cold tea.

Paj relented under Auster's reproach, opening the maps on top of the ship log Holland had given me. "The midnight was found in Yuri's Constellation. It had to be. According to the logs, Holland's crew had been dredging the islands for over a month when Isolde found it, and they continued in that spot for weeks after." He set a finger on the broken cluster of land masses. "Since then, Holland's crew has dredged the hell out of those reefs. First from the north, working their way south. Then from the south, working north."

"But they haven't found anything," I said under my breath.

"Obviously," Paj answered sharply. "They've been working at it almost twenty years and they've covered every reef that Holland's crew was working at the time Isolde found the midnight. To say this is a fool's errand is putting it lightly."

I sat on the edge of the table. "Where are the geological and topographical charts?"

He sifted through the corners of the maps until he found the one he was looking for, and pulled it free. "Here."

The diagrams unrolled before me. The stretch of Unnamed Sea was labeled in different colors and thicknesses of lines identifying the types of rocks and depths of water. Most of the reefs were encircled by basalt, slate, and sandstone— prime locations to find most of the stones that ran the gem trade. But if my mother had only found midnight in one place and Holland had been unable to find it since, we were looking for something different.

"What is this?" I pointed to two islands at the corner of the map marked with the symbol for quartz.

When Paj only stared at me, Auster snatched the log from his hand. He dragged his finger down the page until he found it. "Sphene Sisters."

I'd heard of it before. It was a pair of reefs in Yuri's Constellation where most of the yellow and green sphene was dredged, known for its wedge shape in the rock.

"Looks like there's also an active cache of blue agate there, but the serpentine is gone. It's all been dredged," Auster added.

"Any others?"

"Just some onyx here and there."

I squinted, thinking. "When was the last time Holland's crew dredged here?"

Paj finally spoke, but his face was still like stone. "Two years ago." He reached over me, moving the map. "This is the one that looks the most interesting." He pointed to the specks of black in between two long peninsulas. "Pretty rich in chrysocolla, and it hasn't been dredged for at least ten years."

That *was* interesting. Chrysocolla was typically found in small caches, spread out over large stretches of water. Enough to be dredged over a period of ten years was unusual.

"Any others that look odd?"

"Not really. Holland's been methodical, careful not to skip anything in between."

But if this was the quadrant they were working when Isolde found it, it had to be there. Somewhere. I took the quill from his hand, marking through the areas that showed the least promise. In the end, we were left with the reefs set atop bedrocks of gneiss and greenschist.

"They've been over these reefs again and again," West said, leaning onto the table with both hands.

"Not with a gem sage, they haven't," I said, almost to myself. "Oskar was gone long before Isolde found the midnight."

"Oskar?"

"My grandfather." The words sounded strange even to myself. "He was a gem sage. If Holland had another, she wouldn't be so interested in the fact that I'm one too." Any gem sage with a lick of sense would avoid a merchant like Holland. I turned to Paj. "You sure you can get around these waters?"

"Do I have a choice?"

"Can you do it or not?" I said, harsher than I meant.

He gave me a good, long look of annoyance. "I can do it."

"We have one week," I muttered. Even with two weeks, it would be a nearly impossible dive.

"We need the course charted by sundown," West said.

"Anything else?" Paj looked between us, a mocking smile plastered on his face.

"Yeah," I said, annoyed. "Tell Hamish I need a gem lamp. And another belt of dredging tools."

"My pleasure." Paj pushed off the table and grabbed his jacket before he started for the doors.

They slammed shut as the barmaid set down a third pot of tea and I slid my cup over the maps so she could fill it.

"Another dredging belt," Willa murmured. "What happened to yours?"

"What do you care?" West glared at her.

Willa shrugged. "Just curious what our coin's being spent on."

Her eyes cut to me and I bit the inside of my cheek. Willa was drawing a line. She was on one side, and she was clearly putting me on the other.

"Something to eat?" The barmaid wiped her hands on her apron.

Auster reached into the pocket of his vest. "Bread and cheese. Stew if you have it." He set three coppers on the table.

"Aren't you going to check with Fable first?" Willa sneered.

I frowned, resisting the urge to topple the tea into her lap. I understood why she was angry. All of them had the right to be. But I wasn't sure West understood what he'd risked by forcing their hands. By the time this was over, I might not have a place on this crew.

I looked again to the window with a sigh. When I sent Clove to the docks, I'd told him to be back by noon.

"He said he'll be here," West said, reading my mind.

I pulled my attention from the street and placed it back on the maps. "We start in the eastern section of the quadrant, where Holland's ships were dredging when Isolde found the midnight, and stick to the reefs I've marked. There's no way to know if it's the right call until I get down there, but they have the best conditions for a diverse gem cache. There's warm water from the southern current, a gneiss bedrock, and a pocket of reefs old enough to hold a few secrets." It was the best place to start, but something told me it wouldn't be that easy.

The door to the tavern swung open again, and I squinted against the bright light. Clove pulled the cap from his head, unbuttoning his jacket with one hand, and I let out a relieved breath when I saw Koy behind him.

"Took half the day, but I found him." Clove sat down, taking the pot of tea without asking and filling one of the empty cups.

Koy was still wet, and the raw cuts on his fingers told me where he'd spent the last two days since Zola's ship was commandeered. He'd been scraping hulls. His face gave no trace of shame as he watched me inspect his hands. It was an undignified job, one that Koy hadn't likely done in years, but Jevalis had done a lot worse for coin.

Beside me West sat straight-backed, studying him.

"What do you want, Fable?" Koy finally said, sliding his hands into the pockets of his jacket.

"I have a job, if you want it."

His black eyes glinted. "A job."

Willa leaned forward with her jaw dropped open. "I'm sorry, are you now hiring crew without our permission, too?"

"Shut it, Willa," West growled, silencing her.

I looked back up to Koy. "That's right. A job."

"The last time I saw you, you were a prisoner on the *Luna*, dredging under the thumb of Zola. You spend two days in Bastian and now you're running your own jobs?"

"It appears so." I shrugged.

Across the table, Willa was fuming. She shook her head, gritting her teeth. Koy stared at me with the same sentiment.

I leaned back into the bench, looking at the maps. "Seven days, twelve reefs, one gem."

"That doesn't even make sense. What do you mean one gem?"

"I mean we are looking for one gem, but we don't know where it is."

He huffed. "Are you serious?"

I nodded once.

"And how exactly are you going to do that?"

I rolled up the map between us, tapping it on the table.

"I knew it," he muttered, shaking his head. "You're a gem sage."

I didn't deny it.

"I told everyone on that island there was a reason you were dredging more than Jevalis who'd been diving for fifty years."

He'd never accused me outright, but I'd known Koy was suspicious. The only thing I'd had to hide behind was the fact that I was so young. No one was going to believe him unless they knew who my mother was.

"I'm not interested," he said. "I only got half my pay from Zola before his body was dumped into the harbor by whoever cut his throat. I'm going to spend most of it getting back to Jeval."

And that's what I was counting on. Koy had a family on Jeval who depended on him, and that was the reason he'd taken the job from Zola in the first place. His brother was probably running his ferrying trade while he was gone, and in a few days they'd be wondering where he was.

But I'd have to get him to trust that I was good for the coin if I was going to convince him to come with us.

"We'll double the pay Zola promised you. And we'll give it to you now," Clove grunted between sips of his tea.

"What?" I turned in my chair to face him. It was a much better offer than the one I was prepared to make.

Clove looked uninterested, as usual. Not a single feather ruffled. "You heard me."

"We don't have that kind of coin, Clove. Not here." I lowered my voice. Even if we did, the crew would have my head for spending that much from the coffers.

"I do." He shrugged.

He was talking about the bounty for Zola. The one he was going to use for his own fleet.

"Clove . . ."

"You need it," he said simply. "So take it."

That was the Clove I knew. He'd have stolen the coin for me if I asked.

I gave him a weak, grateful smile. "I'll pay you back. Every copper."

Across the table, I could feel Koy's eyes slide to me. He was clearly listening now.

"We'll also give you passage back to Jeval, free of charge when we head back to the Narrows," I added.

Koy bit his bottom lip, thinking. "What have you gotten yourself into?"

"You want the job or not?"

He shifted on his feet, hesitating. It was an offer he couldn't refuse, and we both knew it. "Why?"

"Why what?"

"Why are you offering it to *me?*" His tone turned bitter, and I realized he'd figured me out. I had to handle him carefully if I was going to keep him on the line.

"You're the best dredger I've ever seen. Besides myself," I amended. "This is a job that's next to impossible, and I need you."

He turned toward the window, staring out at the street. Beside him, West was looking at me. He didn't like this. The last time West had seen Koy, he'd been chasing me down the docks in Jeval, ready to kill me.

When Koy finally spoke, he set both hands onto the table, leaning over me. "Fine. I'll do it. I want the coin now and I need a new belt of tools. Those bastards took them when they pieced the *Luna.*"

"Done." I grinned.

"One more thing." He leaned closer, and West got to his feet, taking a step toward us.

"What is it?" I met Koy's eyes.

"We're not trading favors, Fable. Understand?" His voice

deepened. "I told you. I didn't cut the rope. So, if this has anything to do with what happened on that dive, I'm *out*."

And that was the thing about Koy. His pride was more stubborn than his hunger for copper. If I so much as breathed a hint that I owed him, he'd walk away from the coin.

"Fine. You didn't cut the rope." I reached out a hand between us. "We leave at sundown. I'll have your tools and your coin on the ship."

Koy took my hand, shaking it. He looked at me another moment before he turned on his heel, headed for the door.

Willa stared at me incredulously. I handed her the maps and she shook her head once before she got to her feet.

West watched her go. "What favor is Koy talking about?" he asked.

"That bastard saved my life when Zola's dredger tried to kill me."

"That's what this is about? A debt?"

"No," I said, standing. "I meant what I said. He's a skilled dredger. We need him."

I could see in West's eyes that he wanted the whole story. It was one I'd eventually have to tell him, but not today.

Clove leaned back, looking at me.

"What?"

He shrugged, a wry smile playing at his lips. "Just thinkin'."

I cocked my head to the side, glaring. "Thinking *what*?"

"That you're just like him," he said, taking another sip of tea.

I didn't have to ask who he meant. He was talking about Saint.

TWENTY-THREE

What else needs doing before we leave?" Clove asked, setting down his cup.

"You're not coming," I said.

His bushy eyebrows pulled together. "What do you mean I'm not coming?"

"If Holland finds out that you didn't go to the Narrows, she's going to want to know why. We can't risk it. And I need you to tell Saint what's going on."

"Saint's not going to like that. Me leaving you here. That wasn't the plan."

"Nothing's really gone to plan, if you haven't noticed. I need you in the Narrows, Clove."

He considered it, his gaze floating from me to West. This wasn't just about Saint. Clove didn't trust West. He didn't trust any of them. "This is a bad idea. That navigator of yours will have you run aground before you even get to Yuri's Constellation."

"That navigator will do just fine," Auster snapped.

"There will be hell to pay if Fable doesn't make it back to Ceros." Clove was talking to West now.

"Fable got herself off that island you left her on. I think she can get herself back to Ceros." West's words were like acid.

"I suppose you're right about that." Clove smiled. "Guess I better find a ship headed to the Narrows." He stood, giving me a wink before he started for the door.

"One of Holland's," I said. "We need her to know you're gone."

The barmaid set down two large plates of bread and cheese, followed by another pot of tea. Auster didn't waste any time, reaching for the dish of butter.

He lathered a thick layer onto a piece of bread and handed it to me. "Eat. You'll feel better."

I eyed him. "Why aren't you mad like the others?"

"Oh, I'm mad," he said, reaching for another piece of bread. "What you did was wrong, West. When you took us on, you said we'd each have an equal say. You went back on your word."

"Then why are you playing nice?" I asked.

"Because." He looked past me, to West. "If it was Paj, I'd have done the same damn thing." He tore the bread and popped a piece into his mouth.

West leaned onto the table, letting out a heavy breath. The defensive, rigid set of his jaw was gone now and I knew the reality of what he'd done was setting in. Maybe Hamish would forgive the slight, but Willa and Paj wouldn't be so understanding.

West stared at the table, mind working. "You know we can't give the midnight to Holland if we find it. Don't you? She's the most powerful trader in the Unnamed Sea. If you find the midnight for her . . ." His words trailed off. "She could ruin everything. For us and for the Narrows."

He was right. I'd been thinking the same thing.

"If she gets license to trade in Ceros, everything we planned is over. None of it matters."

"Saint won't let that happen." I tried to sound sure. But the truth was that there was no telling what Saint would do.

Auster reached across the table for another piece of bread, and the tattoo of tangled snakes peeked out from beneath his rolled sleeve. Two knotted serpents eating each other's tails. It was the same one the young man named Ezra had, the one who'd been in Holland's office.

A distant thought whispered in the back of my mind, making me still.

The midnight would save Saint, but it wouldn't save the Narrows. If Holland opened her route to Ceros, it would sink every trader posted there.

"Auster?" I said.

He looked up from his plate, his mouth full of bread. "Yeah?"

"Tell me about that tattoo."

His gray eyes sharpened, his hand freezing in midair. On the other side of the table, West was silent.

"Why?" Auster asked warily.

"What are you thinking?" West leaned closer to me.

"You were right about Holland. This isn't going to be as simple as trading midnight for Saint. If she gets license to trade in the Narrows, it doesn't matter. All of us will be working the docks by the time she's through."

West nodded. "I know."

"No one can touch her. She controls the trade in the Unnamed Sea and she owns the Trade Council."

West shrugged. "The Narrows Trade Council has held out this long. There's nothing we can do except hope that they don't grant her the license."

"That's not true," I said, my mind still unraveling the tangle of thoughts.

They both looked at me, waiting.

"We know that Holland wants to take out the traders posted from Ceros." My gaze drifted, landing on Auster. "She's got a commission with an unlicensed merchant to sweeten the deal with the Council. A commission she doesn't want anyone to know about."

Auster's mouth went crooked. "With who?"

"When we were with Holland, she made a deal with someone who had that same tattoo."

Auster looked suddenly uncomfortable, shifting in his seat. "What was his name?"

"Ezra," I said.

Auster's eyes snapped up.

"Do you know him?"

"I know him," he answered.

"What can you tell us about him?"

"Nothing, if I know what's good for me. You don't want to get involved with the Roths. Trust me."

"Wait. You're a Roth?" My voice rose.

But West didn't look at all surprised. He'd known exactly what that tattoo was.

"You think we can use them?" West said, keeping his voice low.

"No," Auster said evenly.

"Why not?"

"They're dangerous, West," Auster answered. "Henrik would sooner cut you than invite you to tea, like Holland."

I pushed up the sleeve of Auster's shirt, studying the mark. "How do you know him?"

Auster seemed to be deciding how much he would tell me. "He's my uncle. We're not exactly on good terms," Auster added. "When I left Bastian, I left the Roths. And no one leaves the Roths."

"And Ezra?"

When he could see I wasn't going to give up, Auster sighed. "He wasn't born into the family. Henrik found him working for a smith when we were just kids. He took him in because he was talented. Henrik got him the best training there was, and by the time we were fourteen or fifteen, he was making the best silver pieces in Bastian. But Henrik couldn't sell them."

"Why not?"

"For years, the Roth family was the single largest producer of fake gems from the Unnamed Sea to the Narrows. The trade had made them rich, but it also cost them any chance they had at getting a merchant's ring from the Gem Guild. It's illegal for anyone to do business with them."

That hadn't stopped Holland from giving Henrik a commission, and I understood why. The sketches Ezra had shown Holland looked like something out of a myth. Only someone truly gifted would be able to cast a piece like that.

"So he's using Ezra to get a ring."

Auster nodded. "That's what he wants, but he's never going to get it. The Roths' reputation is known at every port in the Unnamed Sea. No one's ever going to trust Henrik, much less give him their business."

"Holland did."

"But she'll never tell anyone who made it. Ezra will never get the credit for whatever she commissioned. Neither will Henrik."

If Auster was right, then Henrik was a man trying to legitimize himself.

I tapped my fingers on the table. "Do you think they'd help us?"

"They don't help anyone. They help themselves."

"Unless there's something in it for them." I thought aloud. I leaned back into the booth, thinking. I didn't know exactly what Holland had planned for the Narrows, but West had been right about her. She couldn't be trusted. And I had a feeling that she was waiting to make her move. "Will you take us to him?" I asked.

Auster looked as if he couldn't believe what I'd just said. "You don't want to get tangled up with them, Fable. I'm serious."

"Will you do it or not?"

Auster met my eyes for a long moment before he shook his head, letting out a heavy breath. "Paj isn't going to like this."

TWENTY-FOUR

"Crazy bastards." Paj had been cursing from the moment we left the harbor, and it had taken all of Auster's will to ignore him as we walked into Lower Vale.

When I asked Auster to take us to the Roths, I hadn't expected him to agree.

Auster didn't say exactly how he'd escaped his family when he and Paj left Bastian, and I didn't ask. But it was clear that it was a past Paj didn't want to revisit. He forbade Auster from taking us to Lower Vale, and only relented when he realized that Auster would go without him.

Now Paj had another reason to be angry, and I was more convinced by the minute that the break among us might be too great to be repaired. I hadn't meant to pull them into Holland's war on the Narrows, but West had made sure of it when he commanded them to Yuri's Constellation. The only thing to do now was to see the plan through and hope we could salvage what was left of the crew after.

If Bastian had a slum, Lower Vale was it, though it was nothing to the stench and filth of The Pinch or Waterside in Ceros. Even the pigeons perched on the rooftops looked cleaner than the ones in the Narrows.

West walked shoulder to shoulder with Auster, shooting a warning look to the people on the street around us who were staring. They watched Auster as he passed, whispering to each other, and I didn't know if it was because they recognized him or if it was because he was so striking. Auster had taken care with himself when he got ready in the crew's cabin, brushing through his thick, dark hair until it lay over his shoulder like melted obsidian. His shirt, too, was clean and pressed. He was always beautiful, even after days at sea with no washing. But this Auster was magnificent. He was breathtaking.

Paj looked different too. There was an emptiness in his eyes that I hadn't seen since the day he dared me to fetch a coin from the sea bottom at the coral islands. "I still think this is a bad idea," he grunted.

That pushed Auster over the edge. He suddenly turned on his heel and Paj almost slammed into him as he came to an abrupt stop.

Auster looked up into Paj's face, his mouth set in a straight line. "Are you finished?"

"No, actually, I'm not," Paj growled. "Am I the only one who remembers what it took for us to leave these people behind? I nearly died cutting you from your deranged family!"

"If you're scared, you can wait at the tavern." Auster shoved him backward.

"It's not me I'm afraid for," Paj answered, and it was so honest and plain that it seemed to make the street noise stop around us. Paj's face softened, his mouth turning down at the corners.

Auster took the sleeve of Paj's shirt, as if to anchor him. "If it's Ezra, we're fine."

"And if it's Henrik?"

Auster gave his best attempt at a playful smile. "Then we're screwed." He pulled Paj toward him until he was low enough for Auster to kiss him. Right there in the street, for anyone to see.

I couldn't help but smile.

"Finished?" West said impatiently.

Auster looked at Paj as if he was waiting for him to answer.

Paj sighed. "Finished."

Auster let go of him, satisfied for the moment, and we followed him into the narrow alley between the last two buildings on the street. The opening lay between the signs for a tea house and a launderer, and the bricks turned black, painted with the soot.

Auster walked with his shoulders pulled back. I could see the armor going up around him, the softness of his face changing, and the weight of his steps growing heavier. What-ever he was about to face, he was bracing for it.

The alley came to an end, where an iron door lined with rivets was fit into the brick.

A string of something above it caught the wind, swing-ing. I squinted, trying to make it out, and grimaced when I realized what it was. "Are those . . . ?"

"Teeth," Auster muttered, answering before I'd even fin-ished.

"Human teeth?"

Auster lifted an eyebrow. "The price of lying to Henrik." His hand curled into a fist before he raised it, and he looked over his shoulder to Paj once more before he knocked.

"You should wait out here," he said, keeping his voice low.

Paj laughed bitterly in response, shaking his head once. "That's never going to happen."

Beside me, West's hand went to the back of his belt, ready to take hold of his knife. There was only the soft drip of water filling the silence as we stood before the closed door. I couldn't stop staring at the string of teeth.

Paj tapped the buckle of his belt restlessly, but Auster didn't seem concerned. He crossed his arms over his chest, waiting, and when the latch finally creaked, he didn't so much as flinch.

The door cracked open enough for a young boy's face to appear. The deep valley of a scar curved over his cheek. "Yes?" He looked more irritated than interested in whatever we wanted.

"Looking for Ezra," Auster said flatly. "Tell him Auster's here to see him."

The boy's eyes went wide as he stumbled backward. "Auster?" The way he said the name sounded as if it came with a story.

Auster didn't answer, stepping into the dimly lit entry with the rest of us on his heels. A series of hooks lined the wall, where a few jackets and hats were hung beneath a series of gold-framed oil paintings. They were depictions of the sea in different styles and colors, and completely out of place on the cracked plaster walls. Even the tiles under our feet were fractured, their mosaic patterns tipping and turning where pieces were missing.

The boy's footsteps sounded in the hall after a tense silence, and he reappeared, motioning us into the dark. Auster followed without a moment's hesitation, but I pulled my knife from my belt, holding it ready at my side. The boy led us around a turn, and the warm glow of a lantern reignited the dark ahead.

A doorframe left empty save for its hinges gave way to a large, rectangular room. Rippling wallpaper the color of rubies was smoothed over the walls, the floor stained a deep mahogany where it was visible. Everywhere else, it was covered by a thick wool rug edged in fraying tassels.

The desk set before the fireplace was bare, but the boy straightened it methodically, lining up the quill along the right side. Before he was finished, the door along the back wall was pushed open, and the young man I'd seen at Holland's appeared. Ezra.

His eyes immediately found Auster as he stepped into the room. "You've got to be shitting me."

Auster stared at Ezra blankly before a smile broke on his face.

Ezra came around the desk, opening his arms and clapping Auster on the back as he embraced him. It was a different mask than the one I'd seen Ezra wear the day before in Holland's office. But the warmth between them seemed to irritate Paj. He rolled his shoulders like he had the urge to punch something.

Ezra ignored him, leaning in closer to Auster as he spoke. "Might not have been a good idea to bring him. Henrik will be here any minute."

"Good luck getting him out of here," Auster muttered.

But Ezra's easiness disappeared, his edges sharpening as his attention landed on me. He recognized me almost immediately. "What is she doing here?"

"She's a friend," Auster answered.

"You sure about that? I just saw her at Holland's."

"I'm sure." Auster set a hand on Ezra's shoulder. "How are you?"

Ezra had a hard time pulling his gaze from me. "I'm fine, Aus."

Auster didn't seem convinced, leaning low to catch Ezra's eyes.

"Good," Ezra pressed. "I'm good."

Auster gave a nod, accepting the answer. "We have a commission for you."

Ezra surveyed him skeptically before he went back to the desk. "What kind of commission?"

"One we know you can do," I interrupted.

Ezra's hand froze on the book in front of him at the sound of my voice. The lantern light cast the scars on his hands silver. I pulled the parchment I'd prepared from my jacket and unfolded it, setting it before him.

Ezra's eyes ran over it slowly, widening. "Is this a joke?"

The door behind him flung open, slamming against the wall, and I jolted, taking a step back. The flash of steel glinted in West's hand beside me.

An older man stood in the opening, one hand tucked into the pocket of a leather apron. His mustache was curled up on the ends, his hair combed neatly to one side. Pale blue eyes shone from beneath bushy eyebrows as they jumped from me to Paj, finally landing on Auster.

"Ah," he crooned, a wide smile breaking on his lips. But it was missing the warmth that Ezra's had. "Tru said the lost Roth darling was sitting in my parlor. I told him it wasn't possible. That my nephew wouldn't have the guts to show up here as long as he lived."

"Guess you were wrong," Auster said, meeting his gaze coolly.

"I see you brought your benefactor." Henrik looked to Paj. "Happy to re-break that nose. Maybe we can get it straight this time."

"Only one way to find out," Paj growled, moving toward him.

Auster caught him in the chest with the flat of his palm, and Henrik laughed, taking a pipe from the shelf. "Thought you were done with the Roths, Auster."

"I am. That doesn't mean I can't do business with them."

Henrik arched an eyebrow curiously. "What business could you possibly have that we would want?"

Auster jerked his chin to the parchment on the desk and Henrik picked it up. "What the—"

"Can you do it or not?" Auster barked.

"Of course we can. The question is, why the hell would we?" Henrik laughed.

"Name your price," I said, ready to negotiate.

Henrik narrowed his eyes at me. "Who'd you bring into my house, Auster?" The timber of his voice was verging on dangerous.

"I'm Fable. Holland's granddaughter. And I'm looking for a silversmith."

Henrik looked down his nose at me. "There is no price I'd take for that commission. Crossing Holland will put an end to our business in Bastian. For good."

"What if I told you that Holland won't be your problem anymore?"

"Then I'd tell you that you're as stupid as you are pretty," Henrik taunted. "I'd make more coin telling Holland you were here than I would off of your commission."

It was exactly what I'd been afraid he'd say. There was no reason for him to trust me and there was nothing I could offer him that would be more valuable than what Holland could. He'd be taking more than one chance by helping us.

My eyes trailed around the room. Peeling wallpaper, expensive candlesticks, the finest tailored jacket hanging on a rusted hook. Henrik was like Zola. A man trying to be something he never could. Not until he had one thing.

"Do this commission and I'll give you what Holland can't," I said.

Henrik's smile faded, replaced by a tick in his jaw. "And what is that?"

I stared at him. "A merchant's ring." The words withered in my mouth as I said them. There was no way to know if I could actually deliver. But if anyone could get one, it would be Saint.

Merchants had to apprentice for years before they could make a bid for a ring. And there were only so many rings to be given from each guild. Often, merchants were working beneath an older one, waiting for them to die or give up their trade.

His hand stilled on the match until the flame was so close to his fingertips that he had to put it out. "What?"

"I can get you a merchant's ring if you deliver. And only if it stays quiet."

"You're lying." The words dripped with fury.

But I could already see that I had him. The desperation of the prospect was all over his face. "I'm not. One merchant's ring from the Trade Council in the Narrows."

"The Narrows? We live in Bastian, sweetheart."

"We both know that a ring from one guild makes it easier to get one from the other. Which do you want more? Holland's favor, or a ring to buy your own?"

Henrik lit another match, puffing on the pipe until smoke

was billowing from the chamber. "Did Auster tell you what will happen to you if you lie to me?"

"He did."

"Your grandmother will be finding pieces of you all over this city," he said softly. "And I'll have to take my nephew off your hands in the spirit of restitution."

Paj's fists clenched. I was sure that at any moment, he was going to tear across the room and break Henrik's neck.

Henrik picked up the parchment, studying the rendering. I'd done it only by memory, my skill not even close to what it should be. But they knew exactly what I was looking for. "Only a Narrows-born urchin would be this stupid."

"Only Saltbloods would be this soft," I shot back. "Will you do it?"

Henrik looked to Ezra, who stood stoically against the wall. Whatever he was thinking, he kept it to himself.

After a moment, Henrik reached up, taking hold of Auster's shoulder. He squeezed it. A little too tightly.

"We'll do it."

TWENTY-FIVE

The sails of the *Marigold* unrolled in unison, slapping against the masts as the sun set over the water. In only a day we'd pulled together everything we needed for the dive at Yuri's Constellation and in minutes, we'd be sailing into the dark.

Henrik agreed to accept our commission, but taking him at his word was like putting faith in the ability of adder stones to protect from sea demons. In the end, there was no way to know what the Roths would do.

The only thing that seemed sure was the fact that our days were numbered. One way or another, Holland was going to make her move. And if she did, the Narrows would never be the same.

I watched Clove standing at the end of the dock with his jacket buttoned up to his chin. I slipped my hands into my pockets and breathed into the scarf wound around my neck as I walked toward him. The sea was gray and blustery, fighting dusk.

He said nothing as I came to stand behind him. His cheeks were reddened by the wind, the tip of his nose rosy.

"Do you think Saint can do it?" I watched his face as he stared out at the water, thinking. His pale blond hair had come out from under his cap, blowing around his face.

"I don't know," he said. Clove hadn't been happy when I told him that we'd gone to Henrik. He was even angrier when I told him what I'd offered him.

I didn't know what my father would say when he found out what I'd been up to. I could only hope he'd play along. Getting a merchant's ring for a criminal was next to impossible. But if I wanted the Roths to come through with the safety net we needed, I had to have it. "Six days."

"Six days," he repeated.

The Trade Council meeting in Sagsay Holm would bring together every licensed trader from the Unnamed Sea and the Narrows. If Holland had her way, she'd secure approval from the Council to open her trade to Ceros. If I had mine, she'd never get the chance to sail our waters.

Clove would have to move fast if he was going to get to Ceros and back to Sagsay Holm with Saint in time.

"What do you know about the midnight, Clove? Honestly."

He sighed. "Nothing. I only know that your mother took it when she left Bastian and that she didn't want it found."

"She told you about it?"

"After one too many glasses of rye." He smirked. "I wasn't sure it was true until Holland told the same story."

If Isolde had taken it, she'd done it for a reason. The only thing that made sense was that she didn't want the midnight in Holland's hands. Midnight's worth was in its rarity. After it was unveiled to the Trade Council of the Unnamed Sea, it vanished, making it no more than a myth.

"I don't even know why I'm doing this," I whispered, watching the water flash silver in the rising sunlight. "Saint would never do it for me."

Clove turned slowly, looking down at me. "You can't really believe that."

"Why wouldn't I?"

He snorted, shaking his head. "That man would sink his fleet for you, Fable. He'd walk away from everything."

A lump curled painfully in my throat. "No, he wouldn't."

Clove pulled the cap back on his head, casting his face in shadow. "*Isolde* isn't the only name we aren't allowed to say." He kissed the top of my head. "You be careful. And you watch that crew."

"Watch them?"

"They look about ready to throw that helmsman overboard. And you with him."

I clenched my teeth, looking past him to the *Marigold*.

"I'll see you in Sagsay Holm."

I watched him go, breathing through the sting smarting behind my eyes. The words he'd said about my father were dangerous things. They held the power to crush me. Because the most fragile hope I'd ever held was that somewhere in the flesh and bone of him, Saint had loved me.

There was a part of me that was terrified to find out if it was true. And an even bigger part that knew it would destroy me.

I climbed the ladder hand over hand until the sound of shouting made me still. I looked over my shoulder to see Holland coming through the archway of the harbor, wrapped in a blood-red cloak. I jumped back down, watching as she floated toward us, her sterling hair flowing behind her.

She was flanked by three guards on each side, taking up the width of the walkway. The dockworkers had to move out of her way, pushing down the slips as she passed.

"West!" Willa called out. She was watching with wide eyes from the railing.

He appeared beside her a moment later and as soon as he spotted Holland, he climbed over the side, landing beside me. "What is this?"

"I don't know," I whispered.

Holland turned down our dock without looking up, her eyes on the sea. The colors of the sunset danced over her face, making her cloak glow like a hot blade held to fire. She lifted a hand into the air and the guards stopped, leaving her to make the rest of the way down the slip on her own.

She smiled warmly as she stopped before us. "Thought I'd see you off."

West glared at her. "Just in time."

Hamish came down the dock behind Holland, marking in his log. He nearly crashed into her before one of her men took him by the collar and yanked him back. When his eyes finally lifted from the parchments, he looked as if he might fall over with shock. He stepped around Holland carefully, coming to stand behind us.

"We'll see you in Sagsay Holm," I said, turning back to the ladder.

"All I require of you before you leave is your deed." She opened her hand before us, grinning.

"What?" I snapped.

"The deed. To the *Marigold*."

West took a step toward her, and her guards instantly drew closer, hands on the hilts of their short swords. "You're out of your mind if you think I'm going to—"

"You don't trust me," she said, eyes narrowing. "And I don't trust you. I have no way of knowing if you'll show up in Sagsay Holm or give me the midnight if you find it. I require the deed to the *Marigold* or the deal's off."

West turned to fire beside me, the line of his shoulders hardening, his skin flushing red.

"We're not giving you the deed," I said.

"There's no reason to worry if you plan to hold up your end of the deal, Fable. What do you have to lose?"

But we both knew the answer to that question. I stood to lose Saint.

West turned to Hamish, who looked stunned.

"You can't be serious," he said, his eyes wide behind the lenses of his spectacles.

West held out a hand, waiting. Up on the deck of the ship, the rest of the crew was at work, readying the *Marigold* to shove off.

I watched in horror as Hamish reached into his jacket and pulled a worn envelope from inside. "West, don't." I reached for him, but he pushed past me, taking the deed from Hamish and handing it to Holland.

Holland opened it, pulling the folded parchment free. The stamp of the Narrows Trade Council was pressed into the top right corner of the document, the black ink penned in an expert hand. West's name was listed in its ownership.

She slipped it back into the envelope, satisfied.

Behind me, West was already climbing the ladder. He disappeared over the railing as his voice echoed out. "Raise anchor!"

"See you in Sagsay Holm." Holland turned, picking up her cloak as she made her way back up the slip.

I cursed, climbing the ladder. When I came onto the deck, Koy was draped lazily over a stack of piled rope, his hands clasped like a hammock behind his head. Willa slid down the mizzen, glaring at him before she went to the bow-anchor to help Paj with the crank.

Hamish muttered something under his breath when he made it up the ladder, and we both watched West to see what he would do. He looked over Paj's notes in the navigator's log, but the cold I could feel creeping toward me from him made me shiver.

Hamish gave me a wary look.

"You just going to stand there?" Willa clipped.

I turned to see her standing over Koy.

He gave her an easy smile. "Yeah. Unless you want to pay me extra to crew this ship."

Willa's cheeks flushed with rage as she went back to the crank. Koy looked pleased with himself, tapping his fingers on his elbows as he watched her from the corner of his eye.

Clove's warning echoed in my mind. By the time we got to Sagsay Holm, the *Marigold* might not even have a crew.

"What was that?" Paj asked, looking down at the dock, where Holland was walking through the archway.

West went to the helm, his attention on the sails. "It was nothing."

The rest of the crew had no idea what had just happened. And West wasn't going to tell them. Hamish looked utterly confused, holding the coin master's log before him.

West handed the helm off to Paj, jerking his chin to the starboard side. "Keep an eye on him."

He was talking about Koy, who was still reclined over the ropes, watching Willa tie off the lines.

Paj answered with a reluctant nod, and West unbuttoned his jacket and disappeared into the breezeway.

I looked back to Hamish, who raised his eyebrows. He was worried. Wondering where the line of his allegiance was. Cover for West or tell the crew about the deed?

I followed West into his quarters, closing the door behind

me. He stood at the table beside his cot, recording a series of measurements into the navigator's log. His lips moved silently around the numbers as he wrote. When he finally looked up at me, it was with the same distance that he'd had that morning in the tavern.

"Looks like we can be there by nightfall tomorrow if the wind holds," he said, closing the book. The quill rolled across the table.

I nodded, still waiting for whatever else he was going to say. But he was quiet, going to his desk and pulling open the drawer to drop the book inside. He absently fidgeted with the maps on the desk and I stepped to the side to meet his eyes, but he turned another inch away from me.

I sighed. "You shouldn't have done that. Given her the deed." The sight of the muscles in his neck surfacing under the skin made me feel suddenly like my stomach was turning, my skin flashing hot. "I won't let you lose the *Marigold*, West. I swear."

He huffed, shaking his head. "You can't promise that."

"I can." I caught my bottom lip with my teeth when it began to quiver.

West crossed his arms, leaning into the wall beside the window. The string of adder stones clinked together as they swung in the wind. Whatever thoughts whispered in his mind darkened the light in his eyes, making him tense all over.

"You have to tell them about the deed," I said.

"That's the last thing they want to hear."

"It doesn't matter. They deserve to know."

"You don't understand." The words were just a breath.

"I do."

"No, you don't. You have Saint. Now you have Holland." He swallowed. "But us? Me, Willa, Paj, Auster, Hamish . . . all *we* have is each other."

"Then why did you force them to do this?"

He swallowed. "Because I can't lose them. And I can't lose you."

I wanted to reach out and touch him. To pull him into my arms. But the walls around him were built up high. "I'm going to get the deed back," I said again. "Whatever it takes."

West stepped toward me. Even in the cold cabin, I could feel the warmth of him. "We do this, and then we're done with Saint." He reached up, taking hold of my jacket with both hands and holding me in place. "Promise me."

I looked up into his face, not a hint of hesitation in my voice. "I promise."

TWENTY-SIX

The night sea stretched out around the *Marigold* like a black chasm, melting into a clear, dark sky.

Paj and Auster were gathered on the quarterdeck with bowls of stew clutched in their hands when I came up the steps from below. The silence crept over the ship, making the crush of the hull cutting through the water sound like whispers.

Hamish had been asleep in the crew's cabin since the sun went down, and I wondered if it was because he was still undecided on what to do about the secret West was keeping. It would only be a matter of time before Hamish came clean.

The sound of Koy snoring lifted from the shadows at the bow. I could only see his crossed bare feet in the moonlight.

A shadow moved over the deck beside me, and I looked up to where Willa was perched high on the mainmast. She was settled in her sling, her head tipped back and looking at the stars.

I hesitated before I took hold of the pegs and climbed, rising up above the *Marigold* and into the rush of cold wind. It had the bite of frost in it, stinging as it slid over my skin.

Willa ignored me as I found a place to sit beside her. Her long, twisted, tawny locks were braided back from her face, making the cut of her slender face more severe.

"What do you want?" Her voice was hollow.

I wound my arm around the mast, leaning into it. "To say thank you."

"For what?"

I followed her gaze up to the sky, where the clouds threaded together in wisps. "For coming to find me." Emotion bent the words into different shapes.

If Willa noticed, I couldn't tell. "A lot of good it did."

"I didn't ask him to do this. I was going to do it alone."

"I don't care, Fable," she said. "You made all of this about you. The same as you've been doing all along."

"What?" I sat up, leaning forward to look her in the eye.

"Since you first stepped foot on this ship, we've been doing what you want us to do. Actually, we were doing it before then, bleeding coin on our route to come to Jeval."

"I never asked for that."

"It doesn't matter. West was never going to stop going to

that island as long as you were there. And when you almost got yourself killed, we were on the hook, taking you across the Narrows to find Saint."

"I—"

But she wasn't going to let me get a word in. "When that fell apart, who came and scraped you off the floor of the tavern? Me. Who risked their necks taking you to Tempest Snare? All of us."

"You weren't doing me any favors with the *Lark*, Willa. If it weren't for me, the *Marigold* would still be anchored in Ceros with no sails."

"I wish she was!" she shouted.

It wasn't until the moonlight caught her face again that I could see she was crying. And they weren't the kind of tears that fell in anger. They were sad. Broken.

"If West had lost the *Marigold*, I would have been able to leave," she choked. "But you saved it. And I thought again, once he was out from under Saint and he had you, that I was free. But we cross the Narrows to find you and you're already making deals. Going your own way. Like it all meant nothing."

My heart sank, realizing that in a way, she was right. I hadn't considered the cost for Willa. Not once. She'd told me that she had finally found a way to leave the *Marigold*. That she'd found a way to be free. And I'd taken it away from her, whether I'd meant to or not.

"You didn't tell him that you're leaving, did you?" I asked.

"No."

"Why not?"

She sniffed. "You don't know what he was like before. When he was working for Saint. I thought once we were done with him, that the West I knew was back. But when you disappeared in Dern, he was that person again. He . . . he just vanished."

"I heard about the ships. What happened?"

"It doesn't matter. That's not my brother. That's what Saint made." She wiped her cheek. "He was willing to leave everything in the Narrows to find you. He was willing to put you before the entire crew," she said. "What else is he willing to do for you, Fable?"

I didn't know what she wanted me to say. I understood it. In her eyes, I'd made West into the same thing my father had. And I could hear in Willa's voice that she wished she'd never come to the tavern that night. That she'd never told me to ask the crew to take me on.

"He was wrong in forcing the crew to come to Yuri's Constellation," I said. "He was just afraid."

"You've given him something to be afraid of." She finally looked at me. Her eyes met mine, and I could see a thousand words she wasn't saying in them.

It was the truth. And this was exactly why Saint lived by his rules and why he'd taught them to me.

Below, the door to the helmsman's quarters opened, flooding lantern light onto the deck. West came out of the breezeway, and even from high up on the mast, I could see the exhausted look on his face.

"I need to talk to you," he called up to us before looking up to the quarterdeck. "All of you."

Willa studied her brother before she unfolded herself from her sling and climbed down. The crew gathered around the helm quietly, all shooting glances to one another as West tucked his hair behind his ear. He was nervous.

"I need to tell you something."

They all waited.

"When Holland came to the docks, she took the deed to the *Marigold*." He said it all in one breath.

"She what?" Paj's voice didn't sound like his own. It was desperate.

Tears were welling in Willa's eyes again.

"She demanded the deed and I gave it to her."

Auster grimaced, as if the words didn't make sense. Beside him, Hamish stared at his boots.

"When we get to Sagsay Holm, we'll get it back from her."

"And then what?" Paj's deep voice echoed.

"Then we go home," West answered.

"Just like that? As if nothing happened?"

West was silent for a long time and they waited for his answer. When I was sure he would finally speak, he turned on his heel, headed back to his quarters.

The crew stared at each other.

"So, we work for Holland now?" The edge came into Willa's voice.

"We don't work for her." I ran a hand over my face.

Auster cleared his throat awkwardly. "Sure sounds like we do."

"We'll get it back," I said, desperate for them to believe me. "Holland wants me, not the *Marigold*."

Hamish fidgeted with the thread unraveling at the hem of his vest. "I'm tired of getting caught up in your family's business, Fable."

"Me too," I muttered.

I could hear it in Willa's words. See it on each of their faces. They'd spent years being controlled by Saint, and now Holland held the most precious thing in the world to them— their home. I hadn't saved them with the *Lark*. I'd trapped them. With me.

TWENTY-SEVEN

Yuri's Constellation was invisible in the dark. I stood on the railing at the bow of the ship, watching the moonlight on the surface of the sea. Even from above, I could feel them—the soft songs of the gemstones hidden in the reef below.

The chain of islands was famous, supplying a major portion of the stones that made up the gem trade in the Unnamed Sea and the Narrows alike. From above, their crests looked like a tangle of veins, pulsing with a steady heartbeat.

The clang of metal rang out and I turned to see Koy at the stern, slinging his belt over his shoulder. He'd slept through the hours it had taken to get to Yuri's Constellation and the moment he woke, the crew's eyes were on him. He pretended not to notice as he came down the steps to the main deck.

The dredging tools I'd had Hamish track down for him gleamed in his hands as he slid them into the belt one at a time. We would be dredging from sunrise to sunset, without a chance to have picks sharpened or broken mallets repaired on shore. Hamish had purchased more than enough tools to last all three of us.

Koy fit the belt around his hips and tightened the buckle absently, his eyes on the water. "Looks tame enough."

"Yeah." I nodded.

He was talking about the currents and I'd thought the same. The tides were meticulously documented on the charts Holland had given us and we'd dealt with far more unpredictable water on Jeval.

"You going to tell me what I'm looking for down there?" he asked.

I'd been dreading this moment. In fact, I'd been sure that if I'd told Koy the truth at the tavern, that he wouldn't have ever stepped foot on the *Marigold*. I pulled Holland's ship logs from inside my jacket and slipped the parchment from under the leather cover.

Koy plucked it from my fingers, unfolding it. His eyes narrowed as they moved over the diagram. "Midnight." He scoffed. "You're even more insane than I thought."

I ignored the insult. "Opaque black stone. Violet inclusions. That's all you need to know."

"Good thing you paid me in advance." He handed me the parchment.

Auster came up from belowdecks with two steaming clay cups, and I jumped down from the railing to meet him. He set one into my hands, and the bitter scent of strong black tea rose to meet me.

I took a sip, wincing. "Better keep them coming."

"I figured as much." He smirked.

Paj untied one of the baskets from the railing on the quarterdeck and tossed it down to Hamish, who was stacking them. He glanced at me over his shoulder, eyeing the cup.

Of everyone on board, Paj would be the most difficult to make peace with. His love and his hate seemed to be intrinsically tied together, with little in between.

"What did Henrik mean when he said that Paj was your benefactor?" I asked, taking another sip.

Auster leaned onto the railing beside me, lowering his voice so that Paj couldn't hear. "I met Paj down on the docks while I was working a job for Henrik. Paj was crewing as a deckhand for a mid-level trader, coming and going from Bastian nearly every week." He swirled the tea in his cup. "Not a month had gone by before I started waiting for his ship at the harbor." Even in the dark I could see him blushing.

"And?"

"And not long after, Paj started putting together that I worked for the Roths. When things got . . . ." He trailed off, glancing over his shoulder again. "Henrik found out about us, and he didn't approve. We were together for maybe a year when I almost got my throat cut stealing inventory from a rye merchant for my uncle. Paj had told me before that he wanted me to cut ties with my family, but he hadn't drawn a line in the sand. Not until then. He came and found me one night before he left port, and he asked me to leave Bastian and the Roths behind. If I didn't, we were done."

"You had to choose. Between him and your family."

"That's right." Auster's eyes paled to the faintest shade of silver. "Paj heard there was a sailmaker willing to pay a lot of coin to be smuggled out of Bastian, and he took the job. Nearly got himself killed, but he pulled it off."

"Leo?" My voice rose.

Auster smiled in answer.

Leo was the sailmaker-turned-tailor who'd set up shop in North Fyg in Ceros. He'd also been the one to save the *Marigold* by making us a set of sails when no one else would.

"He'd gotten into some kind of trouble with Holland and needed to disappear. Paj showed up at my door a few days later with three purses of coin and said he was leaving the Un-named Sea and not coming back. He gave me a day to decide."

"And you just disappeared? Without anyone knowing?"

"No one except Ezra. He was there the night I left, but he let me go. Pretended like he didn't see me climbing out the window. If he'd told anyone I was gone, I wouldn't have made it out of the harbor."

So there was more to Ezra than Henrik and the Roths. "Would you ever change it? Go back and stay with your family?"

"The Roths share blood, but they're not a family."

I didn't press. Something told me if I did, it would un-earth whatever Auster had buried when he left Bastian be-hind.

"But I wouldn't." He leaned toward me, pressing his shoulder to mine. "You know, go back. Change it."

I swallowed down the urge to cry. He wasn't just talking about Paj or the Roths or Bastian. He was also talking about me. Auster had been the first one on the crew to trust me. Somehow, he still did. I shoved back into his shoulder with mine, not saying a word.

"Ready?" West's voice sounded behind me and I turned to see him standing before the helm, both of our belts in his hands.

I handed Auster my cup before West tossed my belt into the air. I caught it, eyeing the straight line in the distance. Daylight was already swelling into the inky black sky, and in a few minutes the sun would appear like liquid gold, waver-ing on the seam of the horizon.

Up on the quarterdeck, Paj and Hamish were loosening the lines that secured the tender boat and dropping it into the water.

"I'll mark, you follow," I said, repeating the plan as I buckled my belt around me.

I'd work my way down the reefs in order, flagging areas that could hold the midnight with strips of pink silk I'd torn from Holland's frock. West and Koy would follow, dredging. When we were finished with one reef, we'd start the next.

But there were over twenty in the tangle of banks and ridges below. We'd have to get through at least six a day if we were going to finish in time to meet Holland.

"When I get to the end, I'll double back to dredge." I raked my hair to one side, braiding it over my shoulder and tying it off with a strip of leather.

Willa came down the steps with the oars to the tender boat. When Koy reached for them, she dropped them on the deck between them.

He grinned at her before he bent low to pick them up.

I'd been worried that problems would arise between the crew and Koy, but he looked more amused by Willa's antics than he was annoyed. Still, I couldn't afford for any of them to get under his skin. The last thing I needed was for him to draw his knife on someone.

Koy climbed the railing as the glow of sunlight bled up into the sky. He stood against the wind, pulling the shirt over his head before dropping it to the deck next to Willa. She stared at it, dragging her incredulous gaze up and pinning it on him.

West waited for me to climb up before he followed. We stood shoulder to shoulder, the three of us looking down at the dark water.

"Ready?" I looked to West, then Koy.

Koy answered with a nod, and West didn't answer at all, stepping off first to drop through the air and plunge into the sea. Koy and I stepped off together and the warm wind whipped around us before we hit the water side by side.

West was coming up when I opened my eyes beneath

the surface, and I blinked furiously against the sting of salt before kicking after him. Already the sky was lighter, and in minutes, we'd have enough visibility to start working the reef.

The tender boat was floating just near the stern, and as soon as the oars hit the water beside us we swam toward it, lifting ourselves over its side. The reef system grew more twisted beneath us as Koy rowed toward the island and the crew watched us silently from the portside above. These waters were too shallow for the *Marigold*, so they'd have to stay anchored in the deep.

When we reached the first reef on our list, West dropped anchor and jumped back out.

The water was warmer in the shallows and the buzz of gemstones was heavier. I could feel it over every inch of my skin as I took the first of a series of deep, quick breaths, working my lungs to stretch. I was already dreading the deep chill that I knew was waiting for me after hours of diving. It was the kind of cold that lingered for days.

West treaded water beside me, tipping his head back to take a last sip of air into his throat before he disappeared. I did the same, sinking into the ink-blue water after him.

Below, he was already kicking in the direction of the farthest edge of a reef that disappeared into the darkness. His hair rippled back from his face as he wove between beams of sunlight, and I let myself float down until I felt the pressure of the water rise.

The reverberation swelling around us was like the chorus of a hundred singing voices, blending in an unsettling tone.

I'd never heard it before, like the sharpest strike of metal felt deep in the bones.

This was an old reef, wrought with time, and the color of the rock bled one to the next like the haphazard patchwork of the rye fields north of Ceros.

West reached the tip of the reef and I watched his hand drift out to touch the shelf of ancient coral gently. There was evidence of dredging all along its ridges, but this reef was a monster, regenerating at a pace that made each break in the rock glow white with new growth. Fish swarmed around pointed crests, where delicate sea fans, bubble coral, and purple death anemone were scattered in brilliant shapes and colors.

Somewhere in the tangle of shoals, Isolde had found midnight.

The tips of West's fingers grazed my arm as I sank below him to the tip of the ridge. The color of the sea bottom told me that the bedrock was limestone. Caches of calcite, fluorite, and onyx would litter the reef in pockets, and I could hear their distinct calls all around me, humming from where they lay beneath the rock.

I set my hands on the shelf before me and closed my eyes, letting a string of bubbles trail up from my lips. The place between my eyebrows pinched as I listened, sorting through the sounds one at a time until I found the deep, resonant ring of something that didn't belong. Some sort of agate? Maybe tiger's eye. I couldn't tell.

My eyes opened and I swam over the ridge, trying to find it. The sound grew, more a feeling in my chest than something I could hear, and when it was so close that I felt as if it was writhing within me, I stopped, touching the bulbous piece of broken basalt that eyed me from beneath a growth of branching coral.

I pulled at a strip of pink silk from my belt and tied it loosely around the frond so that its ends rippled in the pull of the current. Koy came down beside me, getting to work. He inspected the spot before he chose a pick and a chisel. When he slid his mallet free, I kicked off, making my way farther down the reef.

West's shadow followed mine, and when I found another suspicious cache, I stopped, fitting myself into a corner of the ridge so I could tie another marker. West watched me, taking a pick from his belt, and when I turned to start again, he caught my hand, pulling me back through the current toward him.

The edges of the silk kissed my feet as he looked up at me and his fingers tightened around my arm. It was the first time he'd touched me since I'd made my deal with Holland and I could see that he was waiting. For what, I didn't know. West was adrift, lost without the anchor of the crew and the ship. The guilt of knowing I'd been a part of that made it feel as if the air in my chest was on fire.

I threaded my fingers into his and squeezed. The corners of his mouth softened and he let me go, letting the tow of water take me over the shelf, away from him. In another moment, he was gone.

I looked down as the tide carried me over the coral, watching the reef run past me until another gemstone song caught

my ear. Then another. And another. And when I looked back
to the end of the reef where Koy and West had been, it vanished in the murky blue. It was the color of a sleeping sea, my
mother would say, because the water only ever looked like
that before dawn.

The labyrinth of reefs held everything from black diamonds to the rarest of sapphires, and most of the stories my
mother had told me about dredging in the Unnamed Sea
were born in these waters.

This place had known my mother.

The thought made a sinking feeling drop between my
ribs as I tied another strip of silk and kicked off, letting the
current take me again. She'd never told a soul where she'd
found the midnight. What other secrets had she left here?

TWENTY-EIGHT

F able."

I was still floating in the deep, infinite blue illuminated around me. The reef stretched out below, the ripple of sunlight dancing on the surface above.

"Fable." My name was soft on West's gravelly voice.

The length of him pressed against me, and I felt his fingers slide through mine. The blisters on my hands stung as he pressed my knuckles to his mouth.

"Time to wake up."

I opened my eyes just enough to see a faint light spilling through the slats of the closed window shutters of the helmsman's quarters. I rolled beneath the quilts to face West and set my head on the crook of his shoulder, fitting my hands beneath him. They were still a bit numb, even after a few hours of sleep in the warm cabin.

The smell of him filled the room and I pulled it in on a deep, relieved breath. He'd thawed, acting more like himself than he had since we were at Azimuth House. I didn't know if it was being back at sea or if it was the long hours spent underwater in the quiet that had done it. I didn't care.

"Sun will be up soon," he said, pushing the hair back from my face.

The first day of the dive had been brutal, with shifting tides that slowed our progress over the reefs. And though we'd found cache after cache, none of them had been anything close to midnight. Worse, we didn't have time to dredge what we did find. We'd have to leave all those stones where they were buried in the rock.

I curled up closer to him, not wanting to surrender to the rising sun. I took one of his hands and held it to the beam of light. His fingers were cut up and rubbed raw from the coral. "You never told me how you learned to dredge," I whispered.

The first time I'd seen him put on a belt was when we dredged the *Lark*. It was unusual for a helmsman to have ever been a dredger because it was considered one of the lowest rungs on a crew.

"I learned when I was a kid."

"But who taught you?"

He looked as if he was trying to decide how much of the story to tell me. "No one, really. I just started following the dredgers into the water on dives and watching them work. I figured it was better than staying on the ship and giving the helmsman a reason to notice me."

I pressed his hand to my face. Imagining him like that, so young, and being afraid to stay on the ship made my stomach turn.

"And it gave me more than one skill when I went to the next crew."

Saint's crew. It probably wasn't long after he'd left me on Jeval that my father took West on. While I was finding a way to survive on that island, West was finding a way to survive on that ship. I wondered how long it had taken Saint to ask West for his first favor.

I tensed when I felt the vibration of the cot ringing in tandem with a distant rumble. West, too, went rigid, listening.

I sat up onto my elbows, staring into the dark. A few seconds later, it moaned again. The roll of thunder.

"No." I threw the quilts back, going to the window and unlatching the shutters.

West's footsteps hit the floor behind me, and my heart sank as the wind tore through the cabin. Sweet, drenched in the smell of wet earth. The sky was almost completely black, the sparkle of stars still lit above the ship, but there was no mistaking the scent.

It was a storm.

West stared at the sky, listening. I pushed past him, plucking my belt from where it hung beside the door, and went out onto the deck barefoot.

Paj was standing at the helm, watching the water. "Figured

that would get your asses out of bed." He grunted, flinging a hand toward the east.

I leaned over the side, cursing when I spotted what he saw. A crest of white broke on the waves as they pressed diagonally toward us, the chop on the water visible even in the low light.

"Well?" Willa appeared at the top of the steps, thumbs hooked into her tool belt.

I raked both hands into my hair, holding it back from my face as West came out of the breezeway. "We don't have time to wait it out. We can dredge before it hits."

Paj lifted both eyebrows. "You're going to dredge? In this?"

West watched the clouds, thinking. "Have you ever done a dive during a storm?"

I sighed. "Once or twice."

"And the ship?" West asked, looking to Paj and Willa.

Willa was the one to answer. "We'll see. The winds don't look that bad. We're in deep enough water and we've dropped sails. She should be fine."

I didn't like that she'd said *should*.

West thought for another moment, his eyes going back to the sky. The dive was mine, but he was still the helmsman. The call landed with him. "What about the current?"

"It'll get stronger," I admitted. "I'll know when we need to get out of the water."

"All right." He tugged his shirt over his head. "Then let's get down there."

I took the steps belowdecks, knocking hard on the door

of the cabin as I pushed inside. Koy, Auster, and Hamish were still asleep in their hammocks. The snore dragging in Hamish's throat was interrupted by the sound of the door slamming against the wall. I took Koy's belt from where it was hung on the bulkhead and dropped it into his hammock.

He jerked awake, half-sitting up as he sucked in a breath. "What the—"

"Storm," I said. "Get up."

He groaned, rolling from the swinging canvas, and his feet hit the ground behind me.

Willa was grumbling to herself as I came back up to the main deck. She climbed the mainmast with a cord of rope draped over her shoulders, ready to reinforce the lines.

Koy pulled his hair into a knot, looking up at the sky.

"Scared, dredger?" Willa taunted from above.

"I've dredged in storms that would eat this ship alive." Koy smiled wickedly.

We'd finished twelve of the reefs, with twenty-two left to go, and the progress would be slow going in the churn of the water. It would definitely put us behind schedule, and I wasn't sure how we'd make it up.

A bleary-eyed Auster appeared at the top of the steps a moment later, scanning the deck.

"Tender," Paj directed him.

He obeyed without question, jogging with heavy feet up to the quarterdeck to help West drop the small boat into the water. It drifted in the wind, pulling against the line as I balanced on the railing. I could feel every one of my muscles tightening, dreading the jump. After a full day of diving and very little rest, there wasn't an inch of my body that wasn't sore, and hours in the tossing water of a storm would be the worst of it.

Before I could think better of it, I pressed both hands to my tools to hold them to my body and jumped. I sucked in a breath as I fell, crashing into the sea as the first of the waves rolled into the ship.

I kicked hard to draw the blood into the muscles of my stiff legs and pulled in my first breath as soon as I surfaced. West and Koy dropped in behind me, and above the crew stood at the railing, their wary eyes on the clouds in the distance. They were worried.

We climbed into the tender and West took up the oars, setting the paddles into the rings and pulling them to his chest. The wind was getting stronger by the minute and he strained against the tow of the water as I steered the rudder.

When we were in place I jumped back in, not wasting any time. The anchor fell into the water and I pressed my hands to my sore ribs as I started to fill my lungs.

"Stay on the west side of the ridge so the current doesn't throw you into the reef," I said between breaths. "And watch the eddies. They'll get stronger." I tipped my chin up to the right angle of water in the distance, where the sea was already starting to pucker. By the time the storm hit us, the eddy would be a maelstrom, pulling anything that touched it into a whirlpool.

Koy and West both nodded, working their breaths almost in tandem. My chest stung as I sucked in the last of the cold air, and I plunged below the surface.

My arms drifted up over my head as I let myself sink, reserving my strength for the current. It touched my feet first, and my hair whipped away from my face as it swept around me. The reef ran beneath us as we floated over the ridge, the pink silk flags fluttering. But the sand was already clouding the water, casting everything in a green haze that would make it difficult to see. Koy caught the edge of a rock when he reached the place he'd left off the day before, and he sank into the thick sediment, barely visible as we pulled away. West was next, kicking from the current when he spotted the next mark.

He was swallowed by the haze and when I reached the last flag I swam down, letting myself fall to the reef. The sounds of the sea had already changed, deepening with the roar of the storm that was still miles away.

I took the mallet from my belt and chose the largest chisel, tapping in swift strikes to chip the crust of coral. As soon as the rock beneath it was exposed I pressed a thumb to its edge, watching it crumble. The stone was a strange one, the feel of it thick in the water around me. If it was what I thought it was, it had been missed because of the unusual rock formation that had hidden the shape of the cache. Elestial quartz was rare and valuable, but it formed in feldspar, not basalt, which was exactly what this reef looked like. No one had come looking for elestial quartz here, and no one had stumbled upon it. And if the quartz had managed to hide, maybe midnight had too.

When I could see the faded orange face of the basalt, I dropped the chisel back into my belt and switched to a pick.

It only took a few drives of the mallet before the purple gemstone appeared, but five dives later, there was no midnight to
be found. I chipped the last of the feldspar from the ridge, my
teeth clenched. But as the sand cleared, my hand tightened
on the handle of my mallet. Nothing.

Fronds of coral swayed back and forth in the rough
water, the fish swimming wayward as they pushed against the
tide. The noise of the storm radiated through the sea like the
drawn-out sound of thunder, disorienting me. If there was
any midnight on this reef, I wasn't going to find it like this.

I turned, letting a bubble escape my lips as I pressed my
back to the rock and watched a dim spread of pale green
swirling in the distance. In a few minutes we would lose
what little light we had left and we'd be forced to wait out
the winds.

A sharp ping shot through water and I looked up the
ridge to see Koy floating over the top of the reef. He was hitting together two chisels, trying to get my attention. As soon
as I caught his eyes, he sank back down and disappeared.

West rose from where he was working, swimming after
him, and I followed, carving through the water with my
heart hammering in my ears.

Koy's black hair floated up in twisting strands as he hit
the handle of the chisel. I came down beside West, going
rigid when I saw the deep slash of red wrapped around his
shoulder. It looked like he caught the corner of the reef.

I gently touched the broken skin, and he looked back at
me, giving a flick of his fingers to dismiss my concern before
he turned back to Koy.

His hands were working fast, and I eyed the constriction in his chest, pulling beneath the muscle. He needed to surface, and fast. He leaned back when another piece of basalt broke free and my mouth dropped open. The taste of cold and salt rolled over my tongue and I floated closer, eyeing a glossy spread of black.

West looked to me, his brow furrowed, but I couldn't tell through the dim light what it was. I took the chisel from my belt and pushed Koy aside, signaling for him to go up for air before he blacked out. West worked at the other side and we moved the tips of our chisels closer together until the smallest corner of the stone chipped off, falling between us. West reached out, catching it in his palm and closing his fingers around it.

I rubbed the sand from my stinging eyes, my vision blurring. When a fish darted between me and the reef, I looked up. Something wasn't right.

The water turned around us, shifting back and forth quietly. But the reef was empty, every fish and crab suddenly gone. I watched the last of them skitter away, into the murky distance.

West froze beside me, seeing the same.

It could only mean one thing.

I looked up, eyeing the surface, where the ripple of light had been just moments ago. Now, it was only black.

TWENTY-NINE

I broke through to the roar of wind, gasping, and West came up beside me as lightning tangled in the black clouds overhead.

I sucked in a breath as a wave barreled in toward us, and I sank back down before it hit. West disappeared as the water crashed and rolled above, sucking me deeper in its retreat. I kicked in the opposite direction, but another one was already coming in, slamming into the rocks ahead.

I came back up, choking on the burn of saltwater in my raw throat. Down the reef, West was swimming toward me over another wave.

"We have to get back to the ship!" I shouted, turning in a circle to search the rough water.

In the distance, Koy was pulling himself up into the tender boat. We swam toward it, diving under each time another wave crested and when we finally reached him, Koy had both oars in hand.

"Come on!" he shouted into the wind.

I held onto the edge and lifted myself inside, slipping on the wood and falling into the hull. West came up behind me, going for the rudder.

Beyond the shallows, the *Marigold* rocked on the swells, masts tipping back and forth as each wave slammed into the hull.

Koy dropped the paddles into the water and rowed, growling as he fought the current. The wind was too strong. The water too swift.

"We're not going to make it!" I yelled, shivering. The rain was like glass, biting my skin as it blew in sideways.

West's eyes were fixed on the ship. When he opened his mouth to answer, the boat suddenly stilled, the water calming. All around us, the gray sea was beginning to settle, but the clouds continued to roll overhead, like a plume of angry smoke. The hiss of my breath was the only sound. Until I saw it.

Down shore, the water was kicking up, an invisible gale racing toward us. It was dragging a wall of water behind it.

"Row!" West howled.

Koy turned the boat and headed for the beach, screaming as he jerked at the oars. But it was too late.

The wave raced toward us, its crest spilling down as it loomed over us. I watched, a gasp trapped in my throat, as it came crashing down.

"Fable!" West's voice vanished as the water collapsed on top of us.

The boat disappeared and I was plummeted beneath the surface, dragged through the water like hands pulling me into the deep. I thrashed, fighting its strength, twisting and turning, looking for the surface.

A flashing glow appeared below me as the water let me go, and I launched myself toward it, kicking hard. It wasn't until I got closer that I realized it wasn't below me. It was above. The world was tossed and spinning beneath the water.

I broke the surface, screaming West's name and a cry escaped my throat when I spotted the boat pushed up onto the shore ahead. Beside it, West was calling out to me. I frantically swam for the beach and when I felt the sand under my feet, I stood, trudging up out of the water. West caught me in his arms, dragging me from the surf.

"Where's Koy?" I panted, looking up and down the beach.

"Here." He waved a hand into the air. The rope to the tender was pulled over his shoulder as he hauled it higher up the beach.

I dropped to the sand when we reached the cover of the trees. "West," I croaked, "the stone."

"I've got it." He had one hand clenched around the small purse tied to his dredging belt.

I let out a tight breath, looking past him to the *Marigold*. She was just a shadow in the mist. West stood at the water's edge, watching helplessly as she tipped and swayed, his chest rising and falling with heavy breaths.

The storm had come in fast. Too fast. And the winds were stronger than we'd predicted.

Another gale swept over the island, bowing the trees until their branches touched the sand. The thunderous resonance of another wind swelled, skipping over the surface of the sea, and it slammed into the ship.

The *Marigold* heeled, the masts reaching out over the water on the starboard side, and then suddenly she righted, snapping back up.

West took a step into the water, his eyes widening.

"What is it?" But I realized as soon as I blinked the rain from my eyes what had happened.

The *Marigold* was moving. Drifting.

"The anchor line," West said, his voice almost inaudible.

It snapped.

Another strike of lightning cracked overhead, and another, until the wind slowly calmed. The water steadied with each softening wave until they were pushing up around our feet in a final gasp.

West was already towing the tender back into the water.

I jumped in with the oars and handed them to Koy as soon as we were afloat. We glided over the shallows as the *Marigold* drifted farther. I could already see Willa up on the mast, a bronze scope shining in her hands.

By the time we made it past the break, she'd spotted us.

The crew was already waiting when we finally reached the ship, and I caught the lowest rung of the ladder and pulled myself up, my hands so numb that I couldn't feel the rope against my skin.

West was right behind me, his hair stuck to his face. "Anchor?"

"Yeah," Willa answered gravely. "Lost it in that last gust."

He cursed as he went to the rail, peering into the water.

"Hamish?" I said, pulling the small purse from West's belt. "I need the gem lamp."

His eyes went wide as I opened it and dumped the gem into my palm. I turned it over before picking it up between two fingers.

"Is it . . . ?" Auster stared at it.

I didn't know. I couldn't tell what it was. It looked like onyx, but there was a translucence to it that didn't look right. And the vibration it gave off wasn't familiar. It was a stone I didn't know. But without ever having seen a piece of midnight for myself, there was only one way to be sure.

"I need the gem lamp," I said again, pushing through them to the helmsman's quarters.

I came through the door, setting the stone into the small bronze dish on the low table and West set the lantern on the desk, filling the cabin with light.

"What do you think?" Koy leaned into the wall next to me, drops of seawater glistening as they slid down his face.

"I don't know," I admitted.

Hamish came through the door with Paj on his heels, the

gem lamp in his hands. He set it down onto the desk carefully, looking up at us through the fogged lenses of his spectacles.

I sat in West's chair and lit a match, hovering its tip over the oil chamber beneath the glass. But my fingers shook furiously, quenching the flame before it took to the wick. West caught my hand with his, turning my fingers toward the light. They were the faintest shade of blue.

"I'm all right," I said, answering his unspoken question. Somehow, his touch was still a bit warm.

He took the quilt from his cot and set it over my shoulders as Hamish took another match and lit the lamp with nimble fingers. The glow ignited beneath the glass and I opened my hand to let West pick up the stone. He crouched down onto his heels beside me before setting the small gem onto the mirror.

I sat up, holding my breath as I peered through the eyepiece, and adjusted the lens slowly. Everyone in the cabin fell silent and I squinted as it came into focus. The faintest glow lit in its center, surrounded by opaque edges. I turned the mirror, trying to manipulate the light, and the lump in my throat expanded.

No inclusions. Not one.

"It's not midnight," I muttered, biting down hard onto my lip.

Willa set her hands onto the desk, leaning into them to hover over me. "Are you sure?"

"I'm sure," I answered, defeated. "I don't know what it is, but it's not midnight. Some kind of spinel, maybe."

Koy was hidden in the shadowed corner of the room. "We got through two reefs today."

He didn't need to explain his meaning. We only had one more day before we were supposed to be on our way to meet Holland. At our best, we'd still be close to eight reefs shy. If we didn't find the midnight, we'd be sailing back to Sagsay Holm empty-handed.

"It'll be dark in a few hours." Paj looked to West, waiting for orders.

"Then we start again at sunup," West said.

Auster caught Paj by the waist, pulling him toward the door without a word. Hamish and Willa followed them, leaving West and me with Koy. I could see on Koy's face that he was frustrated. He couldn't have had many failed dives in his life and by now, he was nearly as hungry to find the midnight as I was. He stared at the floor silently for another moment before he stood up off the wall and walked out the door.

"The anchor?" I asked, so tired I could cry.

"Willa's on it." West blew out the flame on the lamp before he opened the drawer of the chest and pulled out a clean shirt. Then he ducked out, leaving me alone at his desk.

I stared at the puddle of water on the floor that he'd left, the light flitting over its smooth surface as the lantern swung on the bulkhead.

There were enough stones in these reefs to last the gem traders of the Unnamed Sea another ten years.

So, where the hell was the midnight?

I couldn't ignore the nagging feeling that I wasn't going to find it in Yuri's Constellation. That it was no accident that

Holland's crews hadn't run across a single piece of midnight in the years since Isolde brought it up from the depths.

But the ship logs were clear, without so much as a day left unaccounted for. The crew had been diving in Yuri's Constellation for nearly thirty-two days before they went back to Bastian for supplies. A day later they'd returned, with no deviations off course.

I sat up, staring into the shadows, my mind working. The thin threads of an answer glimmered to life, taking shape in the dark.

If I was right, and Isolde hadn't found the midnight in Yuri's Constellation, then someone had lied. But how?

If the navigator had forged the logs, there'd be at least thirty people on Holland's ship, including the helmsman, who would have been able to report the discrepancy in the days and weeks after the dive.

But maybe it was my mother who'd lied. If Isolde had any suspicion about the value of her discovery, maybe she'd kept the stone's origin to herself. Maybe she'd found it when she was alone.

I stood abruptly, sending the chair tipping back. It clattered on the floor behind me as my hands slid over the maps, looking for the one I'd seen days ago. The one I hadn't even looked twice at.

When I found it, I pulled it from under the others. The Bastian Coast. I took the lantern from the wall and set it at the corner, moving my fingers over the thick, soft parchment until I found it.

Fable's Skerry.

"West!" I studied the depths and charts noted along the shore, the map of currents that slid around the little islet. "West!"

He appeared in the dark breezeway with a dry shirt pulled over one arm. "What is it?"

"What if she didn't find it here?" I panted. "What if she lied?"

"What?"

"Why would Isolde steal the midnight? Why would she leave Bastian?" My voice sounded far away. "She didn't trust Holland. Maybe she didn't want her to know where she found it."

He was listening now, sliding the other arm into the shirt as he walked toward me. "But where? She would have had to have a ship and a crew. The log says they were here."

"They were," I breathed, flipping through the parchments in the drawer until I found the log. I dropped it between us. "Except for one day." I set my finger on Bastian.

"There's no way she found it in Bastian. There are no reefs in those waters. There isn't even so much as a sandbar for miles."

I pointed to the islet.

"Fable's Skerry?"

"Why not?"

"Because it's just a rock with a lighthouse on it," he said.

"What if it's not just a rock?"

He picked up the chair, setting it upright before he looked at the map again, thinking. "It's just offshore of Bastian. Don't you think if there was something there, someone would have found it?"

I let out an exhausted breath. "Maybe. Maybe not. But I can't shake the feeling that we're looking in the wrong place. I don't think it's here, West."

I didn't know if I was making any sense. The lack of sleep and hours in the cold water had cast my mind in a fog. But still, that feeling was there. That doubt.

"Are you sure?" West said, studying me.

I clutched the quilt tighter around me. "No."

It was a feeling, not a fact. I paced the floor in front of him, the warmth finally beginning to return beneath my skin as my cheeks flushed hot.

"I don't think it's here," I said again, my voice a whisper.

His eyes jumped back and forth on mine and I watched as he weighed out my words. After a moment, he was walking toward the open door. And as soon as he disappeared into the breezeway, his voice rang out on the deck.

"Make ready!"

THIRTY

It had only taken Willa an hour to figure out our anchor problem. She sent Koy and West back into the water to fill one of the empty iron-framed crates from the cargo hold with rocks from the seafloor. Once it was rigged, we hauled it up and secured it to the ship.

It was a temporary fix, one that wouldn't hold against another storm. When we got to Sagsay Holm we'd have to use the last of our coin to replace the anchor, giving everyone yet another reason to be angry about West's orders.

I sat curled up in the netting of the jib with the quilt from West's cabin pulled tight around me. I hadn't been able to sleep as we sailed through the night, headed for Fable's

Skerry, abandoning our last day of dredging at Yuri's Constellation. The reefs we'd spent the last four days diving were hours behind us, and even if we turned back now, our time would be up. It was a gamble. One that put Saint's life on the line.

Trailing footsteps slid over the deck below and I leaned forward to see Koy at the bow. He pulled a small amber bottle from the pocket of his trousers and uncorked it, taking a sip.

"No rye on the ship," I said, smiling when he jolted, almost dropping it.

He looked up at me, taking another drink before he climbed up and sat beside me on the jib. He handed me the bottle and I gave it a sniff, holding it up to the moonlight.

"Too good for Jevali rye?" He smirked.

It was the homebrewed stuff, and the scent called to life countless memories of Speck, one of the dredgers who ran a ferrying trade on the island. I'd wrecked his skiff the night I bartered for passage on the *Marigold*.

"You still haven't told me why you took the job on the *Luna*," I said, taking a swig. The burn of the rye raced down my throat, exploding into my chest. I winced, breathing through it.

"Coin," Koy answered.

"Sure." I laughed. Koy made more coin than anyone in Jeval, and his family was taken care of. If he was taking jobs on ships, he was after something else too.

He looked at me as if he was sizing me up. Weighing the risks of telling me. "Rumor has it trade between the Unnamed Sea and the Narrows is going to expand."

"So?"

"That means more ships coming through our waters on Jeval."

I grinned, understanding him. Koy wanted to be ready if the ships from the Unnamed Sea and the Narrows multiplied at the barrier islands, and they would.

"I figure it's only a matter of time before Jeval is turned into a port."

I handed the rye back to him. "You're serious."

He fit the cork back into the bottle, going quiet. "You think it's stupid."

He immediately wished he hadn't said it, embarrassed. I'd never seen that look on Koy. Not ever. "No, I don't. I think it's brilliant."

"You do." He sounded skeptical.

"I mean it."

Koy gave me a nod, leaning back into the ropes.

"Can I ask you something if I swear to never tell a soul your answer?"

His eyes narrowed at me.

I took his silence as a yes. "Why'd you cut the rope?"

He scoffed, pulling the cork from the bottle again. He was quiet a long time, taking three sips before he answered. "If anyone's going to kill you, it's going to be me."

"I'm serious, Koy. Why?"

He shrugged. "You're Jevali."

"No, I'm not."

His gaze was pinned to the sky. "I figure if you've ever

fallen asleep on that island not sure if you'll wake up again, that makes you a Jevali."

I smiled in the dark. For the first time, my memory of those years didn't make my heart ache. He was right. We'd survived together. And that was a bond not easily broken. In a few days he'd be headed back to Jeval, and I was surprised to find that I felt the faintest feeling of regret. I'd uncovered a part of Koy in the last two weeks I'd never seen in my four years on Jeval. I was overwhelmingly glad I'd pulled him from the water that day on the reef, even if it had ended with me running for my life on the docks.

"Get down here." Willa's sharp tone cut the silence.

Koy looked between his feet to see her.

She dropped a coil of knotted rope at her feet.

When she walked away, Koy arched an eyebrow at me. "I think she likes me."

I laughed, and a look of triumph lit in his eyes. If I didn't know better, I'd say that it felt as if we were friends. I thought maybe the same thought occurred to him before he dropped the bottle in my lap and climbed down.

"Fable." Auster called my name from where he stood beside Paj at the helm. He tipped a chin up toward the horizon and I sat up, looking for what he saw.

Fable's Skerry came into view as the moon set, almost invisible on the black sea. The old lighthouse was a pristine white that glowed in the dark, sitting on a thin peninsula that reached out into the water from the east side of the islet.

I jumped from the jib as West came out onto the main

deck. "Reef the sheets!" He pulled his cap over his unruly hair.

I climbed the mainmast, unwinding the lines so I could slide the canvas up. My heartbeat fluttered as the grommets sang against the ropes. On the foremast Hamish did the same, watching me from the corner of his eye. He was thinking the same thing I was. I was either brilliant or stupid for making the call to leave Yuri's Constellation. We were all about to find out which it was.

As if he could hear my thoughts, he smiled suddenly, giving me a wink.

I smirked, climbing back down the mast while the crew unlatched the anchor crank. Every bit of my body screamed with the ache of the last four days as I pulled my shirt off. West took it, handing me my belt, and I fit it around me silently. I was nervous, and that was something I never felt on a dive.

Willa's makeshift anchor splashed into the water. When West started to buckle his own belt around his waist, I stopped him. "Let me take a look first."

Dark circles hung beneath his eyes and the cut on his shoulder was swollen despite Auster's best attempt at cleaning it. He was exhausted. And if I was wrong about the skerry, I didn't need West there to see it.

He didn't argue, giving me a nod in answer. I pulled myself up onto the side and stepped off before I even had time to think about it. I hit the water, and every dull pain resurfaced in my arms and legs as I kicked. When I came up, the entire crew was watching.

I turned away from them, trying to smooth the hitch in

my breath. I wasn't just letting Saint down if I screwed this up. I was letting all of them down. Again.

I dropped down into the water with my chest full of air, and froze when I felt it.

When I felt *her.*

All around me, the warm, melting drip of some whisper fell to the back of my mind, winding around me in the cold deep. I could feel Isolde. Feel her as if she was right there, diving beside me.

My heart raced as I swam, carving through the still water with my arms. The sea was an eerie calm, protected by the rocky, curved shores of the skerry. From what I could tell, the storm hadn't come this far east, leaving the water clear and crisp. It shimmered in the folds of light piercing the soft blue.

The sea bottom was nothing but pale silt that lay in parallel ripples far below. There wasn't a reef or anything like one in sight. The expanse of sand was hedged in by the walls of black, craggy rock that climbed up toward the surface at an angle, where the waves foamed white.

If there were any gemstones to be found here, I had no clue where they would be. And I couldn't feel them. When I made it almost halfway around the skerry, I peered into the distance only to find more of the same. I followed the tide, coming up for air when my lungs twisted in my chest, then sinking back down. Instantly I felt it again, that familiar hush, like the sound of my mother's voice humming as I fell into sleep. I let myself sink to the bottom, the pressure of the depth pushing against my skin as I inspected the rim of rock encircling the island.

It opened to a wide cavern that dropped off into deeper waters. The color bled to black, where the shadows seemed to shift and curl. Above it, the wall of rock crept up in harsh, jagged ridges.

A trail of cold water skimmed past, and I reached out, feeling it. The thin slip of a wayward current. Soft, but there nonetheless. My brow pulled, watching the water around me, and something moved in the corner of my eye, making me still.

Over the lip of the rock's edge, a wisp of dark red hair flashed in the moonbeam casting through the water. The air burned in my chest as I turned, spinning in the current so that I could look around me. Frantic. Because for a moment, I could have sworn she was there. Like a thread of smoke thinning into the air.

Isolde.

I found the rock beneath my feet and pushed off, my hair waving away from my face as I swam back toward the surface. The underwater cliff jutted straight up, and when I made it to the ledge, I reached out to catch the corner of the rock. The outcropping opened into a cavity, but there was nothing inside but darkness. No gem song. No glow of distant light.

If Holland was telling the truth, Isolde had found a refuge on this rock. Away from the shining streets of Bastian and out from under the eye of her mother. Maybe this was the place she'd dreamed of the day she would leave them both behind. Of sun-soaked days on the deck of a ship, and nights in its hull. Maybe she'd dreamed of me.

My pulse hammered in my ears, the last of my breath threatening to flicker out. The heat burned in my face despite the cold, and I pressed my lips together, watching the light skip on the surface above. She was here, somehow. My mother's ghost was bled into these waters. But even in Tempest Snare, where she'd found her end, I hadn't felt *this*.

There was nothing here but an echo of some part of Isolde that I hadn't known and never would. I stared into the black water, feeling so alone that it seemed as if that darkness might pull me into it. As if maybe my mother was waiting there for me.

THIRTY-ONE

I stood in front of the window in West's cabin, every eye on me. The water dripped from my hair in step with my heartbeat, and I watched it pool at my feet.

West had called the crew into his quarters, but Koy had the good sense to stay belowdecks.

"So that's it?" Willa said lowly. "This was all for nothing." She and Paj had the same quiet resentment painted on their faces.

I watched my reflection ripple in the puddle on the floor. She was right. I'd made a deal with Holland and I hadn't come through. And Saint wasn't the only one who stood to lose. We still had to get the deed to the *Marigold* back.

The only card we had left to play was to trust Henrik.

"We still have the Roths," I said.

"If that's all you've got, then you've got nothing," Paj said flatly.

Auster didn't argue with him.

"When we get to Sagsay Holm, I'll talk to Holland. I'll work something out with her."

West finally spoke. "What does that mean?"

I didn't answer. The truth was, I'd do pretty much anything to get the deed back and Holland probably knew it. I didn't have midnight to barter with, giving her all the power.

"What are you going to do, Fable?" Auster asked softly.

"Whatever she wants." It was as simple as that.

Willa muttered under her breath. "Selfish."

"You're angry with me, Willa. Not her," West snapped.

"Is there a difference?"

"Willa." Auster reached for her, but she shoved him off.

"No! This wasn't what we agreed. We said we would find Fable and go back to Ceros to finish what we started."

"I'm sorry," West said. It was followed by a solemn silence, and every crew member looked at him. "It was wrong for me to order the ship to Yuri's Constellation without a vote."

"You can say that again," Paj huffed.

"It won't happen again," West said. "You have my word."

Willa looked at her brother, swallowing hard before she spoke. "I won't be around to find out if you keep it."

"What?" he said, tired.

"When we get back to Ceros, I'm gone."

West went rigid, his eyes boring into her. He was speechless.

"I'm done, West," she said more softly. "I'm done following you from port to port. Letting you take care of me." The emotion in her voice deepened the words. "I want off the *Marigold*."

West looked as if she'd slapped him.

The rest of the crew appeared to be as shocked as West was. They looked between both of them, no one sure what to say.

It was Hamish who finally stepped forward, clearing his throat. "We have enough coin to replace the anchor and get back to the Narrows. We'll have to stop off at the coral islands to top off our ledgers."

"Fine," West answered. He turned toward the window, making it clear they were dismissed.

They filed out one after the other, feet shuffling into the breezeway. Willa looked back over her shoulder before she followed them.

"West." I waited for him to look at me. When he didn't, I leaned into him, setting my head on his shoulder. He pressed his lips to the top of my head and pulled in a deep breath.

We stood there like that for another moment before I left him alone. I took the steps belowdecks at the end of the passageway; the lantern in the crew's cabin was lit, filling the crack in the door with light. I followed it, peering through the opening.

Willa was standing in front of her trunk with her dagger in her hands. She turned it slowly so that the gems caught the light.

I pushed the door open and sat in my hammock, letting my feet swing over the floor.

"I know," she said unevenly. "I shouldn't have done it like that."

"You were angry."

"It was still wrong."

She set her tool belt inside the trunk and closed it before she sat on the lid, facing me. "I know this is awful, but I think part of me was glad when all this happened." She closed her eyes. "Like I finally had a good reason."

I understood what she meant. She'd been dreading telling West that she was leaving and when he went against the crew, she felt justified.

"I'm the one who's selfish," she whispered.

I kicked her gently in the knee with my foot. "You're not selfish. You want to make your own life. West will understand that."

"Maybe." Willa was afraid. Of losing him. The same way he was afraid of losing her.

"What will you do?" I asked.

She shrugged. "I'll probably get a job working for a shipwright or a smith. Maybe an apprenticeship."

"Maybe you'll build us a ship one day." I grinned.

That made her smile.

We fell silent, listening to the hum of the sea around the hull. "It will be hard on him," I said. "To be without you."

Willa bit down onto her bottom lip, staring into the dark. "I know."

I scooted to one side of the hammock, holding it open for her. She hesitated before she stood and climbed in beside me.

"You think he'll forgive me?" she whispered.

I looked at her. "There's nothing to forgive."

After the *Lark,* Willa told me that this wasn't the life she'd chosen. West had brought her onto a crew to keep her safe. But she wasn't the little girl she'd been back then, when they were Waterside strays. It was time for her to make her own way.

THIRTY-TWO

I could feel West's gaze on me as I stood at the bow, watching Sagsay Holm come into view.

The little village was aglow in the sunset, the red-brick buildings stacked like stones ready to topple. But my eyes were fixed on only one ship in the harbor. Dark stained wood and a bow carved into sea demons. Stretched across the jib was a square of wide white canvas bearing Holland's crest.

The knot in my stomach had only tightened in the hours since we'd left Fable's Skerry. I'd stood across the desk from my grandmother and told her I could find the midnight. I'd struck the deal on the toss of dice, and I'd lost.

If Clove reached Saint in time for him to get a merchant's ring to barter, and the Roths actually made good on their promise, we could have a shot at sinking Holland. But that wouldn't keep Saint from finding a rope around his neck. If there was anything my father was bad at, it was playing by other people's rules. He was as much a wild card as Henrik was.

I took up the heaving lines and threw them out as we neared the dock. The loop caught the farthest post as the harbor master came down the wood plank walkway, his attention on the parchments in his hands. He scribbled the quill from left to right, not bothering to glance up until West was coming down the ladder.

He looked up from beneath the rim of his hat when West's boots hit the dock. *"Marigold?"*

West's gaze instantly turned suspicious. "Yeah."

"Holland's waiting for you on the *Seadragon*." He glanced to our crest and made a mark on the parchment. His eyes raked over West top to bottom, but he didn't say whatever it was he was thinking. "Wouldn't keep her waiting if I were you."

West looked up to me, and I let out a long breath before I climbed over the rail and took the ladder down.

"I'll get the deed back, West."

He looked worried. Afraid, even. "It's just a ship, Fable."

I smiled sadly, my head tipping to one side. "I thought we weren't lying to each other."

The corner of his mouth twitched.

"I still have cards to play. I still have my share of the *Lark's* haul and—"

"*We* still have cards to play," he corrected. "And so does Saint."

I nodded, dropping my eyes to the ground. Not for the first time, West had been lured into the utter chaos that was Saint and me, and I didn't like it. It only reminded me that I'd abandoned the rules I'd lived by before I'd met him. The rules we both agreed to leave behind. But now I wondered if we were fooling ourselves into thinking we could do things differently, like we said.

Four guards stood at the mouth of Holland's dock beneath an archway bearing her crest. Every port in the Unnamed Sea probably had one just like it. At the end of the slip, a wooden staircase rose two turns to the port side of the *Seadragon*.

"We're here to see Holland," I said, eyeing the short sword at the guard's hip.

He looked me up and down before he turned on his heel, and West and I followed. We walked up the dock as the sun disappeared and, one by one, the lanterns above the *Seadragon* flickered to life.

I took the steps up from the dock, my hand dragging on the slick railing. The smell of roasting meat drifted off the ship, and when I made it to the deck, I looked back to the *Marigold*. She sat in the shadow of another vessel, her sails drawn up.

Holland's man was already waiting for us. He stretched a hand toward the passageway, gesturing to an open door, where I could see the corner of a crimson rug on the wood slats. I steadied myself with a deep breath before I walked toward it.

Inside, Holland sat before a small, gold-painted table with three different log books open, one on top of another, in her lap. She was wrapped in a scarlet shawl, her silver hair intricately braided on top of her head. Sparkling rubies the size of copper coins hung from each ear.

She looked up at me through her thick lashes. "I was wondering if you were going to show."

"We said sundown," I reminded her.

She closed the logs and set them onto the table. "Please, sit."

I took the seat opposite of her, but West still stood, crossing his arms over his chest.

One dubious eyebrow arched up over the other as she surveyed him. "So? Where is it?"

"I don't have it," I said, keeping my voice as even as I could.

The tiniest trace of some emotion made the set of her mouth falter. "What do you mean, you don't have it?"

"We covered every reef in that system. It's not there," I lied. But I was still convinced the midnight wasn't in those waters.

"I seem to remember you saying that you could find it. You insisted, really." Her voice went flat and when her eyes drifted to West again, I swallowed hard, remembering Zola's boots in the darkened doorway. The way they twitched. "We had a deal, Fable." The threat was there in the deep tone that lifted beneath the words. "But I know how you can make it up to me."

West stiffened beside me.

She opened one of the logs and slipped a folded parchment from inside. Gooseflesh rose on my arms as she opened it and slid it across the low table toward me. "The Trade Council meeting is in two days. You'll be there. As my representative."

I gaped at her. "Representing what?"

"My new trade route in the Narrows."

I slid the parchment back to her without opening it. "I told you I wasn't interested."

"That was before I held the deed to the *Marigold*," she said, sweetly.

She picked up the document and handed it to me. My hand trembled as I opened it and read the words.

"You'll get it back when I have your signature on a two-year contract to head my new fleet."

My lips parted, the sick feeling returning to my gut. "What?" But I already knew. She'd sent me on a fool's errand with the midnight while she stacked the deck. She'd never counted on me finding it.

From the corner of my eye, I could see West taking a step toward me. Before I'd even finished reading, he snatched the contract from my fingers. I watched as his frantic gaze ran over the scripted writing. "She's not signing anything," West said, crumpling the parchment in his fist.

"She will," Holland said, not a hint of question in her voice. "Sign the contract and you'll get everything you want. The deed to the *Marigold* and an operation in the Narrows. The *Marigold* can even work for me, if you'd like." She picked up the teacup, holding it before her. "If I pitch a Narrows-born trader as the head of my new route to Ceros, the Trade Council will concede."

I tried to slow my breaths, holding onto the arm of the chair. "And Saint?"

"Saint is a problem that neither of us want to have. Trust me." She took a sip of tea from the gold rim. "He'll be taken care of by the time we've set up post in Ceros. Without him and Zola to contend with, I'll be handing you the control of the gem trade in those waters."

I looked to West, but he was staring at Holland, his murderous gaze like fire.

"Meet me at Wolfe & Engel tomorrow night with the contract." Her eyes fell to my shaking hands and I curled them into fists, setting them in my lap. She leaned in, the cold gentleness returning to her face. "I don't know what filthy hull of a ship you were born on, Fable. I don't care. But when you sail back to the Narrows, it's going to be under *my* crest."

THIRTY-THREE

The crew stared at me across the cabin, silent. Even Koy looked speechless.

"You're not signing it," Paj snapped. "We've been bleeding coin since we left Dern so that we could bring you back to the Narrows and do what we said we were going to do."

"You can do it without me. This doesn't change that," I said.

"It changes everything," Willa muttered. Behind the others, she was turned toward the lantern, watching its flame behind the glass. This had a different implication for her. If I wasn't on the *Marigold*, it wasn't likely that she'd leave the crew.

"If I sign the contract, we get the deed to the *Marigold* back. If Saint and the Roths come through, it won't even matter. It'll be void."

"And if they *don't* come through?" Willa asked.

"Then you sail one crew member light for the next two years. It's not that long." I tried to sound as if I believed it. Two years away from the *Marigold,* away from West, sounded like an eternity. But it was a price I'd pay if it meant having a place to come home to after my contract was up.

"Contract or not, we need to decide what our next move is. There's still more than enough coin to get a trade route up and running out of Ceros." Hamish set the open book down on the desk between us. Since we'd left Fable's Skerry, he'd been running the numbers. "We don't need a post, not right away."

Everyone looked to West, but he was silent beside me.

Paj sighed, stepping forward to look at the ledgers. "There's no point in getting a license from the Gem Guild if Holland is moving into the Narrows, so I say we stick with rye for the most part."

"Always sells," Auster agreed. "Mullein, too."

It made sense. There wasn't a port in the Narrows that wouldn't take shipments of both.

"That's what I was thinking." Hamish nodded. "Still puts us at odds with Saint, but that's nothing new. Three ports to start—Sowan, Ceros and Dern, in that order."

"I don't know if we're welcome in Sowan anymore. Not for a while, at least," Auster said.

Hamish glanced at West, but he said nothing. Word had

probably travelled all over the Narrows by now about what West had done to the merchant in Sowan. That was a reputation that would take time to live down. But there was one place in the Narrows where reputations didn't matter.

"What about Jeval?" I said.

In the corner of the cabin, Koy straightened, his eyes finding me.

"Jeval?" Paj was skeptical. "It's a supply stop, not a port."

"If trade is going to open up between the Unnamed Sea and the Narrows, then it's only a matter of time before Jeval becomes a real port. It's the only berth between Sagsay Holm and Dern." I repeated the words Koy had spoken to me only the day before.

Hamish's mouth turned down at the corners as he considered it. "There aren't even any merchants on Jeval."

"Not yet." I glanced at Koy. "But if we're trading rye and mullein, there will always be coin on Jeval for that."

"It's not a bad idea," Auster said, shrugging. "West?"

He thought about it, scratching the scruff at his jaw. "I agree."

"We'd have to find someone trustworthy to set up trade with," Hamish murmured.

"I think I know someone." I grinned, tipping my chin up toward Koy.

They all looked at him.

"That true?" Hamish asked.

Koy stood up off the wall, standing taller. "I think we could work something out." He was playing it down, but I could see the glow of excitement around him.

Hamish closed the book, sitting on the corner of the desk. "So, all that's left is to vote." His eyes moved over each of our faces. "Fable, your vote still counts if your share is going in."

"It is," I said without hesitation.

"All right." Hamish clapped his hands together in front of him. "All for using a third of the coin from the *Lark*'s haul to fill the hull with rye and mullein?" He looked to Willa first.

She opened her mouth to speak, but West cut her off. "She's not voting."

Hamish's mouth snapped shut as he looked between them.

"The only ones voting are those putting in their share of the *Lark*."

"What are you talking about?" Willa finally turned away from the lamp. Its light illuminated only half of her face.

"Willa's share is no longer part of our ledgers," West said, still not talking directly to her.

Willa glanced in my direction, as if waiting for me to object. "West . . ."

"I want you to take it," he said. "Do whatever you want with it. Start your own operation. Buy into an apprenticeship. Whatever you want." It looked as if it pained him to say it.

Willa's eyes filled with tears as she looked up at him.

"Whatever's next for us." West swallowed. "You're not stuck here."

Hamish paused, awaiting Willa's reply. But she said nothing. "All right. All voting members then, in favor of stacking our inventory with mullein and rye. Fable?"

I gave him a nod in answer. "I agree."

Paj and Hamish echoed the same, followed by Auster. But West still stood beside me, his absent gaze on the closed ledgers.

"Has to be unanimous," Hamish said.

West's mind was at work. Whether he was running numbers or sorting through options, I didn't know. But I had a feeling I wasn't going to like what he said next. "We could use the coin to buy Fable out of the contract with Holland."

"You're not doing that," I said, fixing him with my pointed stare. "That is *not* happening."

The others stayed silent.

"Why not?" West asked.

"We said we were going to use the *Lark*'s haul to start our own trade. We're not throwing it away on Holland."

"It's not exactly throwing it away," Willa murmured.

"She's not going to take coin. She doesn't need copper. There's only one thing Holland wants and we don't have it," I said, more irritated than I wanted to be. They cared about me. But I wasn't going to let Holland take the chance I'd given the *Marigold*. The chance they'd given me.

"West, we still need your vote," Hamish said more gently.

West finally looked at me, his eyes running over my face. "Fine." He swallowed, stepping around me and going for the door.

"West." Paj stopped him. "There's still repairs to deal with."

"We'll deal with it in the morning."

Paj let him go, watching him disappear into the breezeway. Willa's mouth twisted to one side as she looked to me, and I answered her silent question with a nod before I followed him.

The night was unusually warm, the air balmy, making the deck glisten in the darkness. West's shadow passed over my feet from the quarterdeck. He pulled a strand of frayed rope from the barrel at the stern as I came up the steps. He didn't acknowledge me as I leaned into the railing and watched him unravel it, shredding the fibers to be used as oakum. It was becoming familiar, the way he instantly went to work on tedious tasks when he was upset.

"It's two years," I said, trying to be gentle with him.

He didn't answer, sliding the tip of his knife roughly between the cords.

"Two years is nothing."

"It's not nothing." He grunted, dropping another wad of rope. "We should try to buy out the contract."

"You know that's not going to work."

"If you step foot on that ship, she's never going to let you go. She'll find a way to extend the contract. To get you under a debt. Something."

"She's not Saint."

"You sure about that?" he snapped.

I bit my tongue. I wasn't going to lie to him. The truth was that I didn't know Holland. At times, I felt like I didn't even really know Saint. But I couldn't pretend that I didn't understand what he was saying. From the moment I first saw Holland at the gala, she'd been working toward handing me that contract. She'd trapped me. And the worst part of it all was that I'd been stupid enough to fall for it.

West stopped with the rope, looking out at the water before his eyes drifted to me. "I don't want you to sign it," he said, his voice deep.

I stepped toward him, taking the rope from his hands and dropping it on the deck. He softened when I snaked my arms under his and wrapped them around his middle. "Saint will come through. I know it."

He set his chin on top of my head. "And the Roths?"

"If Saint delivers, they will too."

He fell quiet for a moment. "None of this would have happened if I hadn't tried to get back at Zola for Willa."

"West, this was always about Holland. None of this would have happened if I hadn't asked you to take me across the Narrows."

He knew it was true. But West's nature was to take the blame. He'd had people depending on him for too long.

I tipped my head back to look up at him. "Promise me you'll do what you have to do."

He took a strand of my hair and let it slip through his fingers, making me shiver. Silence from West was a bad omen. He wasn't a man of many words, but he knew what he wanted and he wasn't afraid to take it.

"Promise me," I said again.

He nodded reluctantly. "I will."

THIRTY-FOUR

When I woke that morning in West's quarters, he was gone.

The shutters of the window had come open, tapping softly against the wall in the wind, and the memory of that morning in Dern flashed before my eyes. The gray sky and the cool breeze. The cast of light through the hazy cabin. But it was the Unnamed Sea out the window this time.

I sat up, sliding my hand beneath the quilt where West had been. It was cold. His boots, too, were missing from where they usually sat beside the door.

Out on the deck, Auster and Paj were eating their breakfasts in the breezeway.

"Where is he?" I asked, my voice still hoarse with sleep.

"He and Hamish went to see the shipwright." Paj motioned toward the harbor.

Auster stood from the crate he was sitting on. "Hungry?"

"No." I shook my head. My stomach had been turning since I'd come up from the water at Fable's Skerry.

I walked to the railing, watching the deck of the *Seadragon*. Holland's crew was already up and working, and the melodic brush of holystoning echoed over the water. I used to sit cradled in the jib on my father's ship, watching the deckhands scrape the white bricks over the deck, grinding the wood pale and smooth. Back and forth, back and forth. My father liked his decks sparkling clean, like any good helmsman, and it was the job dreaded by everyone onboard.

White as bone. Not until it's white as bone.

My father's voice snaked through my mind, like the hum that rattled the hull of a ship in a storm.

Not until it's white as bone.

The grind of sand on the wood was as warm under my skin as every memory I had of those days. When Saint would lean into the railing with his elbows, watching the crystal blue water for my mother to surface from a dive.

I hoped that was how my memories of the *Marigold* would stay, there within reach when I needed them for the next two years.

Willa came up the steps from below, her boots in her hands. Her twisted locks were tied away from her face, falling down her back like cords of bronze. The scar on her cheek was flushed pink in the cold.

"Where are you going?" I asked, watching her button her jacket.

"Into the village to see the smith. Can't get back to Ceros without an anchor."

I looked over the rooftops in the distance. Something inside of me was holding its breath, and I realized it was not being able to lay eyes on West that was bothering me. I'd been thinking about that cool look in his eye since the night before. The quiet that had come over him when I said I was going to sign Holland's contract.

"I'll come with you." I went back to West's cabin and fetched my boots and jacket, raking my hair up into a knot on top of my head.

A few minutes later we were climbing the steps out of the harbor, the sun on our faces.

Willa walked the streets in a grid, looking for the smith's shop, and every time someone caught sight of her scar, their steps faltered a little. She was a fearsome thing to behold, her small frame corded with muscle under her tawny skin. Glinting blue eyes were rimmed in dark lashes, making them almost ethereal.

She was beautiful. And that morning, she looked free.

"This is it." She stopped beneath a red painted sign that read IRON SMITH.

The door jingled as she pushed inside, and I watched her through the glass as she went to the wall, where baskets of nails and rivets were hanging from hooks.

A few seabirds were drifting and turning on the wind blowing up from the harbor in the distance and I sighed as

I watched them, feeling heavy there in the alley. It was as if every inch of sky were pressing down on top of me, driving me into the earth.

It was still morning, but by the time the sun went down I'd be signing Holland's contract.

A twist of brilliant blue flared in the shadow darkening the corner of the building, and I studied the street around me. The people walked leisurely from shop to shop, but I could feel the shift in the air. The trailing scent of spiced mullein smoke.

I watched the corner, where the alley narrowed into a small lane that disappeared between the buildings. Over my shoulder, I could see Willa through the window, waiting at the counter.

My mouth twisted, my hands curling into fists inside my pockets as I stepped toward the alley and took the turn. The flash of blue disappeared around the next corner, leaving the alley empty. Silent.

I walked with heavy, echoing steps, glancing back to the street to be sure no one was following me. When I made the next turn, I stopped short, my chest caving in with the weight of lost breath. There, leaning against the soot-stained brick, my father stood with his pipe clenched in his teeth, his cap pulled low over his eyes.

"Saint." My lips moved around the word, but I couldn't hear it.

The sting behind my eyes instantly betrayed me, treacherous tears gathering so quickly that I had to blink them away. It took every ounce of my will to keep from throwing my arms around him, and I didn't know what to do with that feeling. I wanted to press my face into his coat and cry. I wanted to let the weight of my legs give out and let him hold me.

I'd thought over and over that maybe I'd never see him again. That maybe I didn't want to. And here I was, swallowing down the cry trapped in my throat.

He was beautiful and terrifying and stoically cold. He was Saint.

A puff of smoke trailed up from his lips before he looked at me, and I thought I might have seen something there in his steely blue eyes that mirrored the roaring feeling inside of me. But when his eyes shifted, it was gone.

He took hold of the opening of his coat with both hands and sauntered toward me. "Got your message."

"Didn't think you'd come yourself," I said. It was true. I'd been expecting Clove. But I was so happy to see my father that I was almost ashamed of myself. I stared at the toes of his shined black boots in front of mine. "Do you have it?" I asked.

An amused smirk played at his lips before he reached into his pocket and pulled a small brown paper package from inside. He held it between us, but when I reached for it, he lifted it up, out of my reach.

"Do you know what you're doing?" His voice grated.

I glared at him, snatching the package from his fingers. It was the same question West had asked me. The same one I didn't know if I had the answer to. "I know what I'm doing," I lied.

He took a long drag on the pipe, his eyes squinting as I

tore at the edge of the package, pulling back the thick parchment until I could see the corner of a box. When it was free, I lifted the tiny brass latch and opened it. Inside, the golden tiger's eye of a gem merchant's ring stared up at me. I let out a long, relieved breath.

"You look all right."

I glanced up to see his gaze moving over me head to toe. It was his feeble attempt at asking if I was okay. "You could have told me. About Holland."

He considered me for a moment before he answered. "I could have."

"You may have gotten rid of Zola, but I know you wanted to get me off the *Marigold*. It didn't work."

His eyes narrowed. "I figured your grandmother would offer you a place with her."

"She did. I didn't want it."

He reached up, combing through his mustache with his fingers. I could have sworn I saw a smile buried on his lips. He looked almost . . . proud. "Clove says this ring's for Henrik," he said, changing the subject.

"It is."

Saint let another puff of smoke spill from his mouth. "Not the most reliable of criminals."

"Are you saying you don't think he'll keep his word?"

"I'm saying I think you've got a fifty-fifty shot."

Those weren't good odds. I leaned into the wall beside him, watching the opening of the alley where people filled the street. "I need to ask you something."

His eyebrows lifted. He looked curious. "Go ahead."

"Did she ever tell you?"

He frowned as soon as he realized I was talking about my mother. "Tell me what?"

"Isolde." I said her name, knowing he didn't like it. An uneasiness rippled through him. "Did she ever tell you where she found the midnight?"

He took the pipe from his mouth. "She never told me."

"What?" My voice rose. "In all those years? How could she never have told you?"

He looked away from me, perhaps to hide whatever his face would give away. The shadow of it looked a lot like frailty. "I never asked," he said, but the words were taut.

"I don't believe you," I said, incredulous.

"I—" He stopped. He looked like he was unsure of what to say. Or how to say it. And *that* wasn't Saint at all. He steeled himself before he turned back to face me, his eyes holding an entirely different truth. "I made her swear to never tell me."

I leaned into the wall, letting it hold me up. She had told him about the midnight. But I wasn't the only one who knew the fabric making up the man I called father. He'd known himself well enough to protect Isolde.

From himself.

The thought was so heartbreaking I had to look away from him, afraid of what I might see if I met his eyes. He was the only one who'd loved her more than I had. And the pain of losing her was fresh and sharp, knife-edged between us.

He cleared his throat before taking another puff on the pipe. "Are you going to tell me what your plan is?"

"Don't trust me?" I found a smile on my lips, but it was still wavering with the threat of tears.

"I trust you." His voice was quieter than I'd ever heard it. "Are you going to tell me why?"

I could see that he wanted to know. That he was struggling to understand. He'd been surprised when Clove showed up in Bastian with my message and he wanted to know why I'd do it. Why I'd risk anything for him, after everything he'd done.

I looked up, and the shape of him bent in the light. I gave him the real answer. The whole, naked truth of it. "Because I don't want to lose you."

There was no more to it, and no less. I hadn't known it until that moment in the solarium, when Holland said his name. That I'd loved him with the same fire that I'd hated him. That if anything happened to Saint, a part of me would be taken with him.

His mouth twisted to one side before he gave a sharp nod, looking to the street. "You'll be at the Trade Council meeting?"

I nodded, unable to get another word out.

The edge of his coat brushed against mine as he moved past me, and I watched him take the next turn, leaving me standing in the alley alone. The sea wind whipped around me and the lump in my throat ached as I took the narrow passage back the way I'd come.

Willa was waiting in front of the smith's window when I came back out onto the street, a wrapped package in her arms. When she saw me, she sighed with relief. "Where were you?"

I waited for a man to pass us, lowering my voice. "Saint."

"He's here? Did he . . . ?" she whispered.

I pulled the box from my pocket just enough to show her.

She gasped. "He did it?"

"He did it," I said. "I don't want to know how, but that bastard did it."

THIRTY-FIVE

When we got back to the *Marigold*, there were voices behind the closed door to West's cabin. I let out a relieved breath when I saw it, the steadiness immediately returning to my bones.

But I stopped short when I heard Paj's clipped, angry tone. "You should have asked me."

I didn't knock, letting the door swing open to see West and Hamish around the desk with Paj. All three of them looked up at once, falling quiet.

Hamish fidgeted with a stack of papers, his fingers stained with ink. But there was something in his manner that was off. He was angry too.

"Did you find the shipwright?" I asked, watching Hamish open the drawer and slide the parchments inside.

"We did," Hamish answered, standing up straight. He looked around the room. Everywhere except at me. "I'll have those figures tonight," he said, glancing at West.

West answered with a nod. "All right."

Hamish shuffled past, turning to the side so that he didn't touch me as he slipped out the door. Paj glared at West for a moment before he stalked out behind him. I watched them both disappear onto the deck, my brow pulled. But in the cabin, West looked at ease. More relaxed than he'd been the night before.

"What was that about?" I asked, studying him.

He looked up from the desk. "Nothing. Just reporting on the ledgers." But his eyes dropped from mine a little too quickly.

"Paj looked angry."

West gave an irritated sigh. "Paj is always angry."

Whatever was going on between them, I could see that West wasn't going to tell me. Not now, anyway. "I saw Saint," I said, closing the door.

West's hands tightened on the edge of the desk as he looked up at me. "Did he get it?"

I pulled the package from my jacket pocket and set it on the desk in front of him. He picked it up and turned it over, letting the merchant's ring fall into his hand. It was freshly polished, the gemstone shined.

"Now all we need is the Roths," I breathed.

West reached into his vest, pulling a folded paper from the pocket. He handed it to me. "This came an hour ago. I was waiting for you."

I took the parchment and opened it, reading the hurried, slanting script. It was a message from Ezra.

Leith Tavern, after the bell.

I looked out the window. The sun had passed the center of the sky and it would set in a few hours. Holland would be expecting me at Wolfe & Engel, so we'd have to be quick if we were going to meet Ezra. "All right. Let's go."

West tucked the message back into his vest and grabbed his jacket from the hook, following me out onto the deck. When I came down the ladder, Willa was already working on the repairs, suspended beside the hull from the starboard side. She fit the oakum into an opening along the smaller cracks, pounding it in with the blunt end of her adze.

"We'll be back after sundown," West said, jumping down onto the dock beside me.

"Last time you said that you didn't show for two days," she muttered, pulling another nail from her bag.

Whatever she wasn't saying was alight in her eyes. She'd been granted her freedom from the *Marigold*, but she didn't like the idea of me working for Holland. Soon we would each take our own paths, and I didn't know if they would ever come back together again.

We took the main street that led back into Sagsay Holm, finding the tea house at the top of the hill in the eastern part of the village. It looked out over the water, with a view of the rocky coast.

The sign was painted in a glistening gold, hanging out over the street in an ornate, scrolled frame.

WOLFE & ENGEL

I swallowed, the knot in my stomach resurfacing. The windows reflected the buildings behind us, and I was suddenly aware of how out of place I looked among them. Wind-blown and sun-kissed. Tired.

Beside me, West was the same. He said nothing and I, too, was at a loss for words. By the time I left the tea house, I'd be contracted with Holland, and I had no way of knowing if the Roths would save me.

"I'm going to do this alone," I said. The last thing I needed was West making himself even more of an enemy to Holland. I felt like I was holding my breath, waiting for the stillness around him to rupture.

To my surprise, he didn't argue. He looked over me, through the window. "I'll wait."

"All right."

West's face was still stoic as he watched me take hold of the brass handle and open the door. The scent of bergamot and lavender came rushing out, swirling around me as my eyes adjusted to the low light.

Wood-framed booths covered in red velvet lined the wall, the expanse of the room filled with gold tables. Delicate crystal chandeliers hung from the ceiling, fit with candles that gave everything the look of a dream.

It was no accident Holland wanted to meet me here, somewhere extravagant and luxurious, like Azimuth House. It was exactly like the kind of place she could have things on her terms, like always.

"Fable?" A man stopped before me, his eyes raking over my clothes.

"Yes?" I answered suspiciously.

He looked disappointed. "This way."

I looked back to the window, but West was gone, the darkening street empty. I followed the man to the back of the tea house, where a thick damask curtain was drawn over a private booth. He pulled it back and Holland looked up, her silver hair pinned in beautiful, smooth curls that spiraled away from her face like gentle waves.

"Your guest, madam." The man bowed his head a little, not meeting Holland's eyes.

"Thank you." The same disapproval hung in her expression as she looked me over. "Didn't bother to clean the sea off of you, I see."

I slid into the booth across the table from her, trying to be careful with the velvet. I didn't like this. I didn't like what she was doing by bringing me here, and I hated that I felt small. I set my elbows onto the table, leaning toward her, and she grimaced at the sight.

The server reappeared with a tray set with two decadent cups. Their rims were studded with blue diamonds and inside, a clear liquid made the silver look like it was melted. The man gave another bow before he disappeared.

Holland waited for the curtain to close before she picked up one of the cups, gesturing for me to do the same. I hesitated before I lifted it from the tray.

"A toast." Her cup drifted toward mine.

I tapped the rim of my glass to hers. "To what?"

But she looked at me ruefully, as if I were trying to be funny. "To our partnership."

"Partnership suggests equal power," I said, watching her take a drink. Her lips puckered as she swallowed, setting the cup back down gingerly.

I took a sip, swallowing hard when the burn of it lit in my mouth. It was disgusting.

"Tomorrow." She changed the subject and I was grateful we weren't bothering with pleasantries. She was my grandmother, but I wasn't a fool. I'd worked my way beneath her thumb the same way West had with Saint. If a single thing went wrong at the Trade Council meeting and she discovered what I'd been up to, the entire crew would find the same end that Zola did. Their bodies would be dumped in the harbor and the *Marigold* would be taken apart or sailing under Holland's crest.

"Everything's in order," she began, folding her ringed fingers together in front of her. "The Council will open the floor for trading business and I'll make the proposal, introducing you as the head of my new trade route in the Narrows."

"What makes you think they'll vote in your favor?"

She almost laughed. "Fable, I'm not a fool. The Trade Council hates me. Both of them. They need my coin to keep trade moving, but they've drawn very clear boundaries to keep me from controlling their business. You're Narrows-born, you're a skilled dredger, and you know how to crew." She took another sip from her glass. "You're a gem sage."

I set my glass down a little too hard. "You're going to tell them I'm a gem sage?"

"Why wouldn't I?"

My gaze sharpened on her, trying to read the open, honest look in her eye. "Because it's dangerous."

There was a reason gem sages were almost unheard of now. The days of gem merchants pursuing the title were long over because no one wanted to hold that much value, not when traders and merchants would do anything to control it.

"I'm not a gem sage. I never finished my apprenticeship."

She waved a hand, dismissing me. "Those are exactly the kinds of details they don't need to know."

I leaned back into the booth, shaking my head. Maybe that was another reason Isolde had left Bastian. If I had to bet on it, I'd say Holland had tried to use my mother, too.

"Now, it's important that you act as if you know how to behave if we are going to make the right impression," she continued. "There's no way to pass you off as if you actually belong, but my guess is that will probably work in our favor."

There were those words again. *We. Our.*

"You will not speak unless spoken to. You will let me answer the Trade Council's questions. You will *look* the part." Again, she glared at my clothes. "I'll have a dressmaker come fit you for something tonight."

I stared at her. "What if they don't grant you the license?"

"They will," she said defensively. "With Zola and Saint out of the water, the Narrows will be hard-pressed to raise up another trade operation that can expand its route to the Unnamed Sea. If *you're* running the trade, everyone wins."

Except Saint. Except me.

I tried to relax, pulling in a slow breath as I picked the silver cup back up and took another sip. Holland had set up her hand well. With Zola gone, every crew in the Narrows would be casting their bids to compete with Saint for what little power was left. But if Holland got her license, she'd be holding it all by the time the sun set tomorrow.

"Let's get this over with," I said.

"Get what over with?"

"The contract."

Holland touched her fingertips together before she picked up a leather-bound satchel from the seat beside her and opened it. I watched her sort through the parchments before she found the one she was looking for—an unmarked envelope. She set it onto the table before me.

I breathed, willing my heartbeat to calm. Once I signed it, there was no going back. My fate would lie in Henrik's hands. I lifted a hand from my lap and picked it up, opening the flap of the envelope and pulling the parchment free. My stomach plummeted as I opened it before me.

My eyes ran over the black ink again and again.

Ship Deed

The *Marigold*'s name was listed below.

"What is this?" I stammered.

"It's the deed to the ship. As promised," she answered, closing the satchel.

"I haven't signed the contract yet."

"Oh, it's been paid for." Holland smiled. "I had the changes he requested made at the trade office. Everything should be in order."

"What?" I held the deed to the candlelight, reading over the print anxiously.

Transfer of ownership:

I sucked in a breath, my mouth dropping open when I saw my name. It was written in the same script as the rest of the document. "What did you do?" I panted. The deed shook in my hands.

Cold realization filled my skull, making my head ache as I put it together. "West."

West signed the two-year contract with Holland.

"The terms of our agreement have changed," Holland said. "West signed the contract in exchange for the *Marigold*." She pulled another parchment from inside her satchel. "But I have a new offer for you."

I stared at the document. It was another contract.

"You still want to save your father? This is your chance." Holland beamed with pleasure.

We'd walked right into her trap not once, but twice. When West signed Holland's contract, he thought he was saving me. But Holland had gotten two for the price of one. And she knew it. She had no doubt that I'd sign it.

I picked up the quill and dragged it over the parchment. My name looked up at me, shining in wet ink.

I slid out of the booth, throwing back the curtain with the deed clutched in my fist. Heat pricked beneath my skin as

I stalked through the tea house, headed for the dark window. I threw the door open and stepped out, searching the street for him.

West stood across the path, leaning against the wall of the next building.

"What did you do?" My voice grated as I crossed the cobblestones toward him.

He stood, his hands coming out of his pockets as I stopped before him, seething. "Fable . . ."

I shoved the crumpled deed into his chest. "Why is my name on this?"

West stared at the envelope.

"Is that what was going on with Paj and Hamish earlier? Everyone knew about this but me?"

"Willa and Auster don't know."

"You're just abandoning the *Marigold*? You're just going to leave?" I snapped.

"I'm doing the same thing you were going to do. Two years with Holland, then back to the Narrows."

I was so angry that I could feel it in my blood. "You're the helmsman, West. It's not the same."

West looked as if he was measuring his words. "Paj is going to take over as helmsman."

"What?" I was shouting now, and the people on the street were stopping to stare. I didn't care.

"The crew will set up trade just the way we said. It'll be waiting for me when I get back to the Narrows."

I wanted to scream. I wanted to hit him. "Why is my name on the deed?"

West sighed, exasperated. "I don't want it in my name if . . ." He didn't finish.

"If what?" I leveled my eyes at him.

"If something happens to me and the ship is in my name, ownership would fall to the Trade Council until the crew could pay to have the ownership transferred. If you own it, that won't happen."

Tears burned behind my eyes until the sight of him wavered. "So you're just going to go work for Holland. Do whatever she tells you."

"I'll do what I have to do." He gave me the words I'd made him promise the night before.

"That's not what I meant. You know that's not what I meant."

He had no reply to that.

"How could you do this?" I said hoarsely.

I started walking, but West's heavy footsteps echoed behind me. He caught my arm, pulling me back. "I'm not going back to the Narrows without you."

I could see that he wasn't going to concede. And he couldn't now, anyway. He'd signed the contract. But West was already haunted. His soul was dark. And I didn't want to know who he would be if he spent two more years doing someone else's dirty work.

I could feel it. If I lost to Holland at the Trade Council meeting, I would lose West.

"You won't have to. Neither will I," I said, a tear falling down my cheek.

"What?"

"I signed one, too."

"Why? How?"

"For Saint." I stared at him. "Now we all get what we want. You, me. Holland." I almost laughed at how ridiculous it all was.

West let out a heavy breath, looking past me. His mind was reeling. Looking for a way out.

"You can't keep trying to take control of everything. You can't save everyone, West."

But he didn't know how to stay out of it.

I shook my head, starting down the hill without him.

Now it wasn't just *my* fate in Henrik's hands. It was West's, too.

THIRTY-SIX

*L*eith Tavern sat at the end of Linden Street, bustling with people coming and going from the merchant's house before the closing bell rang out over the village.

West kept watch while I looked through the window, searching for a head of dark, shorn hair. The worst thing that could happen was Holland finding out we were meeting with one of the Roths. If she did, we'd all find ourselves sunk in the harbor, blood or no blood.

If the Roths made good on the deal, it would destroy Holland's operation in Bastian. It wasn't only the Narrows-based traders who stood to benefit. Holland controlled more than the gem trade with her wealth, leaning on the guilds for whatever she needed because she was the only one with the power to return those kinds of favors. But she was also likely the main source of revenue for the Roths, and they stood to lose if she fell from her throne.

I could only hope that what they could gain would outweigh what they could lose.

"He'll show," West said, watching the way I fidgeted with the button on my jacket.

"I know," I said coldly. But I wasn't sure of anything, especially after what Saint had said about there being a fifty-fifty chance. His words gave me the same sinking feeling I had when sailing straight into a storm. I didn't know if we were coming out the other side.

"Fable." West waited for me to tear my eyes from the window and look at him.

But all I could think about was his name on Holland's contract. How I hadn't even seen it coming. West hadn't just kept me in the dark. He'd played me. "Don't," I said, going back to the window.

The tables and booths inside were filled with people. I pressed my hand to the glass, searching for Ezra again.

West tugged on the sleeve of my jacket, his gaze pinned to the end of the alley, where four or five figures stood in the shadows.

"It's him," West said lowly.

I followed the wall of the tavern until I could make him out. Ezra watched me from beneath the hood of his jacket, his scarred hands the only bit of him visible. When I stopped before him, the others stepped out of the dark, lining up at his sides. Three other young men and one girl, none of their faces ones I recognized. The young boy Henrik had called Tru was with them, too. He was dressed in a fine jacket with a gold watch chain tucked into its pocket.

The man beside Ezra stepped into the light, revealing combed chestnut hair over a youthful face. He looked me up and down. The Roth tattoo peeked out from beneath his rolled shirt sleeve.

"Do you have it?" Ezra didn't waste any time.

I pulled my hand from my jacket pocket, holding it before him so he could see the gem merchant's ring on my middle finger.

He shook his head, half-laughing. "How the hell did you get that?"

"Does it matter?"

The brown-haired young man smirked. "I told Henrik there's no way you'd come through." He stepped forward, extending a hand. "Murrow. You must be Fable."

I stared at it, not moving, and he dropped it to his side.

"That makes me wonder if you held up your end of the deal," I said, trying to read his face.

But behind him, Ezra was expressionless, his features smooth. "I did. But I covered my bases." A group of men came out of the tavern's side door, and Ezra watched them from the corner of his eye.

I slipped the ring from my finger and dropped it into his palm. He immediately pulled a monocle from his jacket and fit it to his eye, shifting away from me so that he could check the gem set into the ring. When he was satisfied, he dropped it into his pocket.

"I kept my end of the deal. Now it's your turn," I said, my voice hardening. "How do I know you'll do what you promised?"

Murrow grinned, a spark lighting his eyes. "Guess you'll have to trust us."

West moved beside me, and before I even realized what had happened, he had his hands around Tru's throat, dragging him toward us.

"West!"

Ezra and Murrow already had their knives drawn. Ezra lunged forward and froze when West pressed the tip of his knife to Tru's throat. The boy's eyes were wide, his face draining of its color.

"What are you doing?" I rasped.

I set my hand on West's arm. Despite his cool exterior, I could feel the heavy pulse under his skin. I wanted to believe that it was a bluff. That he wouldn't hurt a child. But looking into his eyes now, I wasn't sure. *This* was the West my father had hired. The one he'd relied on.

"Here's the problem." West's face was smooth. Tru thrashed in his arms, his scream muffled by West's hand over his mouth. "I *don't* trust you."

A drop of beryl-red blood trailed down Tru's neck, staining the collar of his clean white shirt. I watched West's eyes. They were empty.

"So you take the ring. And we'll take the boy," West said.

"You'll get him back tomorrow. After the Trade Council meeting."

"You're not going anywhere with him," Ezra said. His eyes jumped from West to Tru. He looked afraid, and I remembered that with the exception of Ezra, the Roths were family.

But there was something strange about him. Different from the light in Henrik or Holland or Saint's eyes. He looked genuinely worried for the boy, and I realized that Auster was right. Ezra was cut from a different cloth. So, why was he still with the Roths?

"You saw him that night, didn't you?" I asked, the words almost a whisper.

Ezra looked confused. "Who?"

"Auster. You saw him that night, but you pretended not to."

The answer was in the way his eyes narrowed. Whatever his reasons, he'd let Auster disappear when he left the Roths. I could only hope that even a shadow of the same loyalty might extend to all of us.

"I'll deliver the commission tonight." Ezra spoke through clenched teeth. "You hurt him, or ever mention a word about this to anyone, and the cost will find you." The threat was clear in the words. "You don't want to step foot in Henrik's shadow. Understand?"

"I understand." I nodded, feeling the truth of the words cut deep. I could see that some part of him liked the mischief at play, but he wasn't going to go down for me with Henrik or with Holland, and he wasn't going to sacrifice the boy on their altar.

"You'll be fine." Now Ezra was speaking to Tru.

He pulled up the collar of his jacket before he slipped back into the shadows with the others.

The boy's eyes widened, and he let out a terrified whimper when he realized they'd really left. I took hold of his jacket and yanked him from West's hands, wrapping my arms around him protectively. "What the hell are you doing?"

West slipped his knife back into his belt. "We needed leverage. I took it."

I wiped the blood from Tru's neck with the hem of my shirt. "Come on." I put my arm around him and started walking. "You're okay. We're not going to hurt you."

He didn't look convinced, glancing over his shoulder to the dark alley where Ezra and Murrow had disappeared.

West followed on our heels, not looking the least bit phased. This was all so simple to him. Order the crew to Yuri's Constellation. Lie about the deed. Sign the contract with Holland. Kidnap and threaten to kill a child.

What else is he willing to do?

Willa's words echoed in tandem with my footsteps on the cobblestones.

Auster had warned us not to trust the Roths, but I'd still put all the power into their hands. Now, West had taken some of it back.

THIRTY-SEVEN

The color Holland chose was the deepest shade of emerald, the strands of silk moving in the light like threads of green glass. It ignited a memory, like breath on embers, but I couldn't place it.

The seamstress carefully ran her fingers over the edge of the hem, pinning it into place at my waist so the fabric draped over my legs like a sweep of wind.

My eyes kept drifting to the closed door, watching for a shadow. Holland's seamstress was already waiting when we got back to the ship, as promised, and West had gone straight up to the quarterdeck to help Willa fit the new anchor. The crew had looked between us and Tru in question, the icy silence deafening.

I'd left the boy in the care of Hamish, who I figured was the least likely to throw him overboard.

"Almost finished," the seamstress sang, pulling a needle from the cushion at her wrist and threading it with her teeth. She fixed the corner with three stitches and trimmed a few threads before she stood up, standing back. "Turn." I reluctantly obeyed as her eyes scrutinized every inch of me. "All right." She seemed satisfied, picking up the bolt of cloth and setting it onto her hip before she lugged it through the door.

I turned back to the mirror Holland's men had hauled up onto the *Marigold*, running my hands over the skirt nervously. It had the look of melting butter, soft and smooth in the candlelight. But that wasn't what made me uneasy.

I swallowed, remembering. This was the dress my mother wore in the portrait in Holland's study. I looked just like her. I looked just like Holland. As if I belonged at a fancy gala or in the private booth at the tea house.

But the *Marigold* was the only place I wanted to belong.

A knock sounded on the door before the handle turned. When it opened, West stood in the breezeway. "Can I come in?"

I wrapped my arms around me self-consciously, covering the waist of the frock. "It's your cabin."

He stepped inside and let the jacket fall from his shoulders. He didn't say anything as he hung it on the hook, his gaze moving over me. I didn't like the look in his eye. I didn't like the feeling of the space between us. But West was shut up tight. Closed off from me.

I watched him step out of his worn boots one at a time. The wind pouring into the cabin turned cold, making me shiver.

"You're a stubborn bastard," I said softly.

The shadow of a smirk lit on his face. "So are you."

"You should have told me you were signing the contract."

He swallowed. "I know."

I picked up the skirt and stepped toward him, but he kept his eyes on the floor. He was still pulling away. "I'm not one more person you have to take care of. You have to stop doing that."

"I don't know how to," he admitted.

"I know." I crossed my arms. "But you're going to have to figure it out. I have to be able to trust you. I have to know that even if we don't agree, we're doing this together."

"We are doing it together."

"No, we're not. You're trying to make decisions for me, just like Saint."

He bristled at the words.

"When I made that deal with Holland, I did it on my own. You were never supposed to be a part of this."

"Fable, I love you," he breathed, still staring at my feet. "I don't want to do any of this without you."

The anger I'd felt was suddenly washed out by sadness. West was doing the only thing he knew how to do. "Will you look at me?"

He finally lifted his gaze.

"Would you have hurt that kid? Really?"

He bit the inside of his cheek. "I don't think so."

It was an honest answer, but I didn't like it. "We said we weren't going to do this by the rules. Remember?"

"I remember."

"You're not Saint. Neither am I."

His eyes trailed over me, tightening.

"What's wrong?"

He let out a frustrated breath. "This." He motioned to the air between us and then to the frock. "All of it."

I looked down at my skirts, trying not to laugh. I cocked my head to the side, narrowing my eyes playfully. "Are you trying to say you don't like my frock?"

But he wasn't taking the bait. "I don't like it," he said flatly.

"Why not?"

He raked a hand into his hair, holding it back from his face as he scrutinized the shimmering silk. His gaze was cold. "You don't look like you. You don't smell like you."

I couldn't help but smile even though I could see it annoyed him. But I loved the way he looked standing there barefoot by the window, half of his shirt untucked. It was the side of West I only got glimpses of.

I took another step toward him, the length of the skirts dragging on the floor behind me.

"I would be happy if I never saw you in one of those stupid things again," he said, finally grinning.

"Fine." I reached up and unhooked the buttons one at a time until it was loose enough to slide over my shoulders, and West watched as it dropped to the floor in a puddle of green. The underdress was almost as absurd as the frock, tied in tiny white satin ribbons that met in bows at each of my hips. "Better?"

"Better," he conceded.

For a moment, it was as if we weren't in Sagsay Holm. As if we'd never come to the Unnamed Sea or met Holland. But his smile fell again, like he was thinking the same thing.

I wondered if he was wishing he'd made a different decision that night at the barrier islands. I'd freed him from Saint, but I'd dragged him into the Unnamed Sea and put him at the mercy of Holland. I'd nearly lost the *Marigold,* and I could see what it did to him, not having any control over what was going to happen.

The shadows caught the cut of his cheeks, and for a moment he looked like a spirit. I clenched my teeth, a stone sinking in my stomach. Underneath the anger, fear was writhing. I was scared that this was just who he was. That he'd signed the contract because he wanted to be that person Saint made him.

I could love this West. The one with a dark past. But I couldn't tie myself to him if he was walking back into it.

"I need to ask you something."

He crossed his arms over his broad chest, as if he was bracing himself. "Okay."

"Why did you sign the contract? Really." I wasn't sure how to ask it.

"Because I was afraid," he answered instantly.

"Of what?"

"You really want to know?"

"I do."

He blinked, quiet, and I found myself dreading what he might say. "I'm afraid that you're going to want what she can give you. What I'll never be able to give you." The look of vulnerability that flashed in his eyes made me swallow hard. "I don't want you to work for Holland because I'm afraid you won't come back to the Narrows. To me."

Emotion curled thick in my throat. "I don't want what Holland has. I want *you*," I said, unsteady. "She can never give me what *you* can give me."

His cheeks flushed. It had cost him something to be so honest.

"I don't want you to work for Holland, either," I said. "I don't want you to be that person anymore."

"I won't have to if tomorrow goes as planned."

"Even if it doesn't go as planned. I don't want you to work for her." I took a step toward him.

"I already signed the contract, Fable."

"I don't care. Promise me. Even if it means leaving the *Marigold*. Even if we have to start over."

The muscle in his jaw ticked as his eyes met mine. "All right."

"Swear it," I said.

"I swear it."

I let out a relieved breath, the tension coiled around me finally loosening. But West looked miserable. He rubbed his face with both hands, shifting on his feet anxiously.

I knew what that look was. It was the feeling of being trapped. Of having no way out. I knew because I felt it too. "My father said that the worst mistake he ever made was letting Isolde step foot on his ship," I said lowly.

West looked up then, like he knew what I was about to say.

"I think maybe he hated that he loved her," I whispered.

The room fell silent, the sounds of the sea and the village disappearing.

"Are you asking me if I feel that way?"

I nodded, instantly regretting it.

He looked as if he was measuring me. Trying to decide if he was going to answer. If he could trust me with it. "Sometimes," he admitted.

But it wasn't followed by the terror I had been sure would come, because West didn't look away from me as he said the words.

"But this didn't start that night on Jeval when you asked me for passage to Ceros. It started a long time before that. For me."

Tears welled in my eyes as I looked up at him. "But what if—"

"Fable." He closed the space between us, and his hands lifted to my face, his fingertips sliding into my hair. The sensation woke the heat on my skin, and I sniffed, so happy that he'd finally touched me. His mouth hovered an inch above mine. "The answer to that question is always going to be the same. It doesn't matter what happens." His hands tightened on me. "You and me."

The words sounded like vows. But there was a grief that bloomed in my chest as he spoke them, like an incantation that gave flesh to bones.

My voice deepened, waiting for his mouth to touch mine. "How long can you live like that?"

His lips parted and the kiss was deep, drawing the air from the room, and the word was broken in his throat. "Forever."

My fingers twisted in his shirt as I pulled him toward me, and in an instant the space that had stretched between us minutes ago was gone. It vanished the moment his skin touched mine. He could feel it, too. It was in the way his kiss turned hungry. The way his fingers pulled at the laces of my underdress until it was sliding over my hips.

I smiled against his mouth, my bare feet stepping over the pile of silk on the floor as he walked us to the cot. I laid back onto the quilts, pulling him with me so I could melt into the heat of him. I hooked my legs around his hips as I tugged at his shirt, finding his skin with my fingertips, and his breath shook on an exhale as he leaned all his weight into me.

West's lips trailed down my throat until the warmth of his mouth pressed to the soft hollow below my collar bone, then to my breast. A pitiful sound crept up my throat as I arched my back, trying to get closer. When he realized what I wanted, his hands trailed up my thighs so he could take hold of my hips, and he fit me against him, groaning.

Like the flick of wind over water, it all disappeared. Holland, Saint, the Trade Council meeting, midnight, the Roths. It could be our last night on the *Marigold,* our last night on this crew, but whatever happened tomorrow, we were sailing into it together.

You and me.

And for the first time, I believed him.

THIRTY-EIGHT

T he harbor bell echoed like a harbinger in the silence of Sagsay Holm as I stood at the window, watching the fog spill over the docks.

West tucked the wild strands of hair behind his ear. His attention was on the buttons of his jacket, but I was thinking about the way he'd looked in the candlelight the night before, warm light on bronze skin. I could still feel the sting of him on me, and the memory made my cheeks flush pink. But West didn't look embarrassed. If anything, he looked more settled. Steadied.

I pulled in a long, slow breath, trying to calm my nerves.

As if he could read my thoughts, West pressed a kiss to my temple. "You ready?"

I nodded, picking up the frock from where I'd dropped it on the floor the night before. I was ready. West had promised me that even if the Roths betrayed us, he wouldn't honor Holland's contract. Even if that meant leaving the *Marigold* behind and spending the rest of our lives in the rye fields or diving on Jeval.

Truthfully, I didn't care anymore. I had found a family in West, and I'd learned enough from all that had happened to know that I would trade anything in the world for it.

Willa, Paj, Auster, Hamish, and Koy waited out on the deck, each of them straightening when we came out of the breezeway. Tru was at the bow, flicking a coin into the air and catching it.

I walked to the starboard railing and tossed the frock overboard. It fell through the air, green silk rippling before it landed in the slate-blue water.

West was right. Holland didn't understand the Narrows. She thought that wealth and power could buy her way into Ceros, but she'd underestimated us. There was a lifeblood that connected the people who were born on those shores. The ones who sailed those waters. The people of the Narrows couldn't be bought.

More than that, Holland had underestimated *me*.

I watched the dress sink, disappearing beneath the white foam.

It didn't matter how much Holland tried to dress me up. I wasn't my mother.

"You sure you don't want us to come?" Paj asked, clearly

uncomfortable with the idea of West and me going to the Trade Council meeting alone.

"I don't want any of you anywhere near Holland," he answered. "No matter what happens, be ready to set sail by nightfall. And let the kid go." He tipped his head toward Tru.

I looked to Koy, then to the others. "Even if you have to leave without us, take him home."

Hamish nodded, but Willa's apprehension was plain on her face as she looked between us. West gave her a reassuring look, but it didn't seem to help. She climbed the mast without a word.

"She's fine," Auster said. "We'll see you in a few hours."

West took the ladder first, and I climbed down after him. I looked back to the *Marigold* one more time as we made our way up and out of the harbor, saying my own kind of goodbye.

The Council District sat at the bottom of the same hill where Wolfe & Engel was perched. It was ensconced by bronze archways adorned with scrolling vines that held the seals of the five guilds: gem and rye merchants, sailmakers, smiths, and shipwrights. The most powerful people on the water and on the land.

The pier was built with thick beams of oiled mahogany, carved with the same seals that marked the archways. West stayed close to me as I stepped into the crowd of fine frocks, pinned curls, and tailored suits headed into the district. I could spot the merchants and traders from the Narrows easily, their sea-swept hair and clothes standing out among the crisp, clean colors. They all drifted toward the enormous open doors ahead.

Holland was waiting at the entrance, her gloved hands tucked into her fur stole. When she spotted us, she frowned.

She looked sourly at my clothes as we neared her. "What do you think you're doing?"

"No one was going to believe I was a dredger, much less a trader, in that ridiculous costume," I muttered. "If you want to use me to bait the Narrows Trade Council, then I can't look like a Saltblood."

She sneered at me. She knew I was right, but she didn't like it. "I'll have that ship at the bottom of the sea by sundown if either of you get in the way of what I'm doing here." Not even a hint of anger flashed in her silvery eyes. "Do you understand?"

"I understand," I answered.

"About time." A smooth voice spoke behind me, and I turned to see Henrik Roth standing over me. A plum-colored bowtie was tied around his neck, his face freshly shaved.

I tried to read him, desperately hoping that he wasn't about to ruin everything.

"*What* are you doing here?" Holland growled.

Henrik hooked his thumbs into the suspenders beneath his jacket. "Thought I'd come and watch all the fun."

There was something unsettling in his smile. As if at any moment, his lips would spread to reveal fangs.

"Can't get in without a merchant's ring or a trading license," he said. "So I thought you'd invite me as your guest."

I could see Holland weighing her options. She could refuse and risk a scene—one that could reveal her connection to Henrik—or she could agree and risk the same thing happening inside. Either way, she could lose.

She took a step toward him. "You try anything and you won't make it out of the pier alive."

"Fine by me." He smiled.

Holland gave an exasperated sigh before she led us to the threshold of the pier.

"They're with me," she said smoothly as the man at the door studied her merchant's ring.

He answered with a nod, eyeing Henrik. He recognized him, and he wouldn't be the only one who would.

Inside, glass lanterns hung from the rafters, filling the ceiling with what looked like rows of golden suns. More than one set of eyes lifted to land on me and West as we followed in Holland's wake. More than one whisper broke the silence.

Holland wove through the fine suits and frocks until the floor opened to a railed rectangle, where two long, empty tables faced each other, each lined with five chairs. The crowd encircled it, filling every inch of the building, and my throat constricted when I realized what they were looking at.

Ezra's teapots and teacups were set before each chair.

They were exactly as Holland conceived them, their forms astonishing and their grandeur inconceivable. The facets of each gem sparkled, drawing every eye in the room.

Tiered rows of seats marked with trading crests and merchant's insignias overlooked the platform. Holland found her chair on the row closest to the tables.

I searched the other chairs, looking for Saint's crest—a triangular sail wreathed by a cresting wave. But when I finally found his seat, it was empty. Behind it, Zola's crest marked another.

I looked up to West. His eyes were trained on the same thing.

"Do you see him?" I spoke under my breath.

He scanned the room, over the heads around us. "No."

I touched the back of West's hand before I shouldered away from him, finding the stairs that led up to Holland.

I took my place beside her, watching the room. Henrik stood at the side of the platform beside West, a look of pure enjoyment on his face. Ezra hadn't said Henrik was going to be there, and if there was some scheme that betrayed both Holland and Saint, we were about to find out.

A woman came by with a tray of cava glasses, and Holland took two, handing one to me.

The pop of a gavel slamming on the table made me flinch, and the crowd instantly quieted, pressing tighter together as the doors on the balcony flew open.

A single line of men and women filed out, taking the stairs down to the platform and finding their seats. Their newly tailored coats and frocks were trimmed with gold and velvet, their hands covered in jeweled rings. The Narrows Trade Council. Even in their finery, you could see their rough edges. They took their places at the far table before they were followed by the council representing the Unnamed Sea, whose opulence was even more grand.

When they were all in place, they took their seats together. The scrape of chair legs echoed in the silence.

Again, I looked to Saint's seat. It was still empty.

The woman representing the Narrows Smiths Guild leaned into the master of the Shipwrights Guild, whispering as two men with white gloves filled the ornate teacups before them. It looked as if the teapots were floating off the table, and I could see that Holland liked the admiration. That had been the point.

She swirled the cava in her glass, watching both councils study the pieces with a satisfied grin sliding up the side of her face. She was priming them for her proposal.

The gavel fell again as the master of the Rye Guild for the Unnamed Sea stood. He brushed his coat before he turned to the crowd. "I'd like to welcome you on behalf of the Unnamed Sea and the Narrows to the Biennial Trade Council meeting."

The doors to the pier closed, shutting out the sunlight, and the room fell quieter, making my palms sweat. I searched the faces in the crowd for my father, my eyes looking for the brilliant blue of his coat.

Beside me, Holland was relaxed, patiently waiting for her moment.

"We'll open first for new business." The guild master's deep voice rang out and the slide of eyes drifted toward the merchant's seats.

Holland took her time standing, looking out over the room. She was enjoying this. "Esteemed councils, I'd like to put forth today an official request for a license to expand my trading route from Bastian to Ceros."

The silence resounded, the attention of both councils on my grandmother.

It was the Narrows Gem Guild master who spoke first. She stood, teacup in hand. "This is the fourth time in eight years that you've submitted a request for a license, and the answer has always been the same."

The Gem Guild master from the Unnamed Sea stood next. "The successful enterprise of Holland's trade has benefited both the Unnamed Sea and the Narrows. Most of the stones traded in your waters have come from her dredging crews. We support her request, as we have done in the past."

As I suspected, the harbor master wasn't the only one in Holland's pocket.

"It is imperative that traders in the Narrows continue to run their routes," the Narrows Gem Guild master replied.

"Let them," Holland answered.

"We all know that if your ships start sailing the Narrows, it will sink the trade based out of Ceros."

The Gem Guild master from the Unnamed Sea lifted her chin. "What trade? Word has it that half of Zola's fleet has been burned in a petty traders' rivalry and he hasn't been seen in weeks. Saint didn't even bother to take his seat at today's meeting."

My pulse kicked up as I eyed the empty chair again. Where was he?

A sick feeling settled in the pit of my stomach then, the edges of thought coming into focus. If Saint wasn't here, it could only mean one of two things. Either he hadn't made it to the meeting because Holland had made sure of it, or . . . I swallowed.

What if he'd never intended on making it? What if this was another one of his twisted schemes? Looking out for himself. Letting me draw fire from Holland so that it didn't find *him*. Maybe he'd struck his own deal. By now, he could even be back in the Narrows.

I bit down onto my lip and breathed through the pain erupting in my chest. That *bastard*.

"I have a proposal that I think will suit both councils." Holland spoke again.

Both Gem Guild masters sat back down, and everyone turned to my grandmother, listening.

She flicked a finger at me, signaling me to stand, and I got to my feet, the weight of hundreds of eyes falling on me.

My mind raced and I looked to the teapots on the tables before us. If Saint wasn't here, there was only one way to bring Holland down. But if I did what needed to be done, I wasn't the only one who would pay the price with Holland. West would, too.

I found him in the crowd. He stood at the back corner, his eyes boring into me. The set of his shoulders was rigid as he gave the slightest shake of his head in answer.

Don't do it, Fable.

"I would like to put forth my granddaughter as head of my trade in Ceros," Holland crooned.

Silence.

"She was born on a trading ship in the Narrows, where she's lived her entire life. She's a dredger, a trader, and a gem sage."

I blinked. A hush fell over the huge room, and I tried not to move. Holland's attention didn't leave the councils before us, where more than one master on the Narrows Trade Council whispered to their neighbor.

"She will sail beneath my crest with a fleet of six ships and set up a post in Ceros under the authority of the Narrows Trade Council and Gem Guild," Holland continued. "Our inventory will be limited to gems and gems only."

But everyone in the room had to know what that really meant. She'd *start* with gems. As her coffers grew, so would her inventory. Smaller traders would go under and she'd be there to pick up the pieces. In no time, she'd own the Narrows.

"Shall we call for a vote?" The master of the Unnamed Sea Rye Guild stood, tucking his hands into his gold-lined pockets.

The masters each gave hesitant nods and my hands curled to fists inside my jacket pockets, my heart hammering. She was going to win. She was going to get everything.

I took a step forward before I could change my mind, my skin going cold. But as my lips parted, the door at the back of the pier flew open, filling the room with bright sunlight. I blinked furiously, my eyes adjusting to see a sharp silhouette moving through the crowd.

"My apologies." My father's deep voice resonated throughout the room, and I let out a painful breath, swallowing. "I'm late."

The Unnamed Sea Trade Council eyed Saint suspiciously as he made his way up onto the platform between the tables.

He didn't look at me as he walked to his chair, flinging his coat out behind him before he sat. "Now, what have I missed?"

THIRTY-NINE

No one looked more shocked and outraged than Holland. She was carved from ice beside me.

"We're due to vote on Holland's proposal to open her route to Ceros," the Gem Guild master from the Narrows answered. She looked almost relieved to see him.

"Ah." Saint pulled the pipe from his pocket, rubbing the smooth chamber with his thumb, as if he was thinking about lighting it. "That won't happen, I'm afraid."

"I'm sorry?" The surface of Holland's flawless calm suddenly cracked.

Saint leaned forward to meet her eyes down the line of chairs. "You won't have that merchant's ring on your finger much longer. It would be a shame to waste parchment on a trade license."

Holland squared her shoulders to him, fixing Saint with her murderous gaze. "You have got to be—"

"I'd like to submit a formal charge." Saint stood back up, taking hold of the opening of his jacket with one hand.

A streak of bright red streaked up from his collar to his chin. Blood. It looked like he'd tried to wipe it clean. And I didn't see a wound, which meant that it wasn't his.

"Against Holland and her licensed gem trade operation."

"And what is the charge?" the Gem Guild master from the Unnamed Sea screeched.

"Manufacturing and trading gem fakes," Saint answered.

A collective gasp sucked the air out of the room, and the Gem Guild master from the Unnamed Sea sprang to his feet. "Sir, I hope you understand the gravity of this accusation."

"I do," Saint said with feigned formality. "Holland has been systematically leaking fake gemstones into the shipments for the Narrows, and I'd like to request the revocation of her merchant's ring, as well as her license to trade in the Unnamed Sea."

Holland was trembling beside me, so furious she had to reach out for the railing in front of her to keep from falling. "This is ridiculous! The accusation is false!"

"I assume you have proof?" the man at the end of the table asked, looking warily to Saint.

This wasn't just bad for the trade. It was bad for the Unnamed Sea.

"You've already got it." He flung a hand lazily to the tables. "You're holding in your hands the same fakes she's been leaking into the Narrows."

The man set down his teacup and it clattered against the plate sharply. He looked at it as if it had bitten him. "You're not serious."

"You're insane. There isn't a single fake in those pieces!" Holland shouted, her eyes wild. She stumbled forward, catching herself on the arm of her chair. "Check them for yourself!"

The Gem Guild master from the Unnamed Sea poured the tea from her cup onto the ground, stepping to the nearest candle and holding it to the flame.

She inspected it carefully, turning it so the light moved in the stones. "Someone get me a gem lamp. Now!"

"While we're waiting . . ." Saint sat on the corner of the table, kicking his leg. "I have another charge to present as well."

"Another," Holland seethed.

Saint gave a nod, pulling a piece of parchment from his jacket. "Six days ago, the *Luna*, flagship of Zola's Ceros-posted trade operation, made port in Bastian. It hasn't been seen since. Nor has its helmsman."

Holland went still.

"The next night, he was murdered at the gala at Azimuth House."

If there was an ounce of warmth left in the room, it was gone now.

"Last I checked, conspiracy to murder a fellow trader was an offense that requires the revocation of a trade license."

That's what he was doing. Covering his bases. Just in case the Roths didn't come through and they'd put real gems in the tea sets. But Saint was taking a huge risk by making an accusation like that. There wasn't a trader in the room that couldn't accuse him of the same crime.

I froze, my eyes finding West in the crowd. That wasn't true. Because Saint never did his own dirty work. He was never even present for it.

That's why he'd had West.

"I'd like to submit the sworn statement of Zola's navigator, who witnessed the death of his helmsman at the gala himself."

A head of pale blond hair appeared from the crowd, and Clove stepped onto the platform. My mouth dropped open. They were going to take Holland down for the very plot they themselves orchestrated.

"Well?" the Gem Guild master from the Unnamed Sea snapped.

"It's true," Clove answered. "I saw it with my own eyes. Holland ordered the murder of Zola in her study. Then she pieced out and sank the *Luna* in Bastian's bay."

"He's lying!" Holland screamed, panicked now. She shuffled down the steps to the platform, her skirts clutched and wrinkled in her hands. "They've worked this out together. Both of them." Her voice disintegrated.

"No." The word fell from my lips heavily, echoing. I'd spoken without even planning to. I was intoxicated by the show of it. By the sheer genius design of it all. "They're not. I was there." Holland turned to me, her eyes wide and hollow. "It's true," I said.

Shouting erupted as a heaving man appeared in the open doorway of the pier, a gem lamp clutched in his big hands. He hobbled up to the platform, setting it down onto the table.

The Gem Guild master from the Narrows picked up the teacup and slammed it against the table. I flinched as she hit it again, working one of the stones free. The man lit the wick in the lamp and the guild master pulled off her jacket, setting the stone onto the glass. Everyone watched in utter silence.

The gem scraped against the glass as she turned it, the hard set of her jaw tightening. "It's true," she confirmed. "They're fakes."

A roar of protest broke out, enveloping everything in the room.

"That's impossible!" Holland cried. "The craftsman! He must have—"

"They were crafted in your warehouse, were they not?" Saint raised an eyebrow at her.

She had no way out now. She'd lose her ring for commissioning work from an unlicensed merchant if she told the truth about where they'd come from. She was trapped.

Every one of the council members stood then, their voices joining in the chaos as they yelled at one another across the platform. It was a fall that would affect the whole of the Unnamed Sea.

Holland sank to the steps of the platform, her hands shaking in her lap as the Gem Guild master marched toward her. "Your ring has been revoked. And if we don't find Zola by the time the sun goes down, so will your license."

Holland fumbled with the ring, pulling it free before she

dropped it into his hand. "You don't understand. They . . . *they* did this."

He ignored her, signaling the two men waiting behind him. They stepped forward, waiting, and Holland got back to her feet, pushing past them to the doors.

The gavel struck again, calling the voices to quiet, and a flustered Rye Guild master fidgeted with it in his hands. "I'm afraid we'll have to reconvene—"

"Not yet," Saint interrupted, still standing in the center of the platform. "I still have new business."

The man gaped at him. "New business? Now?"

"That's right." He pulled another parchment from his jacket. "I'd like to submit a request for a license to trade at the port of Bastian." His voice echoed. "On behalf of my daughter and her ship, the *Marigold*."

I stopped breathing, every drop of blood stilling in my veins.

My daughter.

I had never in my life heard him say that word.

Saint turned to look at me, his eyes meeting mine. And every face in the room blinked out into black, leaving only him. And me. And the storm of everything between us.

Maybe, I thought, he was paying what was owed. Breaking even after what I'd done for him. Maybe he was making sure that there was no debt to be laid at his feet.

But that was the license. Not the words. That wasn't why he'd called me his daughter.

I sucked in a breath through the pain in my throat, not able to keep the tears from falling. They slid down my cheeks silently as I stared at him. And the look in his eye sparked like the strike of flint. Strong and steady and proud.

He was handing over the sharpest blade to whoever might use it against him. But more than that, he was claiming me.

"Granted." The voice shook me from the trance, bringing me back to the room. Where every eye looked between us.

Helmsman. Dredger. Trader. Orphan. Father.

Daughter.

FORTY

The sea looked different that morning.

I stood at the end of the street, looking out over the harbor of Sagsay Holm. It was still dark, but I could see the dance of blue shifting on the waves.

The *Seadragon* was missing from the docks. A man on a sling hung over the side of another ship, scraping Holland's crest from its hull. As the news reached the other ports of the Unnamed Sea, it would disappear. As if all those years and gems and ships had never existed. But there would be a vacuum left behind when Holland was gone. One that would have far-reaching consequences.

The silhouette of a long coat appeared on the cobblestones

beside my shadow. I watched it move in the wind for a moment before I turned to look at him.

Saint was clean-shaven, his blue eyes bright over high cheekbones. "Tea?"

I smiled. "Sure."

We walked shoulder to shoulder down the middle of the street, our boots hitting the cobblestones in a synchronized rhythm. I'd never walked with him like that. Never stood beside him or talked to him anywhere except on the *Lark* or in his post. People watched us as we passed, and I wondered if they could see him in me or me in him. If there was some visible echo between us that told people who we were. It felt strange. It felt good.

For the first time in my life I wasn't hiding, and neither was he.

He stopped beneath the swinging sign of a tavern and opened the door before we both ducked inside.

The barkeep stood up from the stool where he was writing in the ledgers and tightened the straps of his apron. "Morning."

"Morning," Saint echoed, helping himself to a small table before the largest window. It looked out over the street, just the way he liked. "Pot of tea, please."

I took the seat beside him, unbuttoning my jacket and setting my elbows onto the table. He said nothing, watching out the window with squinted eyes as the gold light swelled behind the glass. He wasn't the awkward knot of tension that he'd always been.

When the barkeep set down a plate of toast, Saint picked up a knife and carefully spread it with butter.

It was an easy silence. A comfortable one. All the questions I ever wanted to ask him swirled in my head, spinning so fast that I could hardly untangle them from one another. But they never found their way to my tongue. Suddenly, it seemed, I didn't need to ask them. Suddenly, none of it mattered.

A blue porcelain teapot landed between us and the barkeep set down two cups and saucers, taking care to straighten them so they lined up neatly. When he was satisfied, he left us with a dutiful nod.

I picked up the pot and filled Saint's cup first. The steam from the black tea curled up before him. He was most familiar that way, concealed behind some kind of veil. Never fully in focus.

"I was afraid yesterday that you wouldn't show." I slid the saucer toward him.

He picked up the spoon beside his plate and stirred his tea slowly. "Did you really think I wouldn't?"

"No," I answered as I realized it.

Some part of me had known he'd come. And I wasn't sure why, because I had no reason to trust him.

In my entire life, Saint had never told me that he loved me. He'd fed me, clothed me, and given me a home, but there were limits to how much of him belonged to me. Still, even in those years on Jeval, there was some cord that tied me to my father. That made me feel like he was mine. And that's what I'd held onto in those minutes, watching the doors of the pier and waiting for him to walk through them.

"It took some doing, getting the logs from the harbor master," he said as an explanation.

I remembered the streak of blood on his throat. "How'd you get it?"

"You really want to know?"

I leaned back into my chair. "Not really."

He was quiet as he sipped his tea. The cup looked so small in his hand, the blue paint catching the light and flashing along the rim. He reached into his pocket before he set a folded parchment onto the table. "Your license."

I stared at it for a moment, half-afraid to touch it. As if it would vanish the moment I read the words. Again, the urge to cry coiled tight in my throat.

"That night." His voice pierced the silence, but he didn't look up at me. "I'm not sure how I lost her."

I straightened and the cup shook in my hand. I set it down.

"She was there one moment, and then . . ." He breathed. "A squall came over the ship and Isolde was just gone."

I didn't miss that he said her name. I didn't miss the way it sounded on his voice. Like prayer. It threaded through my heart, the stitches pulling tight.

"I didn't leave you on Jeval because I don't love you."

"Saint." I tried to stop him.

But he ignored me. "I left you there because—"

"It doesn't matter."

"It does." He looked up then, the blue in his eyes rimmed in red. "I left you there because I have never loved anything in my life like I love you. Not Isolde. Not the trade. Nothing."

The words seared, filling the tavern and wrapping around me so tight I couldn't draw breath. They crushed me until I was taking some strange unrecognizable shape.

"I didn't plan to be a father. I didn't want to be one. But the first time I held you in my hands, you were so small. I had never been so terrified of anything in my life. I feel like I've barely slept since the night you were born."

I caught a tear at my chin.

"Do you understand what I'm saying?"

I nodded, unable to make a sound. His hand unfolded on the table between us, reaching for me, but I didn't take it. Instead, I wrapped my arms around myself tightly, leaning into him. I pressed my face into his coat like I did when I was little and his arms folded around me. I closed my eyes and the slide of hot tears fell down my cheeks. For him. For me. For Isolde.

There was no way to undo it. No amount of coin or power could turn time back to that night in Tempest Snare, or the day Isolde showed up, asking for a place on Saint's crew. It was one long series of tragically beautiful knots that bound us together.

And the most heartbreaking of all was that somehow, after everything, by some stroke of darkness, I was still proud to be Saint's daughter.

His chest rose and fell, his arm tightening around me before he let go. I wiped at my face, sniffing, as he reached into his pocket.

The shine of a silver chain sparkled in his fingers. My mother's necklace.

"She would have wanted you to have it," he said, his voice uneven.

I picked it up by the chain, letting the pendant fall into my hand. The green abalone sea dragon caught the light, turning into waves of blue and purple. I could feel her in it. The ghost of my mother filled the air.

"Are you sure?" I whispered.

"I'm sure."

I closed my hand around it, and the resonant hum wrapped around me.

The harbor bell rang out as I dropped it into my pocket. "Time to go," I said hoarsely. The crew would be waiting.

Saint poured another cup of tea. "You headed to Ceros?"

I nodded, standing. A smile found my lips. "See you there?"

He picked up the cup, staring into the tea. "See you there."

I pushed through the door, pulling the collar of my jacket up against the cold morning. The village was already busy, the street filled with carts and open shop windows. I set my gaze on the water and walked, heading for the harbor.

When the reflection of violet skipped across the glass beside me, I stopped mid-stride, my gaze drawn across the street. Holland stood in the arched doorway of Wolfe & Engel, her sharp eyes on me. The white fur collar of her jacket blew in the wind, touching her jaw, the brilliant jewels hanging from her ears peeking out from beneath her hair.

She was still glamourous. Beautiful. Even if she'd lost her ring and her license, she still had her coin. She'd never want for anything, and something told me she'd find a way to get back her own bit of power in Bastian. Either way, she'd never have a stake in the Narrows.

She was as still as stone, unblinking, before she stepped inside.

When she looked over her shoulder, disappearing into the shop, I could have sworn I saw her smile.

FORTY-ONE

Sagsay Holm disappeared like the fog-cloaked memory of a dream.

I stood at the top of the foremast, tying off the lines as the wind filled the sails. They stretched against the blue sky in round arcs, the sound of the salty breeze on the canvas making me close my eyes. I pulled the air into my lungs and leaned into the mast, thinking I never wanted to leave this ship for as long as I lived.

When I looked down, West was standing on the deck, watching me. He was swallowed in gold, squinting against the light, and the wind tugged the shirt around his form in a

way that made me want to disappear into his candlelit cabin
with him.

I climbed down, landing on the hot deck with bare feet.

"You want to check them?" he asked, rolling up his sleeves.

"Yeah."

He caught my hand when I stepped around him, drawing
me back. As soon as I turned, he kissed me. One of his arms
wrapped around my waist, and I leaned into him until he
let me go. His fingers slipped from mine as I headed to the
breezeway and I ducked into his cabin, where Hamish was
sitting at West's desk, two ledgers open before him.

He looked up at me over the top of his spectacles. "Got
you set up over here."

He nodded to the gem lamp on the table. Beside it, a
small chest of gems was waiting.

With the fallout of Holland's supposed treachery, every
merchant from the Narrows to the Unnamed Sea would tighten
their operations, double- and triple-checking the stones they
sold to keep their necks from the blade of the Trade Council.

I sat down onto the stool, striking a match and lighting
the candle beneath the lens. When it was aglow, I took the
first gem between my fingers, an aquamarine. I held it up
so the light showed through, checking the color the way my
mother taught me. Then I set it onto the gem lamp's glass
and peered through the lens, noting the structure of the gem.
When I was finished, I set it aside and picked up another.

Everything has a language. A message.

It was the first thing my mother taught me when I became her apprentice. But the first time I'd understood what

she meant was when I realized that even *she* had song. It was the feeling I had anytime she was near.

It was there in the dark as she leaned over me in the hammock to press her lips to my forehead. I could feel her, even when I could only make out the flicker of lantern light on her necklace as it dangled over me.

It was something I knew in my bones.

Isolde.

I looked over my shoulder to where the sea dragon pendant hung from a nail beside the bed, swaying with the rock of the ship. I got back to my feet and crossed the cabin, taking it from the hook and holding it before me.

The same feeling had found me as I stood in Saint's post in The Pinch, my mother's spirit calling to me through the necklace from where it sat on the shelf. I'd felt it again diving the skerry, where bits of her seemed to emanate through the blue waters.

I wiped at the face of the abalone with my thumb, watching the violet hues ripple beneath the green waves. The thrumming was so clear, radiating into my palm. As if somehow, Isolde still existed within it. As if—

My breath stopped suddenly, the slightest tremor finding my hand until the silver chain slipped through my fingers.

Hamish set down his quill. "What is it?"

"What if it wasn't her?" I whispered, words frayed.

"What?"

"What if it wasn't her I felt at the skerry?" I looked up at him, but he was confused.

I held the pendant in the light coming through the window, studying the silversmithing carefully. Not a single waver caught along the bevel, the details of the sea dragon perfect. I turned it over.

My mouth dropped open when I saw it. The Roth emblem. It was pressed into the smooth surface. It was tiny, but it was there—something I wouldn't have ever recognized if I hadn't seen it in Bastian.

It was no accident that Saint had it made in Bastian. It was no coincidence that it had been made by the Roths. And it wasn't sentiment that made him go back to the *Lark* to find it.

I opened the drawer of West's desk and rifled through its contents until I found a knife. I sank down to the floor, setting the pendant before me. When I lifted the blade into the air, Hamish reached for me. "Fable—"

I brought it down with a snap, driving the handle of the blade into the face of the pendant. The abalone cracked, and with another hit, it shattered into pieces.

The knife slipped from my fingertips as I pressed my hand to my mouth, my eyes going wide.

The glistening, smooth face of black peeked out at us from beneath the broken shell. Even in the dim light, I could see the sparkle of violet swirling beneath it.

"What the . . ." Hamish gasped, taking a step back.

That feeling that wrapped around me every time I was near my mother wasn't Isolde. It was the *necklace*. The one she never took off.

Saint didn't know where to find the midnight, but he knew *how* to find it. That's why he'd given it to me. It was a clue that only a gem sage would understand.

It wasn't my mother I'd felt at the skerry. It was midnight.

FORTY-TWO

Fable's Skerry was like a giant sleeping in the dark. The outline of the rock islet was barely visible against the night sky as we dropped anchor.

I could feel it, standing at the bow of the ship with the sea wind whipping around me. Fable's Skerry didn't have reefs to dredge, but the midnight was here. It had to be.

Maybe it was an accident that Isolde had found it in the first place. Or maybe she'd followed the gemstone's song like a moth to flame.

I wondered how long it had taken her to realize what she'd done. What the stone was worth. How long it had taken her to decide to betray her own mother.

Saint gave me the necklace because it was a key. If I had midnight, if I knew what it felt like, then I could find it. I knew the song of the gem like I knew the rhythm of my own heartbeat. I could probably find it with my eyes closed.

West pushed my belt into my hands before he fitted his around him. I worked the buckle with quick fingers, not even bothering to check my tools. Every inch of my skin was jumping, the tingle of gooseflesh creeping up my arms.

Willa leaned over the side, looking down into the dark water. "You really think it's down there?"

"I know it is." I smiled.

West climbed up onto the railing, and I followed. I didn't wait. As soon as I was standing beside him, we both jumped. The black swallowed us whole and West's warm hand found me in the water as I kicked back up to the surface. The *Marigold* towered over us, the skerry at our backs.

I measured the height of it in the distance. "There." I pointed to the higher rise of rock. "There's a cavern near the tip of the ridge."

West eyed it, unsure. He was probably thinking the same thing I was. That if we dove the cavern, there was no way to know where it opened or even *if* it opened. But Isolde had done it, so there had to be a way.

"Line!" West called up to the *Marigold,* and a coil of rope landed in the water a second later.

West fit it over one shoulder so it reached across his chest and back. When he started to work his lungs, I followed, pulling full breaths in and out.

In and out. In and out.

The tightness in my chest loosened with each one until my lungs felt flexible enough to hold the air I needed. I sealed my lips and nodded to West before I plunged beneath the water and kicked. The rope made him sink faster, and I swam after him, keeping my pace slow so that I didn't tire too quickly.

Moonlight cascaded in beams through the water, lighting West in flashes below me as we descended. The cavern opened up before us, a huge black hole in the face of the rock. The sound of the gems radiated through the water so loud that I could feel it in my teeth. All this time, it was here. A stone's throw from Bastian.

West took the rope from around him and handed me the end. I fit it behind a boulder, wrenching it back and forth until it was wedged so tight a firm tug couldn't budge it. West tied the length of it around his waist, knotting it before giving me the end, and I did the same.

I squeezed his wrist when I was ready and kicked off toward the wide mouth of the cavern. As soon as we slipped inside, the darkness turned the water into ink. So black that I couldn't even see my hands as I swam with them out before me.

The farther we went, the colder the water became. I let a few bubbles of air escape my nose and kept kicking, squinting my eyes to see, but there was no trace of light ahead.

Something sharp caught my forehead and I reached up, realizing I had hit the top of the rock. The passage was narrowing. I let go of a little more air to let myself sink and pushed away from it just as the soft burn lit in my chest. I swallowed instinctively, but the motion only fooled me into thinking I was breathing for a second and the ache reignited. When I looked back, I couldn't see West, but his weight still pulled behind me on the rope.

I felt along the cold stone wall, listening carefully for the deep thrumming that radiated through the water. It was getting stronger. Clearer.

The acidic feeling erupting inside of me was a warning that time was almost up. My heart pushed against my ribs, begging for air, and the slight numbness woke in my fingertips.

I could feel West stop behind me as I thought. If we went any farther, we wouldn't make it back to the surface in time to get air. But if we weren't far from the opening . . . I squinted, studying the darkness. And then I saw it. The faintest glow.

I pushed off the wall and swam. Green light swelled in the black, and as we got closer, it came down in a slice, like a wall of crystal in the water. I was dragging myself along the wall now, searching for holds to pull myself forward to reach it. When my hands caught the edge, I hauled myself forward and broke the surface with a gasp that brought both air and water into my lungs.

I coughed, clinging to the ledge as West came up behind me. The sound of his ragged breath filled the empty silence. I could hardly see. Only the reflection on his blond hair was visible, and I reached out, feeling for him until his hands found me.

"All right?" he panted.

I answered between breaths. "All right."

Above us, a thin vein of moonlight was drawn in a narrow opening at the top of the cave. The space was only twelve feet wide at most, and the walls tapered as they rose to what looked like a tiny sliver thirty or forty feet above us.

I swung one leg up out of the water onto the smooth stone. My heart was a sprinting, angry thud in my chest, my throat burning all the way down to my stomach. West came up beside me, lifting himself from the water. As my eyes adjusted, the shape of him formed in the dark.

"You're bleeding." West's hand reached up, and he touched my forehead gently, tilting my chin so that the light fell on my face.

I felt the slick skin where it was throbbing. When I looked at my fingers, they were covered in blood. "It's nothing."

The call of seabirds sounded above us, and I looked up to the slice of sky, where their shadows flitted over the opening in the earth.

I got to my feet. The cave was silent except for the sound of water dripping from my fingertips and hitting the stone and I froze when a glint of something blinked in the darkness. I waited, staring into the emptiness until I saw it again. A flash. Like the sweep of a lighthouse. I took a step toward it, reaching out before me.

My hands drifted through the diffused moonlight until I found the wall and I felt up its face until my fingertips caught the sharp, glassy points of something hidden in the shadows.

The vibration of the gemstone coursed through me.

Midnight.

West looked up, turning in a circle, where the facets of

the stone winked in the shifting light above us. It was every-where.

"This is where she found it," I whispered, pulling the chisel from my belt.

I felt the rock before I fit the edge beneath a crease and took a hold of the mallet. It came away in a clean piece with three strikes, falling heavily into my hand. I held it in the beam of moonlight between us.

The violet inclusions danced beneath the surface, and I froze when their reflections lit the cave walls like a sky of purple stars.

The feel of my mother was close. Lurking all around us. And maybe she was. She could have dropped the stone into the sea, but she didn't. She'd kept it even though she never came back to the skerry. And I couldn't help but think that she'd kept it, maybe for me. That maybe she'd given me my name so that one day, I'd find it.

West took the stone from my hand, turning it so it glittered. "I've never seen anything like it."

"No one has," I whispered.

He looked up at me then, a question in his eyes. "What do you want to do?"

Midnight was like the dawn of a new world. It would change everything. I didn't know if the Narrows was ready for that. I didn't know if I was ready for that. A rueful smile broke on my lips as he set the stone back into my hand. "What if we do nothing?"

"What?"

Midnight had called my mother to it. At the right time, it had called me too. "What if we leave it here? Like she did."

"Forever?" Beads of light moved over West's face.

I looked around us, to the sparkling walls of the cave. "Until we need it." And we would.

He thought about it, holding the wet hair back from his face with one hand. "We have the *Lark*."

"We have the *Lark*," I repeated, smiling wider. It was more than we needed to start our trade route. More than we needed to fill the hull of the *Marigold* with inventory, and establish a post.

West took a step toward me, and when I tipped my head back, he kissed me softly. "Back to the Narrows?"

The taste of salt lit on my tongue as I repeated the words against his lips. "Back to the Narrows."

The masts creaked against the push of wind, the sails of the *Marigold* unfolding like wings.

I stood at the bow, watching the deep blue water rush beneath the ship. We were soaring over the sea so fast that when I looked up, Jeval was already upon us.

"Let's bring her in!" West shouted from the helm. "Strike all sails!"

Paj and Auster climbed the masts, letting out the downhauls so the ship would slow, and Hamish unlocked the anchor crank.

I took the length of line at the foot of the foremast and secured it, my eyes on the barrier islands. They were like black, jagged teeth. The blue waves crashed in a spray against them, rolling in with the high winds. The docks I'd known in my time on Jeval were gone, replaced by what looked like a small harbor. Huge beams of wood rose out of the water, making twelve ship bays.

In the distance, I could see a small skiff headed toward it from shore.

West watched from the bow with his hands in his pockets. He was always that way when we made port at Jeval, his shoulders drawn up and his jaw set.

I unwound the heaving lines and came portside as the *Marigold* drifted closer to the rocks. A string of Jevalis were already waiting with their hands out, ready to catch her from scraping.

I balanced on the crates as she came in slow and tossed the heaving lines to the boy at the end of the dock. He secured them one at a time and Auster unrolled the ladder just as Koy appeared up the harbor with a hand in the air.

"*Marigold!*" Koy shouted. "I don't have you scheduled for another week!" He glanced at the log book in his hands.

Paj gave me a knowing look from the helm. Koy was right. But West always had a reason why we needed to head back to Jeval early.

"Don't tell me you came through that storm!" Willa's voice called out. I searched the docks, looking for her.

West leaned over the railing, grinning when he spotted his sister, and he instantly relaxed.

But Willa was incensed, coming through the crowd of dredgers and immediately inspecting the ship. She stopped near the bow, pressing a hand to a poorly repaired breach.

West watched her glower at it. "Got a few things that need seeing to."

"When are you going to get a new bosun?" she grumbled.

"We haven't found one yet," West said.

Below, Koy eyed me, and I smirked. We'd tried six different bosuns in the last eight months and West had fired every one.

I came down the ladder, stepping onto the post to jump down beside Koy. He'd hired and paid only Jevalis to rebuild the docks with his coin from the Unnamed Sea, and now he was running them as the harbor master.

A few weeks after it was finished, he asked Willa to set up shop for ship repairs. Seeing them standing on the dock, they looked as if they both belonged there. Together.

My father had sneered when I told him we were building a three-port route that ended in Jeval. But just like Koy predicted, the barrier islands were filled with ships. In another year, we'd be using our license to trade in Bastian.

No gems. No fancy silver teapots or hair combs or silk for fine frocks.

We were trading rye and mullein—goods made by the bastards of the Narrows.

The sparkle of midnight still glimmered in my dreams. So did the sound of my mother's voice. But we hadn't been back to Fable's Skerry. Not yet.

West and I lay side by side on the beach in the dark, the waves touching our bare feet. The voices of the crew drifted on the wind as they drank rye around the fire, and I watched a single star trace a spark across the sky.

When I turned to look at West, that same starlight glinted in his eyes. I found his hand and held it to my cheek, remembering the first time I'd seen him on the docks. The first time I'd seen him smile. The first time I'd seen his darkness and every time he'd seen mine.

We were salt and sand and sea and storm.

We were made in the Narrows.

ACKNOWLEDGMENTS

All my love to my own crew—Joel, Ethan, Siah, Finley, and River. Thank you for letting me live in the world of the Narrows and the Unnamed Sea while I told this story. No matter the adventure, you are always the best home to come back to.

Again, an enormous amount of gratitude to my team at Wednesday Books. Thank you to Eileen Rothschild, my incredible editor and namesake of the Roth family. Thank you to Sara Goodman, DJ DeSmyter, Alexis Neuville, Brant Janeway, Mary Moates, Tiffany Shelton, and Lisa Bonvissuto for all you do for my books. Thank you, Kerri Resnick, for yet another gorgeous cover.

Thank you to Barbara Poelle, my agent, who keeps my head on straight and my eyes on the horizon.

Thank you to my amazing, weird, hilarious family, especially my mom, who this book is dedicated to. I love you!

This book, like *Fable*, wouldn't have been possible without the input of Lille Moore, who served as a consultant on all things sailing, sea, and trade. Thank you so very much for helping me build these books! Thank you also to Natalie Faria, my fearless beta reader unicorn.

To my critique partner, Kristin Dwyer, you were almost no help on this book at all because you were busy making your own dreams come true. Watching you stand on top of this mountain is a beautiful thing to behold, and I'm counting down the days until we can hold your book in our hands. Don't forget my line break.

Thank you to my author and writing community, the ones who drag me along on this road when I've lost my way. And thank you to my non–book world friends who are tasked with the sometimes delicate job of making sure I stay human. I love you all.